Kila's Ho

By Peter J.

Copyright © 2015 Peter J. Blake

All Rights Reserved

To Henry, for giving me a reason to stay young

Thanks to the Wednesday Nighters for their ongoing ideas, enthusiasm and creativity.

Thanks to my beautiful wife, Louise, for letting me spend hours locked away writing and for giving up her valuable free time to proofread and edit my work.

Table of Contents

Table of Contents 5

-Prologue- 8

-- PART ONE -- 13

-Chapter One- 14

-Chapter Two- 30

-Chapter Three- 44

-Chapter Four- 59

-Chapter Five- 73

-Chapter Six- 89

-Chapter Seven- 105

-Chapter Eight- 121

-Interlude- 138

-- PART TWO -- 140

-Chapter Nine- 141

-Chapter Ten- 158

-Chapter Eleven- 174

-Chapter Twelve- 193

-Chapter Thirteen- 209

-Chapter Fourteen- 227

-Epilogue- 243

LUCARCIA

- Ursum
  - The Head of Ursum
    - Cansar
    - Tunis
  - The Spine of Ursum
    - Lucar (Capital)
    - Providentia
    - Black Sail
    - The Inner Sea
  - The Tail of Ursum
    - Sicile
- Manabas
- Ibini
- Granita
- The Lucarian Straits
- The Southern Ocean

-Prologue-

The autumn rains lashed down on the domed glass roof, the intense noise threatening to drown out the words of those sheltered beneath it. The jungle palace of Lily Jade, the Verdant Queen, had been designed and built over five hundred years ago, before the Lucarcian Empire had been founded. It was not in a good state of repair and a deluge such as this exposed the weaknesses of the structure. Karim Moonleaf turned the collar of his green cloak up and tried, in vain, to snuggle deeper into its protection as he listened to the latest rant of his liege.

"He cannot continue to get away with this!" roared the Verdant Queen from her position on the elevated throne in the dead centre of the room. "First he destroys my fleet, sinking all my ships and killing all their crews. And as if that was not bad enough, he then kills my nephew!"

Karim stole a glance out of the corner of his eye at those assembled next to him. The Verdant Queen's court were a ragged bunch. If any of them had come to court with self-esteem and confidence, it only took a few short months in the vicinity of the rages of the queen to whittle any such self-belief away. She was never happy unless she was telling them how useless and hopeless they all were.

"And who let him?" demanded Lily Jade of her courtiers. "Who?" she continued rhetorically, "You lot did! You who are supposed to be my loyal servants and advisors. You who are supposed to be looking out for my interests and the interests of Ibini. You – you did nothing."

Karim knew that this was not true. His network of spies had been out and about all through the spring and summer. His men had advised the queen's nephew, Nikolai Kester. They had infiltrated the courts of all the noble houses, even the Imperial Court in Lucar. They had turned one of the Trade Lords' major operatives to their cause. They had been successful in everything they had set out to do. Everything, that was, apart from stopping the young noble from Providentia from ruining everything.

"Reynard Ferrand, son of a minor noble from some small town on the south coast of Ursum," the Verdant Queen almost spat his name out. "Somehow he managed to thwart all my plans!"

"Not just him, your majesty," interrupted one of the advisors from the floor. Karim cringed at the sound. Yongo was new in court, having only been here a few weeks. He had yet to learn that you never interrupt one of the Verdant Queen's rants.

"What!?" screamed the queen. "How dare you interrupt me?!"

"I was just saying, it was not only Reynard, ma'am. He was aided by others from around the empire and beyond."

Karim shook his head. Yongo had just interrupted the queen as she told him not to interrupt her. This would not end well.

Rather than the expected frenzy from the queen, instead she fell suddenly still. The abrupt change was more terrifying than her rage. Karim took a deep breath as the rains above briefly stopped lashing down. The whole throne room turned instantly deadly quiet. Next to him, Karim could hear Yongo's deep breathing as the young man realised that he had gone too far. Karim expected the queen's retribution to be swift and terrible.

"You are right," came the unexpected agreement from Lily Jade, softly. Karim blinked, mentally thrown off balance by this twist. "It was not just Reynard who thwarted my plans. He and his friends nearly ruined everything. The Niten warrior with her twin swords; the Nubian Gladiator with his prodigious strength; the priest of the Light with his wisdom; the ex-Thought Guard with his intellect; and Reynard himself with his wit, charm and courage. All came close to wrecking my schemes. But they never guessed. They never stopped to think, to question. They never discovered the full depth of my purpose. At least, not yet."

Karim looked up at the domed glass roof. Beyond it he could see the giant acacia trees waving in the strong winds outside. The weather looked awful, yet somehow he would rather be out there in the soaking rain and howling winds than in here, before the Verdant Queen. At least the autumn weather was predictable and a good oilskin cloak and warm furs would keep you protected. The queen had become more and more unpredictable and unstable since the events of the summer. Now, in fact,

Karim was pretty sure she had cracked. He was pretty sure she had stepped across the boundary from unstable to insane.

"None of you truly know, of course. How could you? I have not shared my plans with you, my worthless courtiers. Why would I? Only my darling daughter truly understands and only with her do I share my secrets," continued the queen. Karim did vaguely wonder if there was something he should be worried about in these latest revelations, but it was impossible to tell. Lily Jade did have a daughter, the beautiful Kululu Jade, but the queen and her daughter had never seemed close as far as Karim was able to tell. And quite what the queen may have shared with her daughter was anyone's guess. Kululu was a cold, manipulative, uncaring bitch. But at least she was sane.

"So, you are right my dear Yongo. It is not just Reynard we have to deal with but all of his little friends too," the queen smiled at her new courtier, who appeared pleased to have dodged the queen's wrath after all. "But how?"

"The way the Verdant Court has always dealt with threats, your majesty – send your assassins after Reynard and his band," replied Yongo, voicing the suggestion all in the room had been thinking.

The Jade Assassins of Ibini were a legendary force. A small unit of highly trained women, skilled in espionage, infiltration, disguise, and of course, assassination. They were subtle and efficient. They were infamous throughout the empire. Everyone had heard of them. Their deeds had been put into story and song, embellished of course – and as such their legend had been formed.

Head of the Jade Assassins was Kululu Jade, daughter of the Verdant Queen and arguably the most deadly woman in the Empire of Lucarcia. She was renowned for her icy personality which would have been more suitable for a member of House Snow. An alluring woman, no man risked trying to win her over after seeing the look in her eyes. Rumoured to have killed over a hundred men at the behest of her mother, she was ruthless, deadly and discreet. No one had ever actually seen her slay a single person, yet her reputation was murderous.

"I could send my assassins, of course," responded the queen. "They are known and feared throughout the whole of the Empire. But perhaps they would be too obvious, too easy to trace back to me, should they fail. And Reynard and his friends have proved extremely resourceful, so I am not certain that even my assassins would succeed.

"So now, spymaster, it is over to you," she continued, her eyes flicking from Yongo to Karim. Karim instinctively bowed deeply as she addressed him. "It is time to activate your sleeping agents around the world. Agents which no one would suspect. Agents which no one can link back to us. Contact them all. Activate them all. I have one instruction for you and them: Reynard and his friends must die by springtime."

Karim bowed again, closing his eyes lest they betray his anger to the queen. His network of spies had taken years to cultivate. They had ensconced themselves in places all across the Empire and out into the far reaches of the known world. Now his queen wanted him to activate them. *All of them.* Activating a spy usually meant one thing for certain: that spy would cease to be useful in the role they had been placed. Activating them, especially with a view to getting them to commit murder, would nullify their position as spies. It would expose them for what they were. And if caught, as some undoubtedly would be, they risked revealing their connection to him.

He had gone to great lengths to ensure that none of his network of spies truly knew who he was or who he worked for. So they could not, he hoped, be traced back to the queen and the Jade house. But the issue was that this one proclamation from the queen was about to ravage his entire network. He would likely lose every player he had in every position. And his situation would become quickly impossible, and quite likely fatal when powerful people across the world realised he had been responsible for so many agents in their midst.

Karim straightened up and with as light a tone as he could muster replied, "It shall be done, your majesty."

"Now," continued Lily Jade, her eyes flicking back to her newest courtier. "As I was saying. How dare you interrupt me, Yongo? I am your queen and your liege. You owe me your fealty and your life. You are an insect and a worm and you will never disrespect me again, do you understand?"

"Of course... your majesty.... I am sorry," stuttered Yongo.

"I would like you to accompany my daughter. She will ensure that you never utter such disrespectful words to me again."

Everyone turned to see a beautiful woman striding confidently into the throne room. Dressed in comfortable looking trousers and shirt of green velvet, with soft brown leather boots on her feet, Kululu Jade moved across the floor with the economy of movement of a dancer. Her long auburn tresses were pulled up into a platted bun and held in place by two 4" hair-pins, the Jade house symbol of a sibilant snake curled around a jade gem on the end of each. Though she carried no obvious weapons, rumour had it she would go everywhere armed with many secret weapons concealed about her person. It was not hard to imagine one of the razor sharp hair-pins in her slender hand. Her green eyes were cold and callous as she regarded the courtier.

"This way, please sir," she invited Yongo, indicating that he should proceed her out of the throne room, her tone anything but friendly.

Everyone knew Yongo would not see the next sunrise.

There was no doubt: the Verdant Queen had definitely tipped over the edge. Who knew what had pushed her, or what her hidden agenda was? Karim certainly didn't and he was in no mood to try and find out. The risks were too great. He would do as he was told and activate his agents. Then, once they were set in motion he would think about escaping the Jade Palace and fleeing the island of Ibini. Things were going to be too dangerous to stay here once his network of agents was activated and his orders were given:

Reynard and companions were to die by spring.

-- PART ONE --

-Chapter One-

The *katana* flashed in the autumn sunshine. Sparks flew as it intercepted the razor-sharp rapier. Kita flicked her wrist to deflect the blow sideways, aiming to draw her opponent off balance, but he was a canny warrior and his blade was back under control instantly. She moved to her left, feet perfectly balanced as they shifted across the slippery dirt floor.

She could feel the sun on her back and moved to put it directly behind her, using every advantage she could to get the upper hand. Her opponent dropped deeper into his relaxed stance and let his rapier blade drop an inch. Another fighter would have seen this opening as an opportunity and would have tried to take advantage of it. However, Kita knew her opponent well and knew he was teasing her.

Around the two combatants, a small crowd was gathering. Guards in the livery of the Iron House stood watching the two fighters, expressions of respect and admiration evident. The courtyard of the Iron Fortress was not normally privy to such impressive displays of swordsmanship and the soldiers were doing all they could to enjoy it.

Kita looked up briefly at the Iron Fortress behind her opponent. It was bathed in autumn sunshine, bringing a warm glow to the usually cold stone structure. The courtyard was empty and bare. The last time she had been here, it had been full of brightly coloured market stalls and jammed with noisy merchants and jostling customers. Today however the yard was empty, apart from the two combatants and the soldiers watching on. The gates to the courtyard from the town where shut and no commoners were being allowed in.

High above her she could see the remains of the stained glass window. Covered with weather resistant cloths and supported by wooden scaffolding, the window was in the process of being repaired, as best was possible. It was a long-term reminder of the events of the summer.

That summer, Kita had been a slave aboard a Guild ship. With four other slaves, she had escaped captivity and the group had killed the captain and taken over control of the ship. The Trade Lords, mysterious and sinister leaders of the Guild of Master Merchants and Sea Farers, had discovered their escape and had summoned them. Rather than punishing them for killing a Guild captain, the Trade Lords tasked the group to track down and kill a daring corsair who had stolen a golden suit of armour from them – the legendary Armour of Lucar, armour of the first emperor.

They had tracked the corsair captain, Nikolai Kester, to this very fortress and had him trapped in the Great Hall upstairs. Kester had smashed the three hundred year old stained glass window when he dived through it to escape. At that time, Kita had been reunited with her father, Heremod. He had gone on to join her in her quest to catch the corsair.

With Heremod's help the group followed Kester and his corsairs to their base on the cursed island of Granita. Here they had defeated Kester and killed him. Sadly, in the conflict Heremod had been killed by the corsair's monstrous first mate, Baku. Baku had escaped and fled into the wilds. Kita was still coming to terms with Heremod's death.

A flash of movement brought Kita rapidly back to the present. Her opponent's rapier thrust in towards her exposed belly and only a swift parry from her short *wakizashi* saved her from being skewered. She moved swiftly backwards aiming to disengage, but her opponent's footwork was exceptional. Fast as she could retreat, he followed, rapier flickering, searching for an opening in her defences.

Suddenly Kita slipped. Her usually sure footing deserted her for the briefest of seconds and she was down on one knee, her scarlet kimono sullied in the mud. Her opponent raised a single eyebrow and stopped his attack, an easy smile appearing on his handsome face.

He was dressed from head to toe in black and his long shoulder-length blond hair was tied up in a ponytail. He wore expensive looking black trousers and shirt, with a black waistcoat of Honshu silk over the top. On his feet were polished leather knee-length boots. He was one of the group who had escaped slavery together. In fact, he was their de facto leader, the captain of the ship they sailed on and the son and heir of the Earl of Providentia, Reynard Ferrand.

"Lost your footing, dear?" he enquired, letting his rapier drop to his side.

Kita said nothing, instead using her position low down to the ground to drive upwards unexpectedly, straight at her opponent's chest, her *katana* driving straight forward like a spear. At the last moment, the man reacted, bringing his rapier to bear, using his footwork to move sideways and just out of reach. Her *katana* missed him by an inch. However, whether this was luck or judgement on his part, she could not tell.

"That's hardly sporting," he chided, "especially after you'd fallen over."

"I had not fallen over, Reynard," she responded simply.

"I'm sure I could have finished you off there and then, had I a mind to," he grinned.

"I *would* have done," she returned sharply, letting her unreadable façade drop for a moment.

Reynard declined to reply with words, instead letting his rapier do the talking. He pressed Kita backwards again, using his superior strength and reach to his advantage. Kita retreated before him. Suddenly Kita realised he was using a pattern of attack. It was a familiar sequence. She knew it well – it was one of Reynard's favourites. He had used it to defeat the captain of the Guild ship they had both been slaves on, and he had used an improvised version to defeat Kester when they finally caught up with him. Now he was trying to use it on her. She knew the pattern well and she knew how to defend against it, and of course, she knew the deadly counter that a skilled swordsman could deliver. However, Reynard knew that she was that skilled, so why would he use it on her? It could only mean one thing: he had a trick up his sleeve. The question was what trick?

Reynard pushed her hard, forcing her backwards. His rapier was a blur as it flashed through the pattern. Kita had an advantage in that she had two swords. This pattern was designed primarily to be used against an opponent wielding a single weapon and was made to keep one blade occupied. Kita had two and so, in theory, had a spare blade free at all times. However, such was the skill and speed of Reynard's assault it needed Kita to use both blades to keep him out.

As the pattern progressed, Reynard drove Kita's swords up high. With a sudden burst of speed, he thrust his blade straight for her head, breaking the pattern. Kita parried desperately, driving both swords up in an X-shape to catch his blade and deflect it high. Reynard stepped in close, grabbed both her wrists with his, lifted her arms above her head and planted a kiss right on her lips.

Shocked, Kita blinked in confusion. She almost dropped her swords as Reynard stepped back, disengaging from the duel. Kita's head swam. What had just happened? Why had Reynard kissed her? What did he mean by it? Looking up she saw he was standing there with his easy smile on his face. She felt confused; not sure if she was annoyed or happy with his actions. A little of both she suspected.

"Reynard! Kita!" The shout came from the main keep. Looking over, Kita saw a short, thin, silver-haired Lucarcian standing in the main doorway to the keep. Dressed in simple clothes typical of his race, Tanithil was another one of her trusted companions, another of the ex-slaves who had escaped with her. He was wearing dark cotton trousers and a green shirt, tucked in at the waist. A brown homespun waistcoat kept the chill out and he had short, soft leather boots on his feet. "It's time," he finished, beckoning to them.

Kita looked at Reynard who was still smiling. "I supposed we had best go in," she said.

"Indeed," he replied. "I was just about to win anyway," he followed up, sliding his rapier into its jewelled scabbard.

Kita bristled inside, but kept her face impassive. "I don't think so," she replied.

"Of course I was. You were all flustered and had dropped your guard. If that had been a real fight, I'd have skewered you where you stood." With that, Reynard bowed a courtly bow, spun on his black-booted heel and strode off towards Tanithil and the keep. The guards moved aside for him as he left the area.

Kita stood for a moment. Reynard was right, she realised. She had been so shocked by the kiss that, if they had been fighting for real, she would have been killed. So was the kiss just a tactic to win the fight, or had Reynard meant it? She was completely unsure.

*

"We need to stop the Writhing Death, or you will have no empire left to fight over," said Kita again. She was beginning to become agitated by the short-sightedness of her friends, but kept her emotions inside, her face and voice calm.

The group were upstairs in the Iron Fortress, in Reynard's chambers. A low fire was burning in the hearth, sending flickering shadows across the walls. Reynard had arranged two comfortable couches, facing each other, and the servants had brought up refreshments for the group. All five of the ex-slaves were there and they were discussing what they would do next.

"I'm sorry Kita, but I need to do this," said Reynard from his position by the window. "I am the heir of the Iron House and our house is in a precarious position right now. With the emperor dead, leaving no heirs, the royal Azure House is looking likely to crumble any time now. Our house is a direct vassal to the Azure House. That was always a strong position to be in, historically, but if the Azure House collapses that leaves us with no protection. I will not leave my family and all the people who count on us, at a time like this. "

"The empire is on the brink of civil war," said the silver-haired Tanithil from his position on one of the couches. Tanithil was a Lucarcian and this was his homeland. Once upon a time, he had even been a member of the Thought Guard, the emperor's personal bodyguard; though they had cast him out for cheating at gambling. He was a telepath and his talents had saved their lives on more than one occasion. They would all listen to what he had to say. "Those of us who were born here cannot sit by and let it fall apart. With the Armour of Lucar in his possession, Reynard stands a good chance of actually helping to keep the empire together. And if he is going to wear it then I need to be with him to make sure nothing untoward happens to him."

The Armour of Lucar was a golden suit of full plate armour. It was the armour of the first ever emperor. Legend told that it was enchanted. Now the armour was theirs. It stood in a corner of Reynard's chamber on a stand, gleaming brightly in the flickering firelight. During the summer months, the group had tracked it down and recovered it from the corsair captain who had stolen it from the Trade Lords. As they had done so, it became apparent that the wearer of the armour was capable of ensorcelling those around him. It was clearly an extremely powerful item to possess.

However Tanithil was concerned that such power may have unforeseen side effects on the wearer. Captain Kester, the last person to wear the armour, was psychotic by the end. Reynard maintained the corsair had been unhinged before he ever came across the armour, but Tanithil was still concerned about the dangers of donning the magical suit.

Kita understood Reynard and Tanithil's loyalty to their country. She respected it greatly. Nevertheless, she found it frustrating that they could not see the greater picture. She tried to convince them once more. "I have great respect for your dedication to your homeland. It is honourable. In this case, however, you need to realise the huge threat that the Writhing Death poses to your lands. The last time this terror was unleashed on the world, the emperor, whose armour you now possess, was forced to unleash a terrible ritual, which ripped the lands asunder. You must not underestimate it."

"I have spent some time in the library studying this curse, since we have been here in your home, Reynard," came in the priest Mosi, sat next to Tanithil, stroking his goatee between thumb and forefinger. "It is an evil thing which comes from the darkness of the Void. I have never heard of its like anywhere in the world, through all the long ages. I believe it is an abomination and we must stop it. By the Light's power, I will help you any way I can, Kita." Mosi was dressed as he always was, in a full-length white, cotton robe. A simple white rope belt cinched the robe at the waist. Mosi had sandals on his feet. Around his neck was a valuable golden pendant, shaped like the sun. Kita knew it to be a symbol of the Light, the god Mosi followed, and had personally witnessed the priest curing many terrible injuries with that focus.

Kita nodded her thanks to the priest of Hishan and turned to look at the huge hulking Nubian sat across from him, filling an entire couch with his bulk. Okoth was sitting forward, listening intently to everything that his friends were saying. Okoth looked up into Kita's dark brown eyes but was unable to hold them for long. "I'm sorry Kita, but I do not know what to do. You make a very convincing argument, but I feel that I owe Reynard my life and that I should travel with him," Okoth's eyes flicked to Reynard, where he stood by the window.

"You owe me nothing Okoth," replied Reynard. "If you ever did then you have paid it back a hundred times. You are a trusted companion and a good friend. I would love for you to accompany Tani and me on our trip around the empire, but you are free to make your own choice."

Okoth looked back and forth between Kita and Reynard, his customary white smile missing from his usually cheerful face. He looked forlorn, something Kita had never seen before.

"I agree with Reynard on this," said Kita. You need to make your own mind up about what you do, and you should not feel that you are letting anyone down. "

"Give me a day or two. I will tell you my decision then," said Okoth miserably. Dressed in the traditional outfit of his homelands Okoth was wearing comfortable leather trousers and boots. In acknowledgement of the growing cold as autumn set in, he had taken to wearing a woollen blanket wrapped around his shoulders. Even sat down it was obvious he was a giant. At just over seven foot tall and ripped with muscles, he cut an imposing figure.

"That is fine, Okoth," replied Kita. "I have to try and work out how I am going to get to Albion. That will take me a while."

"Albion?" queried Reynard. "Where is that? And why do you need to go there?"

"Albion is a small country on the far side of my empire, Honshu," she answered. "It's only a small place but home to a surprisingly large number of important people. One of them is the *wu-jen* Camero. He laid the charge on my father to investigate the Writhing Death. It is to him I need to report. However, I have no idea how I am going to get there. It will take many long weeks to sail and ride there from here."

"I may be able to help there," interjected Mosi. "I know Albion a little. My home country of Hishan borders the Kingdom of Albion on the far side from Honshu. Recently we have had improved relationships with the Kingdom. The faith of the Light is strong there, though their church is structured differently to ours. Reynard, I believe you once told me that the town here has a temple dedicated to the Light, is that correct?" he asked.

"Indeed it is, down near the waterfront, just up from the stevedores' offices."

"Then I will pay them a visit. They may be able to help with swift passage to Albion," he said smiling.

Kita wondered what mystery the priest was hiding but decided not to pry. No doubt all would become clear in time.

*

The Temple of Light in Providentia was an impressive building. Built of local grey granite, it rose above the buildings around it. The temple was fronted by a series of large granite columns, supporting an arched roof. The arched roof had a huge golden sun disk emblazoned on the front of it which was positioned such that at sunrise the sun would catch the disk and reflect out across the area in front of the temple, bathing it in golden light. Steps of sandstone led up to the front and it was a mark of how long the temple had stood that the passage of many feet had worn the steps down severely in places. A lone acolyte was out on the steps, washing the sea salt and fallen leaves from the surface as Mosi approached. The priest from Hishan stopped next to the acolyte and bowed in greeting. "Well met, brother," he began. "I am Mosi, priest of the Light from Shelech in Hishan, at your service."

The acolyte seemed confused and befuddled, clearly not used to being addressed by foreign visitors. He quickly recovered, though. Stopping what he was doing, he rose to his feet and brushed his white robes down quickly, removing some dirt and a stray leaf from his front.

Mosi was struck by the quality of the robes this acolyte wore. Of well-made cotton, the robes looked almost brand new and fitted the young man perfectly. The garment was trimmed with yellow thread in subtle patterns and a faintly seen sunrise was embroidered into the chest. A white leather belt, again trimmed with yellow thread, completed the ensemble. Mosi compared this to the simple robe he wore. His was basic, with no embroidery and was held together by a rope. He had owned his for ten years – since the Haji of Shelech had ordained him. He did not expect to be getting a new one any time soon.

"Well met, brother", said the acolyte with a deep bow. "What can I do for you?" It appeared he had recovered his poise now.

"I seek an audience with the High Priest here. Is he available?"

"Brother Fabian is inside. Would you like me to take you to him?" asked the young man.

"I am sure I can find my way, but thank you all the same," Mosi replied, with another bow. "I would not disturb you from your duties."

The acolyte smiled and bowed again, returning to his knees, his bucket and his scrubbing. Mosi passed on up the last few steps, between the huge granite arches and on into the temple proper.

The interior of the temple was even more impressive than the exterior. If the outside spoke of power and stability, the inside spoke of opulence and wealth. Gold was everywhere. The main doors led directly into the main worship hall. This was rectangular and stretched away from Mosi as he entered. Two neat rows of wooden pews were laid out side by side and an aisle led down the middle towards the High Altar at the far end of the room. The High Altar was dominated by a huge golden sun disk, which hung from the ceiling on golden chains. White cloth, heavily trimmed with gold, covered the white marble altar slab itself. Even the pews were covered with white cloth, embroidered with gold. A thick carpet ran the length of the centre aisle. This carpet depicted scenes of angels and other holy beings, frolicking and playing, all bathed in shining light.

A tall man stood up on the High Altar, behind the marble altar slab. Dressed in immaculate white silk robes, it was instantly clear that this was someone of great importance. Mosi moved down the centre aisle and approached the altar. As he did so, he took in more details of the man ahead. He was greying, with his hair well cropped. What hair he did have, he had oiled down, as if he feared to lose control of it. The robes he wore were sublime. In perfect condition, as if never before worn, they did not have a single crease out of line. They were covered with shining golden thread and a huge sunburst was embroidered onto the man's chest in more gold. Mosi recalled that the acolyte had a subtle sunrise on his chest. Perhaps this was some symbolism of the relative ranks of the two men. Whatever, it was clear this man was far more important than the acolyte outside.

"Well met, brother," Mosi bowed deeply as he approached. "I am looking for Brother Fabian, the High Priest."

"Then you have found him," replied the figure, loftily. "And who, pray tell, are you?" he demanded.

"I am Mosi of Shelech", he replied humbly.

The High Priest frowned, as if thinking hard. "Ah," he exclaimed presently, "you are the one who arrived here with the Earl's son, are you not?" The High Priest looked at Mosi as an owl might look at a mouse.

Mosi had been through a lot over the last year and it would take more than an imperious priest to cow him. "I am," he replied simply, his dark eyes looking straight back at the High Priest's, "and I come here to ask a favour of your temple," he finished.

The High Priest's eyes flashed with annoyance before his face recovered its composure. "What would that be, brother?" he asked coldly.

"I would like to make use of your Translocator," Mosi replied, holding the other's gaze.

The High Priest blinked twice as his brain took in the unusual request. "You want to be translocated?" he asked rhetorically. "Why?"

"Why is my own concern," Mosi replied, deciding that this man did not deserve or need to know any more than the bare minimum. "Perhaps 'where?' would be a more appropriate question?"

The High Priest went red, and looked shocked. Mosi felt that he was probably unused to being spoken to in that way. Mosi had already decided that this man deserved no respect and was not going to give him any more than was needed.

"Okay, then, where?" asked the High Priest after a moment. It seemed to Mosi as if he had completely upset Brother Fabian's balance. As an outsider dressed in what amounted to rags in this temple, yet a trusted companion to the Earl's son, Brother Fabian was clearly unsure what to make of him.

"To the Cathedral in Littlebrook, in the Kingdom of Albion," said Mosi. "Please," he added almost as an afterthought.

"Albion? That is a very long way away – almost the other side of the world. That will take resources. Plenty of resources," said the High Priest, eyes beginning to shine brighter as an idea took hold in his head. "Of course we can translocate you. For a suitable donation..." he finished, smiling.

Mosi understood. Although he himself possessed nothing more than the old robes he was dressed in, Brother Fabian knew he was friend to the Earl's son. And he knew Reynard had money.

The Translocators were an ancient device of arcane origin. Mystical circles dotted about various places around the world, they provided a transportation network for those privileged enough to be able to use them. With the correct ritual, any two Translocators could be linked for a short period of time and anyone or anything could pass between them in either direction. Most of these devices were situated deep inside the Temples of the Light around the world, but some could be found in other locations. In order to link two Translocators, one needed to know the unique key for both the source and destination circle. Knowledge of these keys was a closely guarded secret and only the High Priests of each Temple typically knew the codes.

Powering the ritual to open a portal between one Translocator and another consumed valuable arcane materials and the further apart the two circles were, and the longer the portal was to be kept open for, the more materials would be consumed. Mosi had no idea of the precise details, but he knew Translocation was not cheap.

"How much do you want?" asked Mosi, getting straight to the point.

The High Priest quoted a figure. Mosi was not certain of the relative value of gold here in Lucarcia compared with his homeland, but it sounded like an extortionate amount to him.

"I will see what I can do," he said, bowing perfunctorily to the High Priest and turning to leave.

The Haji of Shelech – the High Priest of his order – had sent Mosi to Lucarcia to find out about the cults and behaviours of the churches that followed the Light in this part of the world. This was his first ever experience of the orders here and he was not impressed. This was clearly an organization which prized gold and wealth above spirituality, and Mosi did not think this was what the Church of the Light should be like.

"I hope you found what you were seeking," the acolyte's voice broke into his musing.

Mosi had passed back outside and was on the sandstone steps. The acolyte was looking up at him from his position on the floor, still cleaning. He appeared to be doing a good job of his work and was nearly complete.

"I think I have done, yes, thank you," he replied. Mosi wasn't sure he was pleased with the results, however.

*

"How much?" demanded Reynard, incredulously.

"I know. I thought it was a lot to ask, but it is hard for me to tell. Lucarcia appears richer than my homeland of Hishan," Mosi replied.

"Well I can tell you not many people would be able to afford that 'donation'," responded Reynard. "But as it is so important, I'm sure my father will agree to it," he said. "If not, I'll just steal it anyway," he finished with a grin.

"Thank you Reynard. Thank you very much. This help will enable Kita and me to reach Albion in a matter of moments rather than weeks or months."

The two had sat themselves in the lounge aboard the *Javelin*, the ship the group had been slaves aboard and which they had commandeered from its Guild captain earlier in the year. The lounge was sumptuously appointed and Mosi had always enjoyed his rare moments spent in the captain's quarters. He sipped at a vintage glass of Pembrose Red, imported from Manabas and closed his eyes. Too soon, he would be back on the road again, off facing adventure and peril. He was determined to enjoy the last moments of relaxation.

"Father has never liked Brother Fabian," Reynard confided, "and from what you have told me I can see why."

"Indeed," agreed Mosi. "It saddens me to see such devotion to wealth and opulence. I feel they have lost their way and are falling into shadow away from the Light. I would have nothing to do with them, but we need their help. There really is no other way."

"Agreed," said Reynard, sipping at his own glass of red. He had his long polished black boots up on the low table in the centre of the room, and he too was enjoying a moment of peace. He also knew they were enjoying the calm before the storm.

"So, what do you plan to do next, Reynard?" asked the priest. "The Trade Lords will be wanting their armour back."

The mysterious and dangerous Trade Lords, leaders of the Guild of Master Merchants and Sea Farers, had tasked the group with recovering the Armour of Lucar. The group had won the prize but had yet to return it to the Trade Lords. The leaders of the Guild were not people to cross lightly.

"I'm not sure, to be honest. I know that the empire must be held together. I will not let it collapse into civil war, yet I don't know what I can do to stop it. The armour could be a powerful tool, but how do I use it? To what ends do I put its powers of persuasion?" queried Reynard. "I need a way to bind the empire together."

Mosi considered this. Reynard and Tanithil, natives of the Lucarcian Empire, wanted to stay here and do what they could to serve the empire in this troubling time. The four major remaining noble houses – the Ebon, Ruby, Snow and Jade Houses – were all plotting and scheming their ascendancy in the wake of the collapsing power of the once ruling Azure House. Without direction, the Empire of Lucarcia would soon plunge into civil war, ripping itself apart from the inside.

Meanwhile a terrible evil – a plague of crawling, biting, stinging and all-consuming insects and aberrations – were pouring onto the cursed island of Granita through a recently reopened portal to the Void. If not checked this reoccurrence of the catastrophic Writhing Death would eventually destroy Lucarcia from the outside.

"Perhaps what the nobles and merchants of this empire need is a common purpose? If you can give them a strong-enough reason to bind together perhaps you can avoid the civil war you fear. Perhaps that common purpose could be the Writhing Death? You are an insightful man, Reynard. You know that what Kita says is true; given time the curse on Granita will be the most deadly and destructive threat your empire has ever seen. You have seen it first-hand. You can explain it to the noble and merchant houses. With the Armour of Lucar, you have the power to make them believe you. That is your cause. Unite them together to stop the Writhing Death."

Reynard considered this. He quickly realised it was a brilliant idea. With this approach, he knew he could save the empire from both the internal and external threats to it, all in one fell swoop. All he had to do was convince the warring factions to stop fighting one another and come together under one banner to save the empire. How hard could it be?

*

The rain was just holding off as the group met down on the Providentia waterfront. Dark clouds scudded in on a brisk wind and there was water in the air. Alongside the jetty, the *Javelin* was at anchor, ready to sail. The crew scampered about in the rigging and Birgen, the boatswain, was ordering them about, making final preparations. The tide was almost full and the group had met to say their goodbyes.

Tanithil hugged Mosi, wishing him well and a safe journey. The priest hugged the telepath back and prayed that he walked in the Light wherever it took him. Tani moved next to Kita and kissed her lightly on the cheek. "Farewell Kita. I hope that fortune follows you and that you are successful in your endeavours. The gods know we need you to be," he finished.

"You too, Tanithil. I still wish you were coming with us, but I understand your reluctance," she replied. "Look after Reynard for me – keep him safe and out of trouble," she said quietly, looking over Tanithil's shoulder at the young noble as he said his farewells to Mosi.

"I will, fear not. We will meet again Kita, I am sure of that."

"I hope so," she said with a small neat bow, which she held for longer than usual.

Reynard and Mosi had embraced and said their farewells. The Earl's son turned to the hulking Nubian stood next to him, and looked up into the giant's face. "What is it to be then Okoth?" he asked the huge black-skinned fellow. "Are you boarding the *Javelin* with Tanithil and me, or staying here to travel on with Kita and Mosi?"

"It has been a really hard decision, little man," said Okoth. "You saved my life when you helped me escape from the slavers, and I really thought I would follow you anywhere you went. But the Writhing Death has changed everything. It needs to be stopped. Kita's father's quest must be completed. I feel my place is by her side, helping to do just that. I'm sorry."

Reynard reached out and hugged the huge man. "Do not apologise my friend. It has been a great pleasure to know you and I consider it an honour to count the great Okoth, Champion Gladiator of Nubia, as a friend. Farewell," he said, "and look after Kita for me please," he finished. "She has a terrible tendency to get herself into all sorts of trouble if not watched." He smiled his easy smile and Okoth broke out into his customary white-toothed grin. Kita could not help but smile at the two friends, even if the joke they shared was at her expense.

Okoth took Tanithil up into a huge bear hug and lifted him high off the ground. The two didn't even exchange a word. There was no need. They knew there was huge shared admiration and affection between them. Tani waved goodbye to them all and strode up the gangplank and onto the *Javelin* where he dropped down a ladder and out of sight.

Mosi and Okoth said one last farewell to Reynard and then set off back along the waterfront. Mosi was going back to the Temple of the Light in order to finalise their use of the Translocator, and Okoth was carrying the considerable sum of money that the Earl had agreed to donate for its use.

Kita and Reynard were left alone on the dock. Rain began to fall, a light drizzle which quickly soaked anything left out in it. Reynard took

Kita's hands in his and pulled her in close, sheltering her from the rain with his body.

"Are you sure you won't come with me?" she asked him one last time. "We could use your skills in the upcoming quest."

"My skills?" he asked, smiling. "Is that all you'll miss of me? I have a plan Kita. Well, to be fair it was Mosi's idea, but it's brilliant." He proceeded to lay out Mosi's idea of using the threat of the Writhing Death as a catalyst to strive for peace and cooperation between the noble houses, in an effort to avoid the civil war he was so concerned about.

Kita looked up into his steel blue eyes and smiled. "I am pleased, Reynard. At least this way I feel we are both working towards my father's quest, even if we will do so apart." The drizzle was really soaking them now and Kita's hair was stuck to her face. Reynard brushed it out of her eyes with a gentle stroke.

"I am sad that we will not be together in this," he agreed. "But I am happy to think that I will be honouring your father's memory, as well as working to protect my family and their interests and responsibilities."

"It is funny to hear you talk of responsibility," she said looking up into his face. "Six months ago, nothing would have been further from your mind."

"Yes," he laughed, "you are right. Things have changed. I have changed. But one thing remains. You are still the same beautiful woman who caught my attention in the depths of the slavers galley – though that feels like a lifetime away.

Reynard leaned in and kissed Kita deeply. This time she did not resist.

-Chapter Two-

The three-masted carrack turned westbound and headed into the prevailing winds, sails flapping noisily in the stiff breeze. Off the starboard rail, the coastline of southern Ursum drifted by as the ship headed out of Providentia. Reynard turned to the boatswain and handed him the wheel. "The *Javelin* is yours, Birgen," he announced formally.

The boatswain, his greying hair pulled back into its customary ponytail, nodded curtly and stepped up to the wheel. "Aye, aye sir," he responded.

Reynard moved swiftly down the ladder to the main deck and crossed to his quarters, where he knew Tanithil was already waiting for him. Around him, the crew diligently applied themselves to their allotted tasks. They were working hard and harmoniously to get the ship up to speed. Reynard pushed open the door from the deck, passed along the short corridor into the tiny complex of three rooms and opened the door to the sumptuously appointed lounge.

Reynard was nervous about this meeting. He planned to tell Tanithil that he was going to wear the magical Armour of Lucar, and he knew Tani would be against his decision. The silver-haired Lucarcian had often warned Reynard of the potential dangers in donning the armour and Reynard knew he would not be happy.

Tanithil was standing with his back to the door, holding onto the wall with one hand for support as the ship rose and fell over the gentle swell beneath it. He appeared engrossed in a book and Reynard wondered if he had heard him enter. "You're right," he said, snapping the book shut and turning to face Reynard. "I'm not happy." Tanithil was a telepath and had a talent for reading people – if not specifically pulling words from their minds, at least for telling something of their emotional state, especially when it was heightened, as Reynard's was now.

"It is the only way we will be able to succeed," responded Reynard, crossing to the drinks cabinet and taking out a bottle of Pembrose Red. Uncorking it expertly, he poured two glasses and handed one to Tanithil.

The telepath declined his offer. "It's a little early for me, thank you," he stated, flatly.

"I have to go out there and somehow try to unite four warring noble houses and the Guild under one cause. I will not be able to do that alone, without help," said Reynard, putting one glass down and taking a sip from the other.

"I will be there to help," replied Tani.

"And I'm going to need you," came back Reynard. "But I think we need more than just us two. We need the edge that the armour can give us." The Armour of Lucar enabled the wearer to influence people. It could completely dominate weak minds, and even those with strong personalities could be temporarily influenced, as Reynard had found out first hand when Captain Kester had used it to charm him back on Granita.

"We don't know what effect wearing the armour will have on you, Reynard," responded Tanithil, his intense violet eyes staring into Reynard's steel grey ones. "Kester was virtually psychotic by the end, and I think the armour could have been at least partially responsible."

"We've been through this before, Tani," countered Reynard. "His diary showed him to be unhinged before he even came across the Armour of Lucar."

"True," Tanithil conceded, "but it certainly seems that the armour may have made things worse."

"You don't know that, Tani. You're guessing."

"At least let me have more time to study the armour, to read of its history," Tanithil pleaded.

"I'm sorry, there is no time. We need to go and visit the Trade Lords and we need to go now. They are waiting for us to return the armour to them and if we don't get to Cansae soon they will send people after us. I would rather avoid that.

"We need to go there and try to convince them to unite with the noble houses against the common threat of the Writhing Death. I need to convince them that I should continue to wear the Armour of Lucar. There is no way I am going to face the Trade Lords without that armour on. I will need every edge I can get for that meeting.

"No, I'm sorry, Tani, but I've made up my mind. I'm going to wear the Armour of Lucar."

"I just hope I'm wrong then," finished Tanithil.

*

A few days later, the *Javelin* skipped west on a following breeze, sails full and prow dipping into each crest as it powered onwards. Amidships, a small group of sailors stood in rows, in deep and well-balanced stances. Standing at the front of this group was Florus, one of the crew. He was barking out numbers in the language of Honshu and as he did so, the group all moved from one stance to another. They snapped out kicks, punches and strikes as they moved, each crewman moving as fast and powerfully as they could, whilst still maintaining balance on the shifting deck.

During her time on the *Javelin*, Kita had slowly built up classes, teaching the crew the skills of the unarmed warrior that she had learnt in her far-away homeland of Honshu. Now she had left the ship, many of the crew had decided to continue on training. Florus had proved to be the most advanced of all her students and when he had asked her what the crew should do now she was leaving; she had said that he should continue to teach them. All agreed to this arrangement and he had taken over her role as teacher.

The classes were smaller now, some of the students deciding that they didn't really want to train under Florus, having less respect for his skills than those of Kita. Some continued to train and about a dozen men would be up on deck every day, going through the routines Kita had taught them. They were definitely improving.

From his position at the front of the class, stood near the door into the captain's quarters, Florus called out the next series of moves he wanted the class to perform. He shouted for them to begin and they sprang into action. Then suddenly the class stopped in mid combination. Florus frowned irritably, wondering what could be so important that it would interrupt his class. The students stood, staring past him with various looks of awe and wonder on their faces. Florus spun, only to find his mouth dropping open and all sense of irritation gone.

Captain Ferrand had just appeared on deck. He was arrayed from head to foot in shining golden armour. The soft autumn sunshine glinted off the polished surface and lit up his face. His was a face of power, the face of a leader. Here was a man the crew were proud to call their captain. Here was a man they were proud to follow.

Reynard moved to the forecastle, quickly and easily climbing the ladder up from the main deck. He could not believe how light the armour was, it was only when he looked down and saw the golden colour that he remembered he was wearing it. Looking across the main deck, Reynard saw that the crew there had stopped training and were all looking up at him. The easterly winds blew his hair out of his face as he looked on. "Carry on, men," he commanded from his lofty position. Instantly the group returned to their training. A bystander would have noticed an improved sharpness to their lesson from that moment on. The men were faster, neater, more concentrated and focussed. Their captain was watching them and they wanted to impress him.

*

The Red City of Cansae was busy. Many carracks and caravels had anchored in the harbour and the *Javelin* had had to wait for a berth. With the ship tied up, Reynard and Tanithil were making their way along the waterfront away from the harbour and up to the stunning white marble building, which was the Guild Hall.

Passers-by stopped and looked in wonder as the two made their way up through the city. They stared openly and even adults could not help but point at Reynard, arrayed in his golden armour.

"Well, we're hardly making a subtle entrance, are we now?" asked Tanithil.

"No, I guess not," replied Reynard smiling. "But that was never the intent, was it?"

"The Trade Lords are going to know we are coming," Tanithil continued. "That will give them an edge."

"Maybe", conceded Reynard, "but they won't be expecting what we are going to tell them. In that respect we will definitely surprise them."

"I couldn't agree more," said Tanithil. "Let's hope they listen."

The two reached the huge white building that was the main base of the Guild of Master Merchants and Sea Farers. The Guild Hall stood at the top of a rise, overlooking the harbour and the Aper Sound beyond. Made entirely of white marble, it was three stories high and shone brightly even in the weak autumn sun of late afternoon.

Two guards in polished chainmail with long spears stood to attention either side of the entrance doors. As the pair approached, the guards dipped their spears and crossed them over the doorway, blocking the entrance.

"Afternoon gentlemen," said Reynard, smiling his easy smile. "We have an appointment with the Trade Lords, your esteemed employers."

Tanithil glanced sideways at Reynard, knowing that they had no such appointment and that they had just turned up here unannounced. The guards looked at each other and back at Reynard, who continued to smile at them in a friendly manner.

"Yes, sir. Right away sir," said the first guard, lifting his spear aside. The second guard looked back from his associate to Reynard and back again. Reynard smiled at him and raised an eyebrow quizzically as if asking why he had not moved out of the way.

"Of course sir, apologies," came back the second guard, swiftly moving his spear aside and opening up passage into the interior of the Guild Hall.

"Thank you, both," smiled Reynard as he and Tanithil entered the base of the Guild.

Tanithil waited until they were inside the entrance hall before he stopped Reynard with a hand on his golden arm. "Was that you being charming or the armour's power?" he asked Reynard.

"I have no idea," said Reynard in reply. "All I did was to be my usual self. I didn't feel anything different to usual, but I have to agree that they did seem to let us in rather easily. They didn't even ask our names. I can see this armour being very helpful in the months to come," he grinned.

"Just don't grow to rely on it," advised Tanithil sagely. "Some minds are stronger than others".

"Gentlemen, welcome to the Guild Hall," came a clear voice from across the entrance hall, breaking into their discussion. Looking up Tanithil saw a tall, blonde Lucarcian woman striding confidently across the white marble floor towards them, a smile of perfect white teeth beaming from her pretty face. Her hair was long, flowing down to her waistline in gentle waves, and her eyes were ice blue and stunning to look into. She moved with grace and poise, with a subtle sway of her hips, which was almost mesmerising. Dressed in black knee high boots, in tight fitting black trousers and a white blouse, which was open low at the front, she cut a very striking and attractive figure.

"Well met, milady," replied Reynard, smiling his easy smile back, and bowing in a courtly fashion as she approached them. Reaching out his hand, he took hers and brought it to his face, kissing the back of it lightly.

"Ah, you honour me, sir. Such gentlemanly ways are rare here in these times," she said blushing. Tanithil was amazed to find she looked even more beautiful with flushed cheeks.

"I am Reynard Ferrand, son of the Earl of Providentia and captain of the *Javelin*," he introduced himself, continuing to hold her hand. Tanithil was aware that the two had not broken eye contact since they had met. A flash of jealousy crossed his thoughts but he steadied his breathing and used an old Thought Guard trick to dismiss the unwanted emotion. This was no time for such feelings.

"I know that," responded the woman, making no effort to remove her hand from Reynard's. "I am Evantia and I am to be your guide here in the Guild Hall. I am Varus' replacement. I have been expecting you for some time now, Reynard. You took longer to arrive than expected." Varus was the last contact the group had from the Trade Lords. He had turned out to be in the employ of the corsair, Captain Kester, and had fought at Kester's side. Reynard had killed him in a duel.

"Apologies, we were delayed. You know how these things are," Reynard said, finally releasing her hand.

"Yes, of course, I know," she said, absently rubbing her hand where Reynard had kissed it. "Now, the Trade Lords are expecting you, of course, but without knowing exactly when you were to arrive it was impossible to determine a meeting time. Therefore, if you would be so kind as to wait, I will arrange an audience. It will take a day or so but I can assure you that you will be my top priority.

"In the meantime, I suggest you check into the Weeping Swindler Inn, just around the corner from here. Despite its name it is one of the premiere inns in the city and definitely suitable for one such as yourself."

"Thank you, Evantia, you are most kind. We will do as you suggest and await your pleasure in the inn," said Reynard, bowing once again. "Until we meet again," he continued, spinning on his booted heel and striding importantly across the hall, back to the entrance door.

Evantia watched him go, never taking her eyes off him, then, once he was out of the doors and out of sight, she too turned and headed off into the crowds inside the Guild Hall and disappeared from sight. Tanithil shook his head, aware that the two of them had hardly even noticed he was there through the entire conversation.

*

"It's too valuable to leave in our quarters, Tani," explained Reynard, defensively. The two were about to head down to the common room of the Weeping Swindler, and Reynard was still dressed in the golden Armour of Lucar. Tanithil was trying to get him to remove it.

"But is it really necessary to wear it to dinner?" came back the telepath.

"I appreciate it's perhaps not traditional formal wear but you have to admit, it does look good," responded Reynard, smiling easily.

Tanithil was concerned. One thing they had noticed about Captain Kester, when they had been tracking him across the empire, was that he was easy to follow, as he was always wearing the golden armour – so people everywhere remembered that he had passed by. As far as

Tanithil could tell, Reynard had not once removed the Armour of Lucar since he had originally donned it a week or so ago out to sea on the *Javelin*. His reasons always had merit and made sense but still, it was disconcerting.

"I'm not sure that the inn keeper will be too pleased with you scuffing up his chair with your armour, Reynard. This is not some cheap waterfront hostel where everyone is armed. This is a plush establishment."

The Weeping Swindler was, as Evantia had promised, a fine inn. Built over two floors, it sprawled across a corner of two main roads. Low wooden beams and warm, deep piled carpets in the halls and rooms made the whole place feel very cosy. The common room was large, also built over two floors. Many staircases led between the floors and there were a few small platforms set up in between floors, which functioned as select dining areas. Here diners could eat in relative privacy, whilst still being close enough to the main area to enjoy the atmosphere and hear the enchanting sounds of the harpist who was playing in a corner.

"Anyway," came back Reynard. "I'm not taking it off now. We're already late. Let's head down to the common room."

Tanithil sighed and allowed Reynard to lead him out of their quarters, down the corridor to the sound-proof door that led onto the main common room. The noble's son pushed open the door and moved into the room beyond. Conversation quickly died away as people became aware of the man in the golden armour, but this inn was upmarket enough that people were well bred and didn't stare for too long. They politely went back to their meals and their conversations, only occasionally stealing furtive glances at the man in the beautiful, ornate armour.

Tanithil and Reynard took a table on one of the raised platforms, half way between the two floors. This one had comfortable wooden couches on three sides, boxing it in. In the middle was a long table, and the open end of the platform fed stairs leading up and down. They were soon settled in place and one of Reynard's easy smiles quickly dispelled any discomfort the waiter may have shown about a man wearing full armour in his inn.

Dinner was delicious. A spicy butternut soup was their starter, served with hot bread, dripping with butter. For their main courses, Reynard chose local lamb, cooked so it was still just bloody and Tanithil feasted on deep-sea lantern fish, cooked in a garlic and cheese sauce, a speciality of the Cansae region. They were just finishing up their deserts – a chocolate and coffee cream mixture from far-off Khemit – and supping on the last of their bottle of sweet desert wine from Ibini, when a voice broke the comfortable silence they were enjoying.

"Hello Reynard. I hope you don't mind me coming to find you here?"

Tanithil looked up to see Evantia standing at the end of their table. She was wearing a figure-hugging silk dress of blue and black, which left nothing to the imagination. Her wavy blonde hair was pulled up into a ponytail on the left side of her head and her hair cascaded down her bare back, over her left shoulder. Her lips shone with a red gloss and her ice blue eyes were bright and clear. Her smile was stunning and she was tiling her head in an enchanting fashion.

Tanithil wrenched his eyes from the vision and turned to look at Reynard. His mouth was split in a boyish grin and his eyes were roving. Evantia was clearly happy with the response her outfit had provoked.

"Of course not my dear," Reynard finally responded. "Please, join us," he continued, indicating that she should sit down.

"Actually, I think I'll retire," said Tanithil, deciding he didn't want to be in the same location as Reynard and Evantia.

"Okay, no problems," said Reynard dismissively, "I'll see you later," he finished, hardly even looking up as Tanithil rose and set off back for their chambers.

Tanithil moved up the stairs and back to the soundproof door that led off the common room. Before opening the door, he looked back and saw Reynard and Evantia deep in conversation, oblivious to everything else around them.

"And I was worried about the Armour of Lucar affecting his judgement," Tanithil said to himself, shaking his head as he pulled open the door and stepped through.

*

"Captain Reynard, it appears you are missing three members of your team. Where are the three foreigners? Moreover, and most importantly, why do you come here wearing the armour we tasked you with retrieving?" the deep voice came from the grey cowl of the middle Trade Lord.

The Trade Lords held court in a large circular room. A long cedar table had been placed so as to make a wall across the room and behind it were twelve large cedar seats, almost more thrones than chairs. The Fox and Scales standard hung behind the table, covering the rear wall section. Five simple wooden chairs were arranged in a line facing the table. The light in the room was dim, almost dark, with only two flickering torches illuminating the whole of the large chamber. Trade Lords occupied all twelve of the thrones.

Each of the Trade Lords was dressed identically. Wearing grey, deep hooded robes with the hoods pulled up over their heads, none of their faces was visible in the dim light. The long arms of their robes hid their hands, removing any possible way to identify the people under the hoods. It was not possible to tell what sex, race or creed each was. The Trade Lords maintained their anonymity and their reputation for mystery and power in this way.

Reynard and Tanithil were standing in front of the cedar table. Reynard was resplendent in the Armour of Lucar and Tanithil stood next to him, feeling a little insignificant, as he often had done since Reynard had donned the magical armour.

"Gentlemen, ladies," Reynard began, spreading his arms wide, his voice echoing around the room. "The Empire of Lucarcia is under threat – possibly the biggest threat since it was formed some five hundred years ago. The last of Lucar's descendants has died leaving no heir. The line of the Emperors is at an end. The ruling Azure House, now leaderless, appears ready to collapse at any moment. Into this backdrop you sent us to find and recover this armour," he continued, indicating the golden armour he wore. "During our search we have uncovered proof that the four remaining noble houses are each preparing for war – civil war. It doesn't take a genius to know the economic chaos a civil war would cause. This is something the mighty Guild of Master Merchants and Sea Farers cannot afford to let happen."

Reynard paused, letting the message sink in a moment, before continuing. "But this is actually the least of our worries. On the cursed island of Granita, the long-thought closed portal to the Void has been re-opened and the Writhing Death is, even as we speak, once more pouring into our lands." Reynard let his hands drop to his sides.

There was a long silence, as Reynard waited for a response from the Trade Lords. Finally, a female voice from the left side of the Trade Lords queried, "You have seen this?"

"With my own eyes," responded Reynard. "Our group have all been to Granita and have seen the open portal at first hand. The Writhing Death has returned and with it the greatest external threat to this empire since its birth.

"The Writhing Death will not quickly overcome us. It will take time to build and grow. But when it comes, it will be unstoppable. History teaches us this. It took the entire Conclave of High Magi to stop it five hundred years ago. Now, we have no such power left in the empire. All that knowledge and power has gone, lost to the ages. Our only hope to survive the Writhing Death is if we work together, the whole empire united under one cause – that of destroying it and closing the portal through which it comes.

"To this end we cannot afford to fight among ourselves. We cannot afford for the Empire of Lucarcia to tumble into civil war. We must unite, not splinter. We must pool our resources, not pit them against one another. We must stand together against the common enemy. We must remain an empire."

Another long silence followed as the mysterious leaders of the Guild pondered on all Reynard had told them. Tanithil stood letting his mind flow out, letting his senses expand. He could feel strong amounts of concern coming from the Trade Lords. It was clear that they had taken Reynard's point seriously. There was a small sense of befuddlement coming from some of the minds arrayed before him, and he guessed that was the effect of the armour. However most were focussed and concentrated. If the Armour of Lucar was influencing this meeting, it was only really going so far as to encourage the Trade Lords to take Reynard seriously. But that was all they could hope for.

"Do you have a plan, Captain Reynard?" asked the leader of the Trade Lords from his position in the centre of the table.

"I do," Reynard replied simply. He then began to lay out his plan to travel to all the noble houses and recruit each to his cause. He explained that it would be a difficult task but he felt that with the backing of the powerful Guild he could convince the noble houses to join forces. "And that is why I need to keep this armour," he finished. "The Armour of Lucar. All the noble houses will recognise it. All the noble houses will see it as a symbol of unity. All the noble houses will unite behind it."

"I see you have figured out exactly whose armour we sent you to find. We know of its reported powers, and we are aware that by wearing it you will be more likely to convince the noble houses to ally with you," came back the response from the Trade Lord. "Yours is a bold plan, captain. Do you think you can succeed?"

"I have to," Reynard said simply. "Unless we unite together against the Writhing Death there will be no empire left to fight over. I, for one will not sit idly by while the empire is destroyed. So, as you can see, the Armour of Lucar is vital to the task."

"Okay. So, other than permission to retain the Armour of Lucar, what do you need from us?" asked the Trade Lord.

"In a nutshell, we need an army. We know you can raise a fleet – you did that before when you helped us defeat the corsair, Kester. This time we need something on a much bigger scale. We need troops to fight the Writhing Death."

"I am no historian, captain, but my knowledge of this curse tells me that mere troops will be of little help against the threat of the Writhing Death. Will the creeping doom not simply consume any who go up against it?"

"This is true of the vast majority of the curse," replied Reynard. "Most of it is an unstoppable blanket of crawling, biting, all-consuming insects. However, this time, it has a force of aberrations at its head. These can be confronted, and we will need manpower to do so. Given the super-human power these creatures wield, it will take a small army to engage them. For that, we need you. Remember, if the empire falls to the Writing Death, you will have nowhere left to make your fortunes."

Again, the audience chamber fell into hush as the Trade Lords considered this request. Tanithil expected the Trade Lords to retire to discuss their options, but he could feel a definite sense of acquiescence in the room, as if the men and women in front of him were all feeling inclined to agree to Reynard's request without further discussion. It was clear the armour was working its magic on the assembled group.

"How do you intend to deal with the bulk of the Writhing Death?" asked a new voice from the other end of the Trade Lords' table. "What is to stop it simply engulfing everything in its path?"

"Well," began Reynard, "as I said to you earlier, the noble houses have spent the last months preparing for war. At least one house has been developing a form of warfare which would be extremely well suited for use against a carpet of crawling, biting insects. The Ruby House have been training Pyromancers, and I intend to use them against the Writhing Death."

Tanithil could feel a sense of surprise and shock in the room, which quickly changed to appreciation. It was clear that the Trade Lords had no idea of the secretive training camps of the Ruby House, but that they liked Reynard's plan to use them in the upcoming battle.

"Okay, then captain. I think we are agreed. We will raise a fleet and as many mercenaries as we can to help fight in your war," said the central Trade Lord. "This will take us some time, however."

"That's fine," replied Reynard. "I have an entire empire to travel around in an effort to gain support for my plan. I think it will take me all winter to do so. I don't expect to be ready to confront the Writhing Death until next spring. Does that give you enough time?"

"Yes, I think it does," responded the head Trade Lord. "Now, there is one last thing. If you are to sail off around the empire, talking to all the noble houses and trying to bring them under your banner, and if you are to take the Armour of Lucar with you to do so, then we have one demand."

"What is that?" enquired Reynard.

"We need you to take an emissary from the Guild with you on your trip."

Tanithil's mind flashed back to the last emissary the Trade Lords had forced onto them. Varus had turned traitor and has almost killed Reynard. He hoped this one would be a better choice.

"Who?" asked Reynard.

"My daughter – Evantia," responded the central Trade Lord.

Tanithil's heart sunk.

-Chapter Three-

"Ah, Brother Mosi, you return to us." The voice came from the tall, immaculately dressed figure stood behind the white marble altar at the far end of the temple. The voice held barely supressed contempt.

"Yes, Brother Fabian, I am here, "said Mosi, striding forward towards the altar with purpose. "Allow me to introduce to you my travelling companions. Okoth of Nubia you met when we came here earlier," he said, indicating the giant who was following. Okoth and Mosi had been to the temple two days earlier to pay the extortionate donation Brother Fabian had suggested would enable them to use the Church's Translocator.

Brother Fabian nodded as the group approached, showing he recognised the hulking Nubian. "Indeed," he acknowledged.

"And this is Kita, student of the Niten Dojo," introduced Mosi.

Kita was aware of Brother Fabian's scrutiny as she approached the altar following Mosi. She felt like she was being weighed and measured by his penetrating gaze. She was not sure if she had passed the test. Fabian's eyes narrowed as he watched her. "Well met," he greeted her. There was no warmth in the words. Brother Fabian moved down from the altar. His movements were sure and confident; his stride purposeful and smooth. "Brother Mosi, I have a task for you," the High Priest said, his gaze flicking to the priest from Hishan. As he moved up to Mosi, his hand slipped inside his immaculate white robe and pulled out a bone scroll case. Thin, delicate and decorated with sigils of the Church of the Light, this scroll case was a small hollow cylinder used to protect important messages that priests wished to pass back and forth safely. The case was sealed and it would be impossible to open it unnoticed. It was rumoured that some High Priests had the power to make these cases completely impregnable to anyone other than the intended recipient. Brother Fabian held it out to Mosi. "There is a priest who serves in the Cathedral in Littlebrook," the High Priest continued. "His name is Brother Coenred. He and I did our training in the Seminary together. I want you to deliver this message to him, personally. See that you put it directly into his hands and no one else's. Do you understand?" Brother Fabian leant forward as he spoke, eyes boring into Mosi's face, expression intent, almost hostile. It was not phrased as a request, but as an order.

Mosi took the scroll case from the High Priest, his expression flat and impassive. Kita was impressed with the control that her friend was showing under the intense scrutiny of the senior priest. "I will do as you ask," Mosi replied simply, taking the bone case and sliding it deep inside his worn white robes. "Now, the Translocator?"

"Of course. Come this way," the High Priest responded. Turning on his heel, he led the three friends out of the main worship hall and into a corridor.

The Temple of the Light was less opulent the deeper into its bowels you went, but only marginally so. Nothing that the companions saw compared to the grandeur and splendour of the main hall, nevertheless the whole building was richly appointed. Soft, comfortable carpets filled the corridors. Valuable art works adorned the walls and expensive items were dotted around the place on tables or cabinets. Their purpose seemed nothing other than to show off the wealth of the temple. As the group followed the swiftly moving priest deep into the temple structure, they passed through a few sets of double doors. A pair of warriors in temple regalia guarded each of these doors. These soldiers were wearing chainmail armour and were armed with heavy broadswords. They wore surcoats emblazoned with a shining sun and regarded the armed companions with distrustful stares. It was clear that random visitors to the temple would not be allowed to get this far into the depths of the building.

Presently the group arrived at a further pair of guarded double doors. Passing through these they descended a long set of stairs which switched back on themselves. Kita counted one hundred and twenty five steps to the bottom. The landing at the foot of the staircase contained another of the ubiquitous double doors and another pair of hard-eyed guards. Brother Fabian ignored them and pushed the doors open grandly. He strode forward into the room beyond. Kita and the others followed on his heels.

They entered into a vaulted chamber. The room was some fifty feet across and lit only by torches, placed in sconces on the walls at regular intervals. A dozen guards stood at attention around the edges of the chamber, hands on their swords. They notably relaxed a fraction when they realised that it was Brother Fabian who had entered the chamber, but nonetheless, they kept their hands on their hilts and their eyes alert.

In the centre of the room was a strange sight. A purple circle was etched into the floor of the chamber, perhaps some ten feet in diameter. As Kita got closer she realised the circle was made up of a myriad of tiny runes and glyphs all carved together to make an intricate and delicate pattern. She had no idea what any of the symbols meant but even she could feel the arcane power emanating from the circle.

Next to the circle, just off to one side, was a marble altar. Not as big as the High Altar back in the main worship hall, this was none the less an exquisitely carved block of stone. Dressed with white silk and covered in a dazzling array of golden artefacts, it glinted in the torchlight. Kita idly wondered what all the strange golden devices could be for. Standing behind the altar were two priests in full ceremonial robes of the Temple of Light.

"Welcome to the Translocator," proclaimed Brother Fabian, opening his arms out wide and spinning in place. "You are greatly privileged to have been allowed to see this sacred place."

"And we paid a fortune for that privilege," noted Mosi, quietly.

If the High Priest heard the comment, he ignored it. "Please, wait here whilst we prepare the Translocator and begin the ritual. It will take us a few minutes to open the connection to Albion. Once open, you will see a shimmering picture of a room appear in the space inside the circle. That will be the interior of the Cathedral in Littlebrook. Once that connection is established you can step through and within the space of a heartbeat you will Translocate over a thousand miles!" He was clearly impressed with the arcane might of the device in his control.

Kita, Mosi and Okoth stood idly by whilst the priests of the Light got to work. One of them opened a large book upon the altar and Brother Fabian went and stood between the two priests already there.

He took up the book and began to chant passages from its pages. As he did so, the inert purple circle suddenly pulsed with an arcane light. The room flickered with a violet glow and the air inside the circle grew hazy.

Suddenly the dozen temple guards stationed around the room drew their swords and took a step forward. Instantly Kita's *katana* was in her hand, her *wakizashi* poised to be drawn too. She spun in place, eyes judging distances and speeds, her mind working out which soldier would reach them first.

"Hold!" The command came from a gruff looking temple guard whose livery was slightly more impressive than those around him. Kita judged him their commander. She turned her gaze on him, whilst maintaining peripheral vision on his men. "Sheath your weapons, foreigners. We are merely moving to protect the Translocator." His steel gaze bore into Kita's, challenging her to obey, but not, she didn't think, in an intentionally confrontational way. Rather, here was a man used to having people obey him. "We have no control over who, or what, is on the other side of the connection. It is my responsibility to ensure no unwelcome visitors appear here. Put away your sword and stand behind my men," he continued. "Please," he added as an afterthought.

Kita was a shrewd judge of men and believed what he said. Plus it made a lot of sense to her. She sheathed her *katana*, her eyes never leaving the leader, and moved deftly between the two soldiers nearest her. Okoth and Mosi followed her lead.

"Thank you," said the soldier. "Please wait for my command before you step through the portal – I need to be sure this end is secure first."

The two priests either side of Brother Fabian joined in his chanting and the intensity of the purple glow in the room grew. The lights cast bold shadows on the walls of the chamber, drowning out the torches in their sconces. The droning of the ritual built slowly, rising gently to a crescendo. Kita felt the hairs on the back of her neck tingle as arcane power filled the chamber. One of the priests picked up a small silk bag from the altar. Untying the golden drawstring, he opened the bag. Reverently he tipped it up gently, carefully pouring small measures of fine sand into a golden bowl in the centre of the altar. From her position nearby Kita could see that the sand was being inexplicably consumed as it fell into the bowl. Peering closer, she saw that the sand glittered as it fell. This was no normal sand, she realised – it was fine cut diamond dust.

The circle flared with a pulse of arcane power and wrenching her eyes from the diamond dust Kita turned to see that she could make out a room through the haze in the centre of the circle. The soldiers gripped their swords tightly, prepared for something – anything – to come through. But nothing did. A few seconds passed and then the commander barked out, "Okay! Get moving!" Kita took a deep breath and moved forward into the circle of soldiers. Hoping Mosi and Okoth were behind her, she stepped into the portal.

*

Kita's head spun, her stomach lurched and her eyes saw stars. She was vaguely aware that she had moved from a dim, torch-lit, stuffy chamber, into a sunbathed, bright and fresh room. She was also dimly aware that she was surrounded by armoured men, but her head was spinning and it was hard to focus.

"Who art thou and what is thy business here?" demanded a controlled voice she did not recognise. The language was that of the lands of Albion, but it was an archaic dialect.

"I am Brother Mosi, Haji of Shelech," came Mosi's voice in response. He seemed entirely in control of his senses. Kita briefly wondered how. "I have travelled here from the Empire of Lucarcia under the control of Brother Fabian of Providentia. These are my companions, Okoth of Nubia and Kita of Honshu."

As Kita's head cleared, she took in her surroundings. She was in a grand, high ceilinged room. The room had several large stained glass windows in it, which reminded her of the huge window in the keep in Providentia. These ones showed signs and scenes of the sun – sunsets, sunrises, and eclipses and so on. Natural light was pouring in through the glass, bathing the room in a soft yellow light. She was standing in the centre of a circle of runes and glyphs, these ones painted on the floor in an azure blue. Mosi and Okoth were by her side. Surrounding the portal were a dozen men in full plate armour with white tabards emblazoned with a huge golden sunburst in its centre. She recognised them instantly: Knights of the Sun.

The Knights of the Sun were an ancient order of warriors sworn to the service of the Church of the Sun and the King of Albion. They were all nobles – only those of noble birth, or those who had risen to the ranks of nobility, could be dubbed a knight. As nobles they were the only men in Albion permitted to wear full armour – this was a right of the nobility and no one of lower birth could wear such apparel without risking imprisonment or worse for impersonating a member of the upper classes. The knights were a holy order. They were stationed in a few Chapter Houses around the kingdom, usually attached to larger churches of the Sun. Ultimately they answered to the Cardinal, the leader of the Church of the Sun in Albion.

Kita also knew that there were only a hundred or so Knights of the Sun left. Their numbers had been decimated in the Chaos Wars of a decade or so ago and they had not yet recovered. The tests to become a knight were very hard and not many wished to even take them. Of those who tried only a small number passed. So with only a hundred knights in the kingdom, to have a dozen of them here in this one room was quite a surprise to Kita. It was obviously a very important place. Then again, given that this Translocator was accessible to anyone with the knowledge and resources to open a portal here, Kita could see why it would be deemed vital to protect this location fiercely.

The knight who had challenged them stepped forward, putting his sword back into its jewelled scabbard as he did so. He extended a hand to Mosi and smiled. "I am Sir Osred," he introduced himself, "Commander of the Translocator Guard. Welcome to Littlebrook." Mosi stepped up to him and shook the offered hand.

*

"It's not often we get visitors arriving through the Translocator", said the grey-haired old man in a soft-spoken voice. Cardinal O'Connor, head of the Church of the Sun and second most powerful man in the

Kingdom of Albion after the king, was sitting in a comfortable old armchair, his posture relaxed but upright. He clasped his hands together on his chest and formed a steeple with his fingers. His chin rested on his fingertips. The Cardinal wore simple white robes, subtly embroidered with golden threads in places. He was clearly a big man, tall and once strong. Now aged, his strength had deserted him, but his eyes shone brightly and Kita could tell his mind was still sharp.

They were sitting in a bright conservatory, overlooking spacious green lawns with well-tended flowerbeds and herbaceous borders. A row of ancient oaks lined the end of the gardens, fencing them off from the city beyond. The conservatory had been constructed almost entirely from glass panes, cleverly held in place by thin bands of white wood. The floor was planks of light ash and various green flowering plants were dotted around the room. A set of chairs of differing types and sizes were placed, seemingly randomly, about the area but every chair commanded an excellent view of the gardens from a variety of angles. The glass magnified the autumn sunshine and the temperature in the conservatory was comfortable, despite the chill winds that were swaying the branches of the oaks outside.

Kita sat on a rickety looking wooden chair, which she had found was a lot more stable and comfortable than it appeared just from looking at it. Nearby the giant Okoth lounged on a big two-seater couch, made from local cows' leather. He almost filled it.

"It was quite an experience, your Eminence," replied Mosi. The Priest of the Light was sitting in another comfortable armchair across from the old man. "That was the first time I have ever used one." Mosi stroked his goatee between thumb and forefinger as he spoke.

"So what was the urgency to travel here so quickly? And please, there is no need to be so formal with me. Only the Knights of the Sun use that honorific, and only because they insist on sticking to their ancient dialect," said the old man. As he did so, he turned to another man, who was clad from head to toe in ceremonial armour and standing at a low table nearby, selecting a sweet meat from the array of food that was set out there. "No offense intended of course, Sir Harken," he smiled at the knight.

"None is taken, your Eminence," replied Sir Harken, bowing formally. "It is our duty as knights to uphold the Code, and part of that is to adhere to the old ways, as from them we find the structure which gives strength to the Order." Sir Harken was a large man, not as tall as Okoth but still imposing. His archaic armour was polished to a bright sheen and his white tabard was immaculate. Sir Harken's full helm sat on a table near his chair, leaving his long brown hair to fall down to the pauldrons on his shoulders. His face was stark but not ugly. Sir Harken was head of the Knights of the Sun in Albion and another very important person in the kingdom.

The Cardinal smiled, turned back to Mosi and prompted again, "So, the reason for your journey?"

"Kita here is our leader," Mosi replied, indicating the young Niten warrior on the nearby chair. "It seems most appropriate for her to explain."

"Of course, yes," agreed the Cardinal. "Please do my dear," he invited to Kita.

Kita waited for Sir Harken to select his choice of refreshments from the table and to sit down, and then she rose from her chair and began. "I am Kita, daughter of Heremod of Waymeet, the Albioner who became the first *gajiin* Niten Master at the school in Sapporo," she introduced herself.

The knight and Cardinal both nodded in recognition. "Thine father is well known and respected here, Kita," said Sir Harken.

Kita felt a lump rise in her throat but suppressed the rising feeling of grief. "I am sad to tell you that my father was killed a few weeks ago," she told them, keeping her voice controlled and level. She would not show these strangers any weakness.

"That is sorry news, milady," replied the knight. "Might I enquire of thee how this evil event occurred?"

Kita was surprised at the knight's directness, but knew that the Albioners' customs were vastly different to those of her homeland, so she decided to answer the direct question with a direct answer. "He was killed in a fight with a powerful aberration from the Void," she told them. She went on to explain how they had been on the trail of the pirate

Captain Kester and had tracked him to Granita where they had fought him and his first mate, Baku. She told of the final battle with the pirate and monster and of how Baku had slain Heremod and escaped.

"I am sorry for your loss, Kita," said Cardinal O'Conner in a soft and comforting tone. "We will pray for his soul."

"Thank you," she replied simply. "My father was not originally trying to find the pirate captain. He was actually in Lucarcia in order to look into rumours of strange happenings on the cursed island of Granita." Kita looked at the two Albioners and realised that what she was saying clearly didn't have any particular meaning to them. "I can see I am going to have to explain," she said. "It's a long tale."

*

Later that day the three companions were relaxing in their quarters when there was a soft knock at the door. Kita rose and went to answer it. Opening the heavy oak door, she found a white robed cleric waiting outside. He smiled affably at her, his deep brown eyes meeting hers.

"Well met Lady Kita," he began. "I am Brother Coenred. You asked to see me?"

"Of course, Brother," she said, stepping aside, "Please, come in. Actually it wasn't me that wished to see you, it was Brother Mosi," she said, as she led the priest into the room.

"May I just say, milady, that I am truly sorry for your loss. I knew your father from the times he had spent here in the capital with Sir Colby. I was terribly upset to hear the news. If there is anything I can do for you, you need only ask. Anything at all."

"Many thanks for your concern, Brother Coenred, but I am fine." Kita had been surprised that so many people here seemed to know her father. She knew that many throughout the lands of Albion had heard of Heremod, but she didn't think so many people would know him personally. Now, however, she remembered Sir Colby. Heremod had often travelled with a very good friend of his who was a Knight of the Sun. The two had grown up together in the village of Waymeet. They had gone their separate ways as young adults – Heremod off to the Niten Dojo to learn the ways of the Niten warrior, and Colby off to the capital to try to become a knight. It was rare for common folk to be accepted as squires in the Order of the Sun, but some promising young men and women were enlisted. Colby had succeeded in being appointed as a squire and after five long and hard years had earned his spurs and been knighted by the king here in Littlebrook, thus becoming Sir Colby in the process. After Colby was knighted and Heremod had graduated from the Niten School, they travelled the lands of Albion together for a time. So it made sense that the knights and priests here would know Sir Colby and by extension his friend Heremod.

Mosi rose from his position near the fire where he had just been contemplating his next move in the game of *gi*, which Kita was teaching him. *Gi* was a simple game of strategy played by placing stones onto a grid. It was extremely popular in Kita's native Honshu and she had been delighted to find a *gi* board here in their quarters and had insisted that Mosi try it. The young woman was not going easy on him – he was losing badly. "Ah, Brother Coenred. Please, make yourself comfortable," he said moving to welcome the visitor, happy to have an excuse for a break from the trouncing. "Do take a seat."

The quarters the group had been given were clean, spacious and comfortable. Like all the rooms they had seen since arriving through the Translocator, it was brightly lit by natural sunlight. They had discovered that the Translocator was sited in a room inside the main Cathedral of the Sun in Littlebrook, the capital of Albion. So far, they had not left the Cathedral complex since their arrival. The complex comprised the Cathedral building itself, large well-tended grounds and a big Chapter House which was the home to the Knights of the Sun when not on duty.

Everywhere in this complex, the sun played an important part of the design and every room had large windows to let in as much natural sunlight as possible. It had not escaped the companions' notice that nearly every room had a west-facing window – when the sun set it would be visible from nearly every location in the Cathedral. This was a building dedicated to the sun and to the worship of the deity it represented.

Brother Coenred was short and slim. His hair was shaved nearly entirely off so it was hard to say what colour it may have been but his bushy eyebrows hinted that it was probably a non-descript brown. He sat himself down on a wooden chair near the *gi* board and looked over the pieces. "I believe black is going to lose this game in two moves," he commented almost immediately.

"Two moves?" queried Kita returning to the board. "I think it will take three."

"You are, I assume, thinking of capturing the south west corner of the board next. That is the obvious move and will take three turns, I agree. But I think two well-placed white stones in the north west will finish black off."

Kita studied the board for a moment and realised the priest was right. He had spotted that obscure finish within seconds of seeing the board. He must clearly be a master. "You are correct, Brother," she agreed. "I had not seen that. You are obviously very skilled in the game. Perhaps you would like to play against me after this game is finished?"

"I would love to, milady."

"Excellent," said Kita, intrigued by the cleric's knowledge of her homeland's game. "I will endeavour to complete this game quickly. In *two* moves," she smiled.

"Indeed," he grinned. "Now, Brother Mosi, what was it you wanted to see me about?" enquired Coenred, turning to the priest of the Light with a friendly smile.

"I have this for you," said Mosi, reaching into his robes and pulling out the bone scroll case Brother Fabian had given him. "It was given to me by the High Priest of the Temple of the Light in Providentia. He said that he knew you."

Kita thought she saw a subtle look of surprise and something else cross the priest's face, but it was gone in an instant, replaced once more by the usual smile.

"Yes, of course!" exclaimed Brother Coenred with a grin. "Brother Fabian and I were trainees in the Seminary in Rodin together. How is the old man? I haven't seen him in many years. Is he well?"

"He seems in good health," said Mosi neutrally. "I really only met him a couple of times and not socially."

"I understand," replied Coenred, taking the scroll case from Mosi. "I wonder what he wants. Anyway, it will soon be Vespers," he said, rising from his chair. "I must head off I'm afraid. It was good to meet you both. I will no doubt see you both again soon." With that, the priest headed out of the door, the bone scroll case clutched in his hands.

Kita watched him leave; wondering what had caused him to rush off so quickly. What was the emotion she had seen flicker quickly across his face at the mention of Brother Fabian? Was it fear?

*

Kita reined her horse in sharply, causing it to skid slightly on the wet paving stones of the King's Road. The persistent rain that had been falling since they left Littlebrook the day before had left the highway slippery, as well as drenching the three travellers as they rode north along it. Behind her Okoth and Mosi cantered up to her and drew to a halt more gently.

"What is it?" asked Okoth. "How come the sudden stop?"

"Look at the stand of beech trees up ahead," she replied. "What do you see?"

Okoth peered through the drizzle into the small copse, but couldn't see anything untoward. "Nothing unusual," he replied, "Why?"

"Just under the eaves towards the left as we look. Do you see a light grey patch?" Kita asked.

"Yes, now you mention it, I do. What is it?"

"A helmet I think," Kita answered. "I think there are armoured men in the trees."

"Then shall we go and ask them what they are doing there?" suggested Okoth, his customary white grin spreading across his face as he hefted his spear.

"Indeed," agreed Kita, hand on the hilt of her *katana*.

"Do not be rash," advised Mosi. "They may simply be travellers sheltering from the rain."

"And they may be bandits," countered Kita. "Let us find out which," she finished as she spurred her grey forward at a trot.

As Okoth and Kita approached the woods, Kita's keen ears picked up the sounds of muffled voices coming from the men lurking inside.

"Is that them?" one asked.

"A woman from the east, a priest from Hishan and a dark-skinned giant from the south," said another. "Seems pretty clear to me. It must be them."

"I think they've spotted us," said the first. "Shall we attack?"

"You are correct," shouted Kita loud enough to be heard by those in the small copse. "You have been seen. Now come out of the trees, show yourselves and let's get this over with".

"Fire!" came the shouted reply from the wood, and a volley of arrows flew at the two riders.

Kita instinctively ducked down behind the flank of her horse as a couple of arrows whizzed overhead. The horse whinnied in pain as one arrow drove into its side. She rose to see Okoth with a cut on his arm where an arrow had clipped him. Kita decided that fighting on horseback, inside a wood, on a horse with an arrow in it was a bad idea so she slipped her leg over the saddle and dropped to the floor, landing nimbly on her feet. She was sprinting for the woods instantly, her two swords flashing into her hands as she ran. She heard Okoth bellow a challenge from close behind her. Then she was in the trees.

A sword flashed in the gloom. Kita parried with her short *wakizashi* and spun in place, her *katana* severing the neck of the bandit. Another stepped in from her right and she plunged her short sword into his heart as she looked for the next assailant. Whipping the *wakizashi* out and letting the swordsman slump to the floor, dead at her feet, she spotted two more men hiding behind a leafy bush. She heard Okoth to her right side noisily dispatching other brigands.

Stepping beyond the bush she was faced with two swordsmen dressed in rough leathers. "Put down your blades and you do not need to die today," she told them as she dropped in to a relaxed defensive stance.

The brigands looked at each other as Okoth stepped in beside Kita, his spear in hand. The wood was quiet now, apart from the odd groan of the injured back through the trees.

Suddenly one of the two bandits leapt forward, his sword arching for Kita's head. There was a flash of movement and his arm flew into the bushes nearby, neatly severed at the elbow, still clutching the pitted sword. The man made a gurgling noise as Kita's *wakizashi* drove into his guts. He slumped to the floor as she pulled it clear, and thrashed in place twice before laying still. The remaining outlaw dropped his sword and raised his hands.

*

"That's all I know," repeated the brigand.

The group were huddled in the shelter of the beech trees as the rain increased in intensity. Mosi had gathered the horses and had tended to the wounded animal as well. Okoth had bound the hands of the captured man with some strong twine from his pack and Kita was asking him questions.

"So let me sum up then," replied Kita. "You are part of a band of ruffians who regularly way-lay travellers on this stretch of the King's Road," she started. The man nodded. "Normally you rob people but do not intentionally kill them. But today your leader, that man over there," Kita indicated one of the dead bandits, "told you that you would be ambushing a specific group of travellers – namely us. And that you were to kill us all. Is that correct?"

"That's right," the brigand confirmed. "He said there was good money in it. Said we would be paid handsomely by his patron. I guess we just figured that twelve onto three was good odds and it would be easy money. Seems we was wrong."

"Let's see what we can find on your leader's body then," said Kita moving to where the bandit chief's body lay. Squatting next to him, she heard the faintest groan coming from his lips. "Mosi! Quick, this one still lives!" she called.

Mosi hurried to the leader and looked down. He was amazed that someone who had taken the wounds he had could still breathe. The man's body was covered with blood and a huge gash split his abdomen. His insides were slowly becoming his outsides. Mosi knew straight away that there was nothing he could do. Even with the Light's help.

"He lives, yes, but not for much longer, Kita. He is beyond my power to help. I'm sorry."

Kita knelt beside the brigand. "You are dying," she told him. "Your intestines are leaking into the floor of the forest. I have seen these wounds before. It may take you hours of agonizing pain to die. I can end it in a heartbeat. Just tell me the name of your patron and I will put you out of your misery. Who hired you to kill us?"

The bandit leader's eyes flicked open. They focussed briefly on Kita's. He beckoned her closer and Kita leant over and put her ear to the brigand's mouth.

"Brother Coenred at the Cathedral," he whispered.

-Chapter Four-

"You want to break in?" asked Tanithil, incredulously.

"I'd prefer to go and look for ourselves, rather than having the official tour where they have a chance to cover things up before we get there," replied Reynard, shrugging slightly.

"Yes, I can see the reasons why we might want to go there unannounced, but it is a big risk."

"Agreed," replied Reynard, "But one I think we need to take."

The couple were sitting in the tiered lounge of the Weeping Swindler, sipping on local coffee and discussing their immediate future. A liveried waiter appeared on their platform and the two stopped their conversation whilst he topped up their pot. The waiter bowed politely, turned and moved off to another level where a group of four merchants were gathered. Reynard poured himself and Tanithil a fresh cup and put the pot back on the mahogany table between them.

"Okay, so what is your plan?" asked Tanithil.

"When we were first here, you said you could feel the Pyromancer training hall, correct?"

Tanithil nodded. He remembered the time vividly. He had been letting his senses float out to feel the town around him. Then his senses had been assaulted by a wave of arcane energy. It had not been hard to find the training hall where the Pyromancers were conjuring flame from the Void. "Yes," he said to Reynard, quietly, "I could feel it."

"Good. Then I propose that we wander the city, looking at the sights, and you see if you can locate it again. I'm assuming, of course that it will be in the same place, but even if they have moved it you should be able to find it, given enough time."

Tanithil couldn't think of any other better idea. "Okay", he agreed.

*

The autumn rain lashed down on the pair as they trudged through the streets of Cansae. The Red City looked glum and gloomy in the grey afternoon rain. A light wind was blowing off the Sound and it was unpleasant to be outside.

Tanithil followed Reynard up a long, narrow flight of steps. The stairs were slick with the rain and the red brick glistened, but Tanithil was only vaguely aware of his immediate surroundings. His mind was detached, pushing gently out into the streets around them. He was letting his thoughts float, not particularly directing them other than to keep them external. He sensed the feelings of families huddled in the warm dry shelter of the houses around him. He felt the affection of a mother for her young child, who was trying to learn how to walk. He felt the anger of a young man, frustrated that his parents did not understand that he was an adult now and that they kept treating him like a child.

Tanithil and Reynard moved on through the drizzle. Soon they came to the top of the town, far above the Aper Sound below. Here the city thinned out with space between the buildings growing larger. Ahead the two saw a large red brick building, looming up out of the mist.

The building appeared to be over two storeys and built of the usual red stone from which much of Cansae was constructed. It sported a sloping, arched roof with dark brown tiles that looked almost black in the dim light. A series of windows surrounded the place, but each was shuttered closed.

Suddenly Tanithil staggered and nearly fell. Reynard's quick reactions saved him, the noble's hand flashing out and grabbing Tanithil's arm as he slipped. Tanithil looked up at Reynard, his eyes struggling to focus.

"Something is wrong," said the telepath. "Something is dreadfully wrong."

"What is it?" asked Reynard, concerned for his friend.

"That hall," Tanithil pointed at the building ahead as he struggled to stand unaided. "That is definitely where they are practicing the arcane arts. I can feel the energies – they are almost overwhelming."

"Well done, Tani. But why do you say that something is wrong?"

"The pain. The screams. I can almost hear them, they are so intense."

"What do you mean?" said Reynard, looking into Tanithil's face.

"The Pyromancers – I think they are testing their powers on people. They are burning people alive in there."

*

Reynard's dextrous fingers twitched once and the lock clicked open. Slipping the lock pick back into its small pouch, he replaced it inside an inner pocket. Taking a quick glance around to make sure no one was watching them, he pushed open the door. It swung open easily. After a quick check that no one was immediately behind the door, he stepped in. Tanithil was close on his heels.

The couple stepped into an entrance hallway. A thick rug lay across the flagstone floor and the room appeared richly appointed. Pictures showing various scenes of the local region, the Head of Ursum, decorated the walls. Two torches were burning brightly in wall sconces. A single door lay ahead of them. Reynard noted that the surface of the outside wall, and the door he had just closed, were covered with thick, red velvet. He was wondering what the purpose of the velvet was when a loud scream pierced the air. Then he realised – it was soundproofing.

Reynard pushed the internal door open a fraction and peaked in. Beyond the door was a large open chamber. The walls were all made of the ubiquitous local red brick. The ceiling was supported with arched buttresses that peaked about thirty feet overhead, filling what had seemed like a two storey structure. This was all in the same red brick. The floor was constructed in a similar manner. The whole chamber was spartan with virtually no decoration at all.

The chamber was full of people wearing deep ruby coloured robes, gathered into small groups, although some were standing alone. All around the people were chanting strange words and making erratic gestures with their hands. The air crackled with energy.

Not far from where Reynard peered in, a line of men was standing. They were bound at the wrists. Three soldiers in the uniform of the Ruby House guarded these prisoners. One of the prisoners was wearing expensive looking black clothes, and Reynard's observant eye spotted the crest of the Ebon House embroidered on his chest. It seemed that the Ruby House had captured one of the nobles of the Ebon House and had him prisoner here.

Slightly apart from the other prisoners, one bound man had been dragged out and was standing alone. No one was near him. Instead, a robed figure was standing opposite him, chanting and gesticulating in an arcane way. Abruptly the robed man stopped chanting and waving his arms. His finger pointed directly at the lone prisoner and he shouted a word of power. Instantly the prisoner burst into flames. His screams rent the air as his clothes ignited. He collapsed to the floor, writhing in agony as the flesh melted away from his body. Within mere seconds he was dead, his body rapidly consumed by the arcane fire, leaving nothing behind but a charred husk. The mystic fire had devoured his body in a fraction of the time it would have taken a normal fire to do.

Incensed at this wanton slaughter, Reynard kicked the door to the chamber open and rushed in. His rapier was in his hand instantly and before anyone could react, he had crossed the short distance to the Pyromancer and thrust his sword into the man's back, impaling him through the heart. Blood fountained from the man's mouth and he slumped on the floor, dead. All eyes in the room turned to the man in the gleaming golden armour.

"Kill the intruder!" screamed a tall robed man who was standing off to one side. At his command, the three uniformed soldiers leapt forward, drawing their broad-bladed swords. Reynard, still furious at what he had witnessed, rushed to meet them. He parried the clumsy swing of the first guard and drove his rapier deep into his chest. Pushing him off the end of his razor-sharp blade with the heel of his boot, Reynard spun in place. The other two guards were now either side of him and he realised that his anger had gotten the better of him and he had lost control. Now he was in danger as the two guards circled him warily.

All at once, both soldiers attacked. These two were well trained and knew that by acting in tandem from flanking positions they would make it very hard for Reynard to hold them off. Reynard knew this too.

He blocked a fast sideways strike from the guard he was facing and flicked his light rapier blade up and across, slicing a thin cut across the man's face as he swayed back.

Reynard felt the soldier behind him step in and, faster than Reynard could react, his broadsword slashed into the noble's side. Such a blow should have opened him in two. But Reynard was wearing the golden Armour of Lucar, and though it felt like it weighed next to nothing, it was incredibly strong. The heavy sword bounced off Reynard's side and the soldier almost dropped it. Reynard used the split second of surprise in his opponent to strike. He thrust his rapier low into the man's thigh, spearing it right through. The soldier dropped his sword and fell to the stone floor, clutching his leg. Blood seeped through his fingers. He was out of the fight.

Spinning on his heel Reynard saw and parried the other man's follow up strike, just ducking under the deflected blade. From this low position, he thrust his leg out sideways, holding it extended, and then swivelled around, flicking his hips as he whipped the legs out from under guard. The swordsman crumpled to the ground and Reynard thrust the point of his rapier at the man's throat. The soldier dropped his sword and held his empty hands aloft. Reynard stepped back, letting the weaponless man get to his feet.

Suddenly the leader of the Pyromancers pointed at Reynard and uttered a word of power. The air around the young noble burst into flames and Reynard was engulfed in a pillar of fire. Reynard could still just about make out the chamber through the heat haze of the inferno; but amazingly, he felt very little effect at all from the fire. He noticed it getting a bit warmer and a small bead of sweat dropped off his nose, but he did not catch fire and he did not burn.

As quickly as it had started the flame was spent. Reynard looked around him at the shocked faces. The Pyromancers had all gathered near and were clearly expecting this intruder to have been cremated by their leader's arcane power, but here he stood, seemingly unaffected. Reynard was about to grin but realized that the entire collective of the Ruby House's Pyromancer community were now facing him, intent on his death. He wasn't sure that even the Armour of Lucar could protect him from their combined power.

"Burn him," ordered the leader in a quiet and ominous voice. "Burn him where he stands."

"Hold!" broke in a new voice, loud enough to be heard by everyone in the room. "Hold or your leader dies." Reynard looked across to where the leader was standing and saw Tanithil just behind him. The telepath had a small silver letter opener pressed up against the jugular of the Pyromancer and was pushing it in, threatening to pierce the skin. It seemed that with all eyes on the intruder in the gleaming golden Armour of Lucar, no one had noticed Tanithil creeping into the hall and up behind the leader. Now Reynard let himself grin.

*

Catulus Ruby was the firstborn son of the Dragon. He was proud of his heritage and proud of his family. The Ruby House had ruled the peninsula at the Head of Ursum since before the time of the Lucarcian Empire and they were a strong and noble house.

When Catulus' father, Ignatius Ruby, had given him the task of researching into the ancient rites and rituals of the Pyromancers, Catulus could not have been more proud. He knew that back in the ancient days of the Rainbow Empire, the Pyromancers of House Ruby had been famed throughout the lands. They had controlled fire. They had summoned fire. They had commanded fire. Then the Rainbow Empire had collapsed and the Emperor had banned the study of the arcane arts. So the skills of the Pyromancer had slipped into disuse. The knowledge was lost.

Until Catulus had rediscovered it.

He recalled with pride the day he had found the ancient tome, deep in the catacombs beneath the Dragon Fortress here in the Red City. He remembered his fingers, trembling with excitement, as he opened the dusty book carefully, trying desperately not to break the crumbling pages as he turned them. He recalled being so absorbed in the writing that before he knew it nearly two days had passed and he was still reading. He had found the long lost secrets of the Pyromancer. And he had begun to understand what was possible.

From that day forward Catulus devoted himself to studying the tome. He took to transcribing it onto fresh pages, learning it word for word as he did so. His aim was to preserve the knowledge to make sure that it would not fade away again. Making sure that this lost tome was not the only source of the arcane secrets it contained.

And he began to practice what it taught.

It took him some time, but after a few months of teaching his mind and fingers the complex rituals, he found himself able to master the simplest of skills. It was only then that he went to his father, Ignatius, and told him of his success. His father naturally wanted a demonstration. So Catulus had given him one. He had had the servants lay out the wood for a fire in the Grand Hall of the Dragon Fortress. He had asked his father to join him there and, after dismissing all the servants from the hall, Catulus had lit the fire – with his mind. With the right gestures and the correct words of power, he had opened a portal to the Void and from there had summoned a minor spark – big enough to catch in the silver birch bark laid at the base of the fire. Big enough to set it alight. Big enough, such that ten minutes later the Great Hall was lit and warmed by the merry burning of a full blown hearth fire. He had done it.

His father was pleased. But he wanted more. He charged Catulus to continue in his discoveries, and to expand on his work. Catulus was to pick people with promise that he could trust. He was to make sure they were dedicated to the Ruby cause and that they could keep a secret. And he was to train them in the skills of the Pyromancer.

Catulus had done so. He had built a small cadre of trusted fellows. He had shared his secrets with them and he had trained them. They had grown into a formidable force, slowly growing in numbers and in power.

Catulus had soon realised he needed a place to train. Fire was a destructive force and after nearly burning down his private quarters, he knew he needed to find somewhere safe. His answer came in the red stone that the entire city of Cansae was built from. It turned out that this stone had a powerful property. It was almost entirely resistant to fire.

Therefore, Catulus had a training hall built from it, up on the top of the hill, away from the majority of the city. Here he had trained his men. Here he had resurrected the lost arts of the Pyromancer.

And now intruders had entered their training hall and slain one of his men. Catulus was livid. Unfortunately, he also had a knife held at his throat.

"Who are you and what do you want?" he asked the man in the golden armour before him.

"My name is Reynard Ferrand, heir to the Iron House," the man said. "And I'm here to recruit you."

*

Ignatius Ruby was an old man, past his prime physically, but he was still sound of mind and his voice had lost none of its power or authority. Dressed in simple but elegant clothes cut from fine Honshu silk and dyed the ruby colour of his House, he still cut an impressive sight. He stood up from his comfortable chair in the back of the Great Hall and moved forward.

Ahead of him stood his son, Catulus, dressed in the robes of the Pyromancer. Next to him was a Lucarcian with silver hair and striking violet eyes. These features would have made him of immediate interest had it not been for the two others who stood with him. Beside him was a stunning woman with long blonde hair and bright blue eyes. Had Ignatius been younger he knew she would have stirred his blood, but his age made him immune to the lure of the flesh of young women. Instead, his eyes passed over her and settled on the man next to her. He looked like a man from a legend. A man in golden armour the likes of which had not been seen in this land in many, many years. In fact, Ignatius had never seen it before – but he recognized it instantly. And he knew of the power it was rumoured to possess. Here was a man he must respect and be wary of.

"Welcome to the Dragon Fortress," boomed Ignatius, spreading his arms wide. "Please, friends, make yourselves comfortable; partake of our hospitality," he added gesturing to a long table piled high with food and drink.

The Great Hall of the Dragon Fortress was the meeting hall for all the nobility of the Ruby House. It was a huge chamber, some hundred feet long and half that in width. Torches lined the walls at regular intervals. The head of the hall was dominated by a massive tapestry depicting a colossal fire-breathing dragon – the crest of the Ruby House. Large feasting tables were spread around the main part of the hall, all looking stained with years of spilt wine and ale. There were two huge hearths, one on each side, and a merry fire burned in one. In the depths of winter both fires would be lit but now in autumn only one was necessary.

"Thank you, my lord," said the man in the golden armour, with a friendly smile on his face, "But I am not hungry right now."

"Suit yourself then," responded Ignatius, sitting himself down in the large mahogany throne which was placed at the head of the hall. He knew that by sitting there he asserted his dominance of the room and he realised he needed every advantage he could get in the upcoming exchanges.

"So what can I do for you, Reynard Ferrand? What brings you to the lair of the Dragon?"

"I am here to ask for your help," began Reynard. The young noble then went on to explain about how the portal to the Void on Granita had reopened and how the Writhing Death was, even as they spoke, starting to pour though once more, threatening the very existence of the empire.

Ignatius listened intently to the fantastical tale. He had no reason to believe any of it was made up but suspected that it was probably exaggerated. It would be in the young courtier's interests to make things sound worse than they truly were in order to gain more help.

"And why should I help you?" enquired the Dragon, leaning forward on his throne.

"It is your chance to prove to the people of the empire that your powerful arcane knowledge can be used for good, my lord," replied Reynard. "Five hundred years ago the High Magi were responsible for creating the gate into the Void from which the Writhing Death poured. Because of that, the emperor banned the study of the arcane arts, claiming they were too dangerous. I have seen first-hand how dangerous the Writhing Death is. And I have seen how dangerous your Pyromancers have become," he continued with a sideways glance at Catulus. "I believe they are the key to destroying the multitudinous numbers of crawling, creeping, biting insects which comprise the majority of the threat. The way we will contain them is with the fire your men command. Lend your Pyromancers to the cause and let the people of Lucarcia know that through the powers of your arcane energy the Writhing Death was halted and destroyed, permanently. In this way you prove that arcane power can be a great boon to the empire, and that its ban should be rescinded."

The young woman spoke then. "My name is Evantia and I am the representative of the Guild of Master Merchants and Sea Farers, my lord," she introduced herself, smiling beguilingly at the Dragon. "All know of the great strength of the Ruby House. It would be a great boon to have you on our side," she said.

"Our side?" queried Ignatius.

"Indeed. For the Trade Lords have already pledged their support to this cause. They have realised the massive danger that the Writhing Death poses to our lands and lives. They are with Lord Ferrand."

"He is not *Lord* Ferrand yet, milady, you forget yourself," corrected the Dragon. Turning to Reynard he spoke directly at the young noble, ignoring the others in the room, as if they were unimportant.

"Reynard, I fully appreciate what you have told me. I understand the threat to our empire is real and serious. And I would like to help. However, if I take my eye off the politics of Ursum then there is a real risk that the Ebon House will take over the island. You know that they are preparing for civil war? I cannot afford to concentrate men and time to your cause and leave the interests of the Ruby House unprotected. So, unless you can convince the Ebon Lord to join your crusade then I am afraid I will have to decline my help and that of my Pyromancers."

"So, you will join me if Lord Barrius Ebon also signs up to the cause?" asked Reynard.

"Yes, I will. But under no other circumstances," Ignatius declared.

"Then it is as well that Selkie and the Ebon Lord are my next port of call," returned Reynard. "I will bind them to our cause and accept your word that on their joining us, your Pyromancers will too."

"You have it," stated the Dragon.

"Then my business here is done," said Reynard. "It was a pleasure to meet you, my lord. I will send word once the Ebon House has joined us."

Ignatius Ruby watched the young man in the golden armour turn and leave. At his side strode the beautiful woman and trailing behind them, almost forgotten in their shining presence, was the Lucarcian with the silver hair. Ignatius had hardly noticed him the entire time.

The Dragon waited until they had left and then turned to his son. "An interesting development," he commented.

"Indeed, father. Very interesting," Catulus replied, lost in thought.

Catulus appeared distracted and his father was irritated. What could be more important than the events of the last few minutes? "Is something on your mind?" he asked coldly.

Catulus looked up, as if noticing his father for the first time. "Yes my lord, there is. I have some bad news. It seems that our prisoner from the Ebon House managed to slip out when we were confronting Reynard in the training hall. In the great confrontation, no one noticed him escape. He's gone."

Ignatius was furious.

*

Back on board the *Javelin*, the crew were working hard to prepare the ship for departure. Birgen was among them, chivvying them here and berating them there. The ship was a hive of activity. The tide was rising, they wished to set sail in less than an hour, and there was much to do. As such, he was slightly annoyed when one of the crew told him that there was someone on the dock wanting to speak with the captain. Captain Reynard was in his chambers and did not want to be disturbed so Birgen, as the ranking officer on deck, went to speak to the visitor.

He reached the port rail and looked down. There on the dockside was a bedraggled figure. Dressed all in black, the man was swarthy looking and had raven hair, which was most unusual in a Lucarclan. Birgen stared down at him. "What is it you want, sir?" he called down.

"Permission to come aboard," the man shouted up.

"I'm not the captain," Birgen replied. "What is it you want? We are about to depart."

"I know you are not the captain, sir. That would be Captain Reynard. I would like to book passage aboard your ship."

Birgen looked closer. The man hardly looked like he could afford a hot meal let alone pay for passage on a ship. His clothes were dirty and ripped in places, and now Birgen noted the man did not even have shoes, but was barefoot.

"I doubt you can afford it, sir", Birgen called back.

"Let me talk to Reynard. He will grant me passage."

"The captain is indisposed," Birgen replied. "I'm sorry."

The raven-haired man looked up at the boatswain and caught his eyes with a menacing stare. There was an unspoken but very real threat in that look which made Birgen shiver involuntarily. "Go and get Reynard. Now."

Birgen went.

Minutes later Reynard arrived at the rail. He looked down and saw the Ebon House noble standing on the dockside. The man looked much as he did when Reynard had last seen him – except that he had lost his bonds. He did not look happy. "We meet again, sir," he greeted the noble. "My boatswain tells me you wish to come aboard?"

"Yes, please captain. As you can appreciate I would like to leave the city," he said, casting a glance around the dockside. "Something about the Red City at this time of year – it doesn't agree with my constitution."

Reynard smiled at the man's manner. Though his eyes were cold there was a glint of amusement behind them which Reynard recognised. "Permission granted sir. Welcome aboard the *Javelin*."

The man climbed the gang plank and stepped on to the main deck. "Thank you captain. You are very kind. I will see to it that you are well rewarded. I am Wiktor of Selkie."

"Where is it you wish to sail to, Wiktor?"

"Anywhere away from here, to be honest. My ultimate destination is home to Selkie, but any port in that direction would be a good start," replied the Ebon noble.

"Well you are in luck I think, as we are about to set sale for Selkie. We will have you home within the fortnight."

*

The *Javelin* had been at sea for a week since departing Cansae. They were making good progress and were ahead of schedule. The ship had just turned north into the Lucarcian Straits and would reach the Inner Sea and the port of Selkie within a few days. Reynard was in his chambers, sat upon his bed, sipping at his last glass of Pembrose Red. He would have to restock when they made landfall.

He had a lot on his mind. They would soon be in Selkie. Once there he would take Tanithil and Evantia and go and seek an audience with Barrius Ebon – known as the Dark Lord. A man who had a sinister reputation. A man who was well known as sadistic and evil. A man who had ordered both Reynard and Tanithil into slavery upon one of his ships. Now Reynard was going to have to ask him for an alliance. It was not an easy thing to come to terms with.

As he considered his fate and his options there was a soft knock at his door. "Who is it?" he called out, wondering what crew issue he would have to deal with.

The reply surprised and interested him. "Evantia," came a soft voice.

Reynard stood up, brushed his shirt down and took a quick look at himself in the mirror on the wall. He grinned and strode over to the door. Pulling it open, he couldn't help but blink.

Evantia was dressed in a clinging blue dress that hugged her curves and showed off her slim, toned body. The plunging neckline drew Reynard's eye. Her long blonde hair was cascading in waves down the side of her face and across her shoulder. She had her head tilted to one side and was looking at Reynard demurely. "May I come in?" she asked, almost purring.

Reynard knew exactly what she was there for and where this would lead if he let her in. "Definitely," he said, stepping aside with a big grin on his face.

-Chapter Five-

Three horses crested a rise on the King's Road and their riders reined in, coming to a halt just as the sun began to set over the tended farmlands to the west. A bushy hedgerow edged both sides of the road here and formed a natural border to the thoroughfare as it wound its way onwards to the small village in the near distance. The three weary travellers could see fields of well-tended crops, and scattered groups of livestock, grazing on fresh grass.

"Waymeet," said Kita, indicating the settlement ahead. "My father's home. I haven't been here in a long time. We should head for the inn. It has comfortable rooms and is the best place in Albion to hear news of what is going on in the country. Not much happens which does not reach Tallisan the innkeeper's ears. You two should go and settle yourselves in. I have to go and see my father's parents."

Neither Okoth nor Mosi had to ask why. They knew Kita had to tell them of their son's death. It would not be a happy reunion.

"We shall await you in the inn," said Mosi. "There is no need to hurry. Take as much time as you need."

"Thank you," she replied, not meeting his gaze. This was going to be a bitter-sweet meeting. Kita had not spent much time with her grandparents – her father and mother spent most of their time living across the border in Sapporo. Those times when her father had returned here to see his parents he had often brought Kita with him. His parents always treated her with great kindness and love, doting on their only grandchild. Kita remembered their small wooden home with great fondness and feelings of safety and security. She recalled her little spot by the fire, where her grandmother would put out a thick blanket for her to snuggle down into and she would fall asleep listening to her father talking with his parents about all sorts of things. It mattered not that she didn't understand the conversations; she was safe, warm and loved. It was a special place for her.

Kita nudged her horse down the hill and into the village, vaguely aware that Mosi and Okoth had turned off and were heading for the inn.

Up ahead she spotted the little cabin which held such fond memories for her. It was a small affair, lovingly constructed by her grandfather. The exterior was timbered, with a tightly thatched roof which was common in Albion. Kita could see small sections of the thatch which needed patching. The little garden outside was still well tended but there were a few more weeds than she remembered. A single wooden door stood closed, keeping the brisk autumn wind out and the only window had a bright blue flower sat on the shelf. The cabin still looked homely and welcoming.

Kita dismounted and tied her horse to a nearby pole, being careful to make sure it didn't have enough head to start chomping on the flower garden. She strode up to the front door and stood for a moment. Taking a deep breath, she recalled the code of the Niten Dojo: *Never show fear. Never show pain.* It was going to be very hard to live up to that code in the next few hours.

*

Later that evening the three reunited in the common room of the inn. They sat at a sturdy wooden bench in a corner of the large hall, near the fireplace. Each had a platter of hot food in front of them. The conversation drifted around without settling onto anything in particular; nobody seeming to want to raise the topic of their current quest.

Once dinner had been finished and cleared away they sat back, wondering what to do next. Moments later a rather fat, middle aged man wearing clothes which were well made and cared for approached the group. He carried a tray with four crystal glasses balanced on it, each of which contained a rich, velvety red liquid.

"Well met, travellers. Allow me to introduce myself. I am Tallisan, owner of the Waymeet Inn. It is traditional in this establishment for travellers to swap stories of their journeys across the country in exchange for a glass of the local port, as distilled by my family here in the Inn for four generations. Would you honour me by upholding our tradition?"

"We would be glad to, Tallisan," replied Kita, smiling. She had been expecting something like this when they arrived. "You don't remember me, do you?"

The ruddy-cheeked landlord stopped, took a step back and looked closer. "It's not? Surely it can't be? But I guess you would be about the right age. Kita? Is that little Kita?"

"Yes, indeed. But not so little anymore."

"I remember when I used to bounce you up and down on my knee singing babies songs to you, and now look at you. How you have blossomed. How are you? How is your father?"

Kita looked him directly in the eye. She knew this would come. "I'm afraid my father is dead. He was killed in the summer, far across the sea."

Tallisan appeared stunned and embarrassed. "I am so sorry, my dear. I had no idea. How are you coping?"

"I am fine," Kita lied. *Never show pain. Never show fear.* "He died defending me and fighting for a cause he believed in."

"If there is anything I can do?"

"Not really, other than tell us how the road to Eastward lies? We had some trouble on the way here and would rather avoid any more."

"May I join you?" enquired the fat innkeeper.

"Of course," Kita gestured.

Tallisan handed out the port glasses, taking the fourth for himself, and easing his large frame into the spare chair at the companions' table. "What sort of trouble did you have on the way here?" he asked.

Kita proceeded to tell of their journey north from the capital of Littlebrook to the village of Waymeet. She told of the attack upon them by the brigands in the wood. She did not tell of their reasons for travelling through the kingdom or of the fact that the brigands had attacked them at the behest of a priest in the Cathedral of the Light.

Tallisan listened intently to the whole tale, politely interrupting on occasion to ask for some clarification or voice an insightful question. As the tale progressed Kita noticed the innkeeper quickly scan the common room to see if anyone appeared to be listening to her story. Kita, always a private sort of person, was not being overly loud in her tale-spinning. So

It seemed that no one was listening in. Kita finished her tale and sat back in her seat, taking a sip from the warming glass of port.

"An interesting story indeed, young Kita," said Tallisan when the tale was complete. He cast another quick glance around the common room. "A word of caution for you, if I may?"

"Certainly," she nodded.

"Albion has unusual laws where foreigners are concerned," he began. "Specifically, as outsiders you have no rights in this country. This means that if someone were to rob you, you would have no rights to complain. Should you hurt an Albioner in the process of trying to defend yourself the law would be on the side of the perpetrators of the attack upon you. So, in fact, legally you have committed murder by killing the brigands who tried to waylay you, even though it was clearly self-defence."

Kita was fully aware of Albion's unusual laws. Her father had explained them to her on many occasions. Even though Heremod was a local, Kita was considered by some to be foreign, as her mother was from Honshu to the east. And Mosi and Okoth were certainly not Albioners.

"Worry not though," said Tallisan, "I will not report you to the authorities for your actions, and indeed Warden Thomas who oversees the village would not punish you for what you have told me. Most people in Albion allow common sense to override the archaic laws which sometimes govern this country. But, take some advice: do not tell this tale so freely in other company as many in this country are less reasonable than the people of Waymeet."

Kita nodded again. "I thank you for your advice and your sound sense," she told him. "We will be careful in future."

"That is good. And now, I must return to the duties my job demands of me. I will return here later to see that you are being well looked after. My daughter Jenna will wait upon you in my absence."

The three companions waited for the fat innkeeper to leave, and then Kita leaned into the middle of the table. "So, what do you make of the brigand attack?" she asked her friends.

There was a pause as both considered the question. Mosi was first to respond.

"Well, clearly the attack was sponsored by Brother Coenred," he began. "What we don't know is who put him up to it? And why? Unfortunately, I can make an educated guess as to the who."

"Brother Fabian of Providentia," replied Kita.

"How come?" asked Okoth. The big Nubian was not best at unravelling the intricate politics and intrigues of the schemes of the world.

"Fabian handed Mosi a note to give to the priest in the Cathedral. It just seems to make sense," replied Kita.

"Yes, I understand," said Okoth, though clearly he didn't.

"Well, actually, it makes no sense at all," continued Kita, "But it is the only answer I can think of. I'm sorry Mosi, to suggest that a High Priest in your order would be so evil," she said, looking at the robed cleric.

"Not at all, my dear," responded Mosi, stroking his goatee between thumb and forefinger. "It is exactly the same conclusion that I have come to. But for the life of me I cannot fathom why Brother Fabian would want us dead."

"I suspect there is nothing we can do about this save continue with our quest and ponder it over time. Until such time as we are ever in Providentia again it is unlikely we will ever be able to make sense of it."

"I concur," said Mosi in response. "We may as well just press on and forget about it for now."

"That's one thing I can agree on," said Okoth, looking somewhat relieved.

Later that same evening the innkeeper, Tallisan, returned to their table. "Good evening again, friends," he began. "I trust your meal was pleasant and that you are enjoying our hospitality?"

"Indeed so, thank you, Tallisan," replied Kita.

"I just remembered that you had said you were travelling on to Eastward and were wondering if I had any advice for you," he said.

"Correct."

"I guess that you are heading home to Honshu. Anyway, I should warn you about the current state of things in the town of Eastward. They are not pleasant. Tensions are high between the locals there and the Easterners – your mother's people. Occasional border skirmishes have started breaking out in the area of No Man's Land in between Eastward and Sapporo. Nothing official you understand but blood has been shed and word has it that people have been killed. I would be careful when travelling through or staying the night in the town."

"Many thanks Tallisan. Your warning is very helpful. I don't think we have any real choice but to go there next though," Kita replied.

"In which case, watch yourselves," the innkeeper warned the companions.

"We shall".

*

Eastward was a fortified town, Albion's frontline defence against the aggressive Empire of Honshu to the east. It was very much a frontier town, in a constant state of readiness for war. The town here was a barracks town and the navy blue uniforms of the Duke's soldiers were a regular sight on the streets.

The Land's End Inn was a well maintained hostelry where mercenary bands and privateers tended to stay. It was just across the main street from the barracks which housed the Duke's army and was not far from the east gate which was the portal out into No Man's Land. Eastward marked the far eastern border of Albion, and the Empire of Honshu officially began on the edge of Kita's home town of Sapporo which was some thirty miles away. The lands in between were technically stateless and this wilderness had long been a place of skirmish and confrontation between the navy blues of Albion and the Imperial Red colours of the forces of Sapporo's *daimyo*.

The inn was busy with quite a few armed mercenaries in town due to the increased tensions between Albion and the Easterners - as the locals referred to the people of Honshu. Where there was friction and fighting, mercenary bands tended to flock, and Eastward was no exception.

Okoth was up at the crowded bar trying to order some more drinks. He was still getting used to the Albion custom of having to stand near one central place to ask for drinks to be refilled. In his native Nubia things were very different. The locals were giving him wide berth due to his huge and intimidating size. The common room was warm with so many people crowded in, so he had forgone his blanket and had stripped to the waist. As well as being black skinned – a trait which was extremely rare in this land – he was also hugely muscled, and the combination made him a very intimidating presence; something he was making use of to help reach the bar.

Meanwhile, at the companions' table across the room, a local youth had approached. He had a half-finished ale in one hand, was swaying slightly and his breath stank of stale beer. One look was all Kita needed to know he was trouble. "You're not from around here, are you?" he slurred.

"Not originally, no," conceded Kita. "Though my father was born and raised in Waymeet."

"Of course he was," laughed the youth. "You look like Albioners – both of you. You're an Eastern slut aint ya? One of them whores, I'd wager," he said as he swayed alarmingly to one side. "And you must be her pimp," he declared, looking at Mosi, squinting to focus. "Definitively not from around here."

"You would have just lost your wager, had you made one, young man," responded Mosi calmly. "I am Mosi of Shelech, Haji of the Light, and not a pimp. This is Kita, student of the world famous Niten dojo of Sapporo, and no whore. And behind you is Okoth, Champion Gladiator of Nubia. But you are right on one thing – we are not from around here."

The youth turned slowly and looked into Okoth's barrel chest which was about at his eye level. Slowly his brain registered what he was looking at and his eyes worked their way up to Okoth's head way above his own and looked at the giant's huge grin. The youth's addled brain obviously just registered who he was facing and the colour drained from his face. He staggered back and weaved his way off into the crowded room, deciding that he probably didn't want any more attention from the three strangers.

However the scene had caused everyone in the area to stop and take notice. Now there were a few muttered comments from the mercenary bands sitting around nearby. Kita thought she heard the phrase, "Eastern whore" from a few mouths. There was definitely an air of hostility in the room.

"I think perhaps we should leave this establishment, and look for somewhere a bit more upmarket," suggested Mosi.

Unwilling to run from any potential confrontation, Kita was forced to go against her nature and agree, as Albion's archaic laws would support the actions of any local mercenary group who cared to pick a fight with the foreigners. "Sadly, I think you are right," she told him. "Let us collect our things and move on."

"I'll get the horses from the stable and meet you out the front," said Mosi.

Kita and Okoth rose from the table and Okoth pushed his way through the crowd. The front door was a long way away and Kita spotted a well-armed bunch of privateers near the front door, talking to the drunken youth who had first accosted them. She tapped Okoth on the arm and directed him to the nearby backdoor. It would be a faster and safer escape route. The giant nodded and changed direction, gently pushing his way to the closed oak door. Opening it he stepped out into an alley which ran down the side of the inn. Turning right he headed for the front of the building and the main street, Kita on his heels.

"Where do you think you are going, Easterner?" asked a gruff voice from behind them when they were about half way to the end of the alley. Kita turned and saw three burly men had followed them out into the alley from the backdoor.

"Somewhere quieter," she responded, "where the air is less … prejudice."

"What you saying?" asked another of the three as they began to advance.

"Okoth, remember, we must not use excessive force here. Be mindful," Kita whispered to her companion who she could feel was standing just behind her shoulder. "As much as we would like to," she added grimly.

"I reckon we should help the war effort, lads," said the third thug. "One less Easterner and her black lover will help our boys out in No Man's Land, won't it?"

"Maybe we can get ourselves from Eastern fun too whilst we's at it," responded another.

Kita dropped back into a defensive stance and waited, blocking the taunts and conversation out of her mind. Three onto two was no issue here. The alley was thin, meaning the thugs would have no chance to surround them and Okoth and her would be more than a match for three street bravos, even without weapons.

"Get em!" shouted the first thug as he rushed in, the other two on his heels.

Kita waited until the first thug was upon her, then dropped low and aimed a spear hand right into his solar-plexus, completely knocking the wind out of him. He dropped like he had been gutted. Spinning on her left heel she then spun her right leg around, fully extended and swept the second bully off his feet. He crashed into some nearby boxes sending bits of wood and garbage all over the place.

Next to her she felt Okoth move forward to intercept the third rowdy. He swung a huge fist at the attacker which the man simply didn't see coming in the darkness of the alley. It connected squarely on the thug's temple, lifted him off the ground and sent him flying backwards into a wooden gate which was closing off a nearby terrace garden. The man crashed into it with great force and Kita saw his head loll forward.

The first attacker struggled to his feet, heaving for air from where Kita's strike had winded him. He looked around him and very quickly realised him and his friends were totally out-matched. "Let's go back inside, Eadfrid," he gasped out to the man sprawled on the wooden crates. Eadfrid picked himself up, plucking some rotten cabbage off his face and scowled. But he too realised the futility of the fight. The two men dropped back to where the third was still laying against the gate.

"Alric?" asked the first, looking at his friend. "Alric? Oh no, Alric. No."

"Murder!" shouted Eadfrid at the top of his lungs, "They've killed Alric!"

It took Kita a moment to work out what they were talking about but then as the clouds shifted she could suddenly see in the moonlight. The thug Okoth had punched was lying at an awkward angle on the gate he had crashed back into. And sticking out of the front of his chest was a wooden slat. Blood was oozing heavily down his shirt front. He had been impaled on the gate.

"Run!" urged Kita as she turned into Okoth. "Run!" she commanded again, pushing the giant, who had frozen in place. "We need to get out of here."

"But I didn't hit him that hard," protested Okoth looking confused.

"I know," she agreed, continuing to push the Nubian backwards towards the main road and the stable where she prayed Mosi was waiting.

Behind her she heard the back door open and more people come into the alley. "Murder!" the cry continued to go out. She knew it would only be moments before the town guard would be here and regardless of what defence the companions tried to use, by Albion law they were guilty of murder. They had to flee and they had to flee now.

Kita and Okoth reached the front of the inn where a few people had started to come out, including the mercenary band who had been standing near the front door. Casting a look over to the stables she saw Mosi leading the first horse out. Kita grabbed the still stunned Okoth by the arm and dragged him to the priest.

"What happened?" asked Mosi, seeing the commotion and hearing the continuing calls.

"No time to explain, but we need to get out of here. Now."

Kita pushed Okoth to his horse and half forced him to mount it.

"But I didn't hit him that hard," the giant repeated, still confounded.

"Ride!" Kita shouted, slapping Okoth's horse's rump and sending it off down the street. She then grabbed the reins of her own mare and leapt into the saddle, turning it sharply and urging it straight into a fast canter. Looking back over her shoulder she saw the two surviving thugs from the alley talking to the mercenary band leader, a woman armed and armoured. Members of the company had got their own horses from the stables and they were starting to mount. Kita had time to see the mercenary leader pointing across the road to the barracks and then her horse rounded a corner and the inn was lost to sight. It was clear that the mercenaries were going to chase them whilst rousing the Duke's soldiers too.

Kita pushed her horse to catch up with Mosi and Okoth. It was then she realised they were going the wrong way. The East Gate and the safety of No Man's Land was the opposite direction. They were headed deeper into town.

The companions rode on as fast as they could. Ahead they could see the impressive Church of the Light which they had passed on their way into the town earlier that afternoon. Briefly Kita wondered about stopping there and seeking sanctuary, but she quickly dismissed the idea, knowing that the priest there would be forced to hand them over to face the law.

Behind them now she could see four or five riders galloping along through the streets in pursuit. In the distance beyond them she could hear the shouts of the rabble rousers. She knew it would not be long until the city watch were added to their troubles. It was hard to think whilst riding at breakneck speed through the cobbled streets but she had no choice. To slow down was to be caught by the riders following and although she had no doubts of the companions' ability to defeat the mercenaries in a fight, doing so would probably lead to more unnecessary death and would delay them enough that the Duke's soldiers would soon be upon them. No, they had to press on and press on fast.

Rounding another bend in the road Kita could make out the high western wall of the town. They were already almost across to the other side of the settlement. The road they were on, the main thoroughfare through Eastward, led on and out into the interior of Albion through the West Gate which she could just make out in the gloom ahead. Then she realised her fortune at coming this way: the West Gate, facing into Albion and not out into dangerous territory like the East Gate was, remained open. It would be closed at midnight, but at this time of the evening the gates were still clear.

Their freedom beckoned.

*

Oswald was seventeen and had been with the Eastern Eagles mercenary company for just a couple of days. Considered a grown man now, he felt very good in his father's old leather jacket. It was far too big for him but he was sure he would soon grow into it and was proud to wear it none-the-less. This was his first real action in the company and he was extremely nervous. His palms were sweating and he was struggling to keep a good grip on the reins. Fortunately his piebald was a well bred horse, one which had even been considered for the Knights of the Sun, and reins were almost unnecessary. Oswald was no great rider but even still it was as if all he had to do was think about where he wanted to ride and the gelding took him there.

Ahead he could see the open Western Gate which led out into the countryside. He knew this area well, having grown up in a small hamlet just north of the town. His father, a local hero called Ethelwulf, had grown up in Waymeet but had moved to a tiny village near Eastward when he had met a local lass on one of his trips to the town here. They had settled down and married and Ethelwulf had eventually given up the life of wandering warrior. Ethelwulf was well known in the region for he wielded a huge double-bladed axe with great skill and dexterity. When he had approached Anna, the leader of the Eastern Eagles, and had asked her to take on his son, she had of course agreed.

The foreign murderers they were chasing were approaching the gates and Sigbert, the most experienced of the five mercenaries who were on the tail of the fugitives, shouted to the gate guards. "Shut the gates! Stop those foreigners! They're murderers! Shut the gates!"

Too late though, the guards seemed to understand and react. The three riders ahead were at the gates when the first guard ran out to try and stop them. The huge black-skinned giant lashed out with a booted foot; hit the guard square in the chest and the soldier crashed back into the dirt. Then the three were through and out into the open countryside.

Oswald held on tight as his gelding seemed to surge to even greater speed. He and the other Eagles were definitely gaining on the outsiders. But what would happen when they caught them? Oswald had trained with his father's sword for years but had never used it in anger.

He had never been in a real fight save the odd scuffle or tavern brawl. His palms began to sweat some more.

Moments later Oswald's gelding broke through the West Gate and out into the countryside. It was dark but in the moonlight he could still make out the quarry. They had turned north, up a rutted lane which led on to Oswald's hamlet a few miles ahead. The mercenary horses were all well-bred and extremely well trained. Anna had a deal with Sir Balain who was the knight in charge of the Eastward Chapter House. This was where the Knights of the Sun trained their war horses, the finest in the kingdom. Anna was given first choice of those horses which were rejected from the Chapter House training grounds so every horse the Eastern Eagles rode was quality. As such Oswald was sure their mounts would be able to run down the regulation riding horses they chased. It was just a matter of time.

*

Kita pushed on, mindful that her horse was already tiring. She knew the way in daylight but had only been down this lane once before and wasn't really certain of her bearings. The light was reasonable – the moon half full and the clouds being broken and not heavy. As such she felt it safe to push her mount a bit more but knew the mare only had so much strength left. And if the mercenaries overtook them, blood would be spilt.

Kita had a specific destination in mind. The village of Hollytree was an altogether insignificant little hamlet on the edge of a sylvan wood. It had just a few houses in it, no inn for passers-by and just a small village hall in the centre. But there was one structure which stood out from all the rest and which marked Hollytree as unique: a huge marble tower which rose high into the sky. Known as the Wizard's Tower, it was home to Camero, the man who had sent her father on the quest which had killed him. That was where she was headed for, and that was where she needed to reach before the mercenaries rode them down.

The three companions thundered into a small hamlet. For a moment Kita thought it was Hollytree but she quickly realised she was mistaken. Though similar in layout, in the centre where Hollytree had a village hall, this hamlet had an inn. And of course this settlement lacked the Wizard's Tower. The three were through the village and out the other side in a matter of heartbeats. Kita didn't notice the huge figure standing in a doorway, watching as they passed. The large man had a great double-bladed axe in hand. Moments later the axe man smiled to himself as the five mercenaries galloped through the village in hot pursuit. His eye was on the lad at the back of the mercenaries in oversized leathers and a half-scared, half-excited look on his face.

Okoth's horse was tiring fastest. The giant Nubian weighed far more than either Kita or Mosi and though his horse was the strongest of the three it was also doing the most work. Looking back over her shoulder Kita wondered when it would collapse, for she had seen this before. A horse could literally be ridden to death if the rider was heartless enough. Kita certainly had no wish to see that happen, but if the choice were the death of a horse or the death of the mercenaries who chased them, she would see the horse die first.

It was possible that the companions could take out five well-armed warriors without killing any of them but if they were as well trained as they were equipped she thought it unlikely. The only true way to be sure an opponent was no longer dangerous was to fully incapacitate them. And in the chaos of a lethal encounter the difference between an incapacitating strike and a fatal one was minimal. It was unlikely they could stop all five without killing at least one of them. And if they were too concerned with keeping their enemies alive they would be putting themselves at serious risk of getting killed themselves. No, the only way to avoid death was to avoid the fight in the first place. But Okoth's horse was about to give in.

Suddenly they broke into another settlement. Kita was not sure how far behind them the last hamlet was but this one had come upon them faster than she had expected. And as she looked up she saw a welcome sight: the soaring white marble edifice that was the Wizard's Tower. They had reached Hollytree.

Reining in, Kita leapt from her horse and rushed up to the tower. A spiral staircase wound around the outside of the tower a little way up to end at a plain looking wooden door. Kita hammered on it with all her might. "Camero! Open up! Please!" Looking back down she saw Okoth and Mosi had gathered the three mounts and beyond them the five mercenaries were charging into the hamlet.

Kita and her companions were just too late.

*

Oswald saw the huge white tower ahead and blinked twice. Oh no. Hollytree. Everyone knew the place was dangerous. It was not a place you went to unless you had a very good reason. He had grown up not more than five miles from the place but had hardly ever been there, such was its reputation. Even his father, the great Ethelwulf, avoided Hollytree. And yet here he was.

Sigbert reined in and Oswald followed suit. The mercenaries dismounted and Sigbert handed the reins of all the horses to Oswald. "Keep the mounts calm when the blood flows," he instructed Oswald.

Oswald blinked and gulped.

"You killed an Albioner in Eastward!" Sigbert accused the foreigners loudly. "And we have come to take you back. Alive, or dead, makes no difference to me," he added, drawing his shortsword and advancing slowly. It was clear to Oswald that Sigbert had no intention of taking them back alive.

Behind Sigbert the others drew their own blades and fanned out. There were four of them and just two foreigners ahead of them, the big black-skinned warrior and the white-robed skinny fellow. Then the pretty looking easterner rushed down the spiral stairs of the tower and joined her friends, two swords appearing in her hands almost instantly.

"It was a total accident and in self-defence," she replied. "We have no wish to kill more of you. Put down your blades and no one needs to get hurt here."

"I think not," Sigbert growled. "The law is on our side."

"Actually, you are wrong there my dear fellow," came a new voice. Melodic and powerful it cut through the night air and stopped everyone in their tracks. Oswald froze in place, not sure if he was scared halt to death or elated. His eyes were drawn involuntarily up to the white tower. There, stood upon the spiral staircase was a figure. The man was dressed in exquisite robes, fashioned from Honshu silk. As he moved they seemed to shimmer and change colour. The effect simply added to the mesmerizing power of the man's voice. Oswald was spellbound.

"This is Hollytree and by Royal Decree of his majesty King Jarrad, the first of that name, this hamlet lies outside the jurisdiction of the laws of the kingdom. So, although these people may be fugitives in your kingdom, here in *my village* they are free."

"But…" muttered Sigbert, and Oswald was amazed that he was able to speak at all, let alone almost seem to complain to the figure before them.

"You will leave this village and return back to Eastward. Tell Anna that you chased your quarry here and that they are now under my protection. I gift you their three horses as reparation for your trouble. You should know that they are horses from the Cathedral in Littlebrook, so treat them well. I suggest you rest the Nubian's before you push it too hard again. Its heart is close to giving out. Now, take the horses and leave. Do not push my patience. I am not in a good mood this evening."

Oswald suddenly felt like a weight had been lifted from his shoulders. He was free to act again. He shook his head and looked up. All was as it had been moments before but the enthralling figure was gone. He looked to Sigbert for guidance.

"Collect their horses and let's get out of here," commanded Sigbert. "I have no wish to cross that one."

Oswald stepped forward and took the reins of the three foreigners' horses from them, once they had removed the saddlebags from their backs. He tied the reins to the saddle of his own horse and mounted up easily. The others had mounted their own horses and Sigbert called for a gentle walk out of the hamlet. Behind them the three foreigners stood, hands still on weapons, watching them leave.

Oswald had been a member of the Eastern Eagles for two days. And he had already met the Archmage. He couldn't wait to tell his father.

-Chapter Six-

The *Javelin* was heading north through the Lucarcian Straits. A stiff breeze was coming out of the Southern Ocean, filling her sails and speeding her on her way. The sun was setting over the cliff tops to the west and the boatswain, Birgen, had the wheel. Captain Reynard was sitting in his study, sipping on a glass of Pembrose Red, contemplating his near future when there was a soft knock at the door. He smiled to himself, expecting his late visitor to be Evantia. The memories of her warmed him more than the wine was doing, but they were tainted with a subtle feeling of guilt. Every time he thought of the stunning blonde beauty his daydreams blurred and faded to be replaced by a dark haired, steel-eyed face with almond-shaped, brown eyes. Kita. What were his feelings for the swordswoman from Honshu? He wasn't really sure but her face would always come back to him.

Forcing her image out of his mind, Reynard rose and moved to the door. A visit from Evantia was just what he needed right now. Anything to take his mind off what the next few days would bring. The *Javelin* was two days out of Selkie, capital of the Tail of Ursum and home of Lord Barrius Ebon. The Dark Lord, as he was known, was a truly dangerous man and if ever someone could be called evil, perhaps he was such a one. Lord Barrius had seen to it that both Reynard and Tanithil had been put into slavery. He was responsible for most of the problems Reynard had endured over the last year. And now Reynard had to go and ask him for his help. It was most distressing, and the chance to spend some time with the distractions Evantia offered him was most welcome.

Reynard straightened out his Honshu silk waistcoat and opened the door with a big grin. Only to find the Ebon noble, Wiktor, on his doorstep.

"Oh," he blurted, the grin dropping from his face in an instant.

"Not quite who you were expecting?" the noble asked, grinning back.

"Of course, come in. Come in," he said stepping back and indicating that the noble should enter his study. Reynard moved back into the room and went to the table where he poured a fresh glass of red for his visitor and topped up his own. He indicated for Wiktor to sit opposite him and took his own seat again.

"Now, what can I do for you?" asked Reynard, putting his boots up on the low table in the centre of the room and crossing his feet.

"We'll, if it is not too much to ask, I was wondering if I could trouble you to a pair of boots," replied the Ebon noble, putting his own feet up. They were bare.

Reynard had the decency to feel ashamed. He had allowed the noble onto his ship almost two weeks ago now and this was the first time he had really spoken to the man - and he hadn't even stopped to make sure he was properly clothed. "Of course. At once," he replied, jumping to his feet. "Let me see. I think these will do," he continued, moving to a corner of the study and picking up a pair of his older riding boots. "They are worn but well cared for."

Wiktor tried them on, finding them to be a reasonable fit and certainly preferable to being bare foot any longer. "Many thanks, Captain Reynard. I am in your debt three times over now."

"Three?" enquired Reynard.

"Three," confirmed the noble. "Once for rescuing me from the clutches of the Ruby Pyromancers; once for taking me on your ship from Cansae to Selkie; and once for the boots. Now what is it that brings you to Selkie?"

"It's a long tale."

"Well, I have a fresh glass of wine, some fresh boots and nothing to do for a day or two," said Wiktor.

Reynard sat back, and swilled his glass of red. "You are aware of the Writhing Death, of course," he began.

"Everyone in the Lucarcian Empire and many beyond are aware of the Writhing Death," replied Wiktor.

"Yes, but you think of it as a history lesson; as something which shaped the empire, in fact perhaps as something which created the Lucarcian Empire out of the Rainbow Empire which came before it. Well, now it has moved from being a part of a history lesson to a present danger and something which threatens to destroy the very empire it was partially responsible for creating. The Writhing Death has returned. Even as we speak it is inching its way across Granita again."

"What? How can this be?" asked the Ebon noble, sitting forward in his chair.

"The gate to the Void has reopened," explained Reynard.

"How do you know?"

"I have seen it with my own eyes. I have witnessed what only a handful of people have seen in five hundred years. But if nothing is done a whole lot more people are going to witness it first hand in the next year or so." Reynard went on to explain the events of the summer and his experience of chasing the aberration Baku across the wastelands of Granita only to find him at the head of the Writhing Death.

When Reynard had finished Wiktor sat back, letting out a long exhalation of air. "That is an amazing story," he said. "That also explains the golden armour you wear," he added.

Reynard felt a brief moment of concern when the armour was mentioned, but a quick peek over his shoulder reassured him. The golden Armour of Lucar was still on the armour stand in the back of the study. Tanithil had finally convinced Reynard to remove the armour when it was not necessary and Reynard had agreed. However Reynard always kept the armour in sight. It was too valuable to risk losing to theft.

"As you know, the recent death of the emperor has left the empire in a state of confusion. The Azure House has no leader and there is no heir. No one really knows what will happen now. As it turns out all the noble houses have been spending time preparing for civil war, knowing this moment was possible, even likely. And now the empire is poised to rip itself apart from the inside, just as the greatest threat in its entire existence is creeping towards it ready to engulf it from the outside. So now, I am trying to unite the noble houses. If they splinter into civil war they will doom the empire. They need to come together to have any chance to defeat the apocalyptic power of the Writhing Death."

"What is your plan then, Reynard?" asked Wiktor, clearly engrossed.

"Well, as you will know I have already travelled to Cansae. There I managed to get the Trade Lords to agree to join us. They agreed to raise an army for the cause. They have sent their representative, Evantia, to aid me," he said, blushing involuntarily.

"Of course," replied Wiktor with a grin. "I'm sure she is."

Reynard coughed and continued. "I have also spoken to the Dragon. As you are extremely aware he has been secretly training Pyromancers."

"So I noticed," commented Wiktor icily.

"The Dragon has agreed to send his Pyromancers to Granita to fight the Writhing Death directly."

"Has he, indeed?" responded Wiktor. "I am somewhat surprised at that."

"Why?" asked Reynard, curious to know how much the Ebon noble knew or guessed.

"Well, I suspect that he would consider the Head of Ursum to be under threat if he sent his powerful Pyromancers away. He is not stupid. The Dark Lord would see that as an opportunity for expansion I am sure."

"Quite. And you are right –he is not stupid, for he voiced that exact same concern. And he has agreed to send his Pyromancers with the condition that the Dark Lord must be committed to the cause as well."

"So now you go to Selkie to petition the Dark Lord to join your cause," surmised Wiktor.

"Exactly," finished Reynard, taking a long draw from his Pembrose Red.

"Exquisite wine," Wiktor complimented Reynard, taking a long drink himself.

"How well do you know Lord Ebon?" asked Reynard directly.

Wiktor shrugged. I am acquainted with him, he responded evasively. "Why do you ask?"

"Well as you will have gathered I am not all too happy to be going and begging for help from him, after all he has done to me in the last year. However I am prepared to put the good of the empire before my personal issues."

"Very noble of you," commented Wiktor.

"I was wondering what you thought the chances are that he will lend his support against the Writhing Death. His backing is absolutely critical to my undertaking. And indeed, to the survival of the Lucarcian Empire itself.

"Then I think you are going to need some help," responded Wiktor.

"That's what worries me," replied Reynard.

"One question does spring to mind," continued Wiktor. "And that is: who opened the gate to the Void?"

Reynard stopped and thought for a while. "You know what? I don't think anyone has asked that question before. We have all been so busy trying to work out how to deal with the problem that no one has stopped to consider how it became a problem in the first place. Maybe it just opened itself?"

"Maybe. But maybe someone opened it on purpose," suggested Wiktor.

"If so then who, and why?" asked Reynard.

Neither of the men had an answer for that.

*

The castle of Selkie was built from imposing black basalt carved at great cost from the Frosthold peaks some forty miles to the south at the edge of the Tail of Ursum. Most of the city had been built of rock from the same range but the castle was constructed of the rare basalt which was found only in the most hard to reach parts of the Frostholds. The Dark Lord of the time, Lord Synistor Ebon, had ordered its construction and, legend told, had not flinched at the terrific toll in lives the castle had taken to build. From the date of its construction to the present day Castle Ebon had a malevolent reputation.

As he approached the castle, Reynard craned his neck to look up at the huge standard which was fully unfurled in the strong autumn breeze. It showed a giant raven on the wing and the way the flag rippled in the wind it looked like the raven was truly in flight. Behind the standard dark storm clouds billowed and the air was thick with the promise of a powerful storm. If the Dark Lord had wanted an ominous backdrop to someone approaching his castle, he could not have asked for much more.

Taking a quick sideways glance at his companions Reynard could see that Evantia was visibly shaken by the experience. Tanithil had a blank look on his face and Reynard guessed that the ex-Thought Guard was using one of his mind-controlling exercises to quell any fear he might have been feeling. Reynard noted that, although he was impressed with the castle, the setting and the reputation of the Dark Lord, Barrius Ebon, he was not as overwhelmed as he might have expected to feel. Perhaps the golden Armour of Lucar was bolstering his confidence. It certainly felt great to be wearing it again.

The three visitors climbed the last few steps up to the huge portcullis which barred the entrance to the castle. Standing stock still outside were four guards, clad in ceremonial black armour with helms made to look like oversized skeletal heads. The guards didn't move a muscle as Reynard and friends approached. The portcullis was closed but a small door was built into the huge metal framework and that door was open. Reynard took a quick look at the guards who were showing no signs of stopping them, and stepped through the small door and into the castle proper.

The entrance corridor was dark, with a vaulted ceiling. It was made of the same black basalt as the outside of the castle. A single torch smoked in a wall sconce a few feet in, doing little to illuminate the passage and more to obscure vision with the smoke it was generating.

From the darkness ahead a large figure loomed. Tall, rotund and smiling the man was dressed from head to toe in bright, garish colours which clashed terribly. His face was split with a jolly grin and he could not have looked more out of place in the gloomy castle entrance.

"Welcome, welcome!" he boomed, his loud voice echoing down the corridor. "Welcome to the illustrious Ebon Castle, home of the Warden of the East, Lord Barrius Ebon. May your stay be a comfortable and happy one," he continued.

"Well met, sir," began Reynard. "I am Reynard Ferrand of the Iron House," he introduced himself.

"Of course you are. You are well known in these halls, young man," replied the round-faced man. Reynard could not help but think that he was well known because the Dark Lord had ordered him thrown into slavery in order to tighten his grip on the lands of Ursum.

"I am Festus, seneschal of the Ebon Castle and your guide and friend in your time here," the smiling man continued. "Allow me to lead you to a reception room where you can make yourselves comfortable until my lord is ready to see you." The large man turned on his heels and strode off along the corridors without even a backward glance and Reynard was forced to push himself to keep up. For a big man the seneschal moved quickly.

Their guide took them along cold and empty corridor after deserted passage. The castle interior was as bleak and foreboding as any Reynard had experienced. There were no tapestries or wall hangings to break up the uniform walls. There were no carpets to soften the floor. The light was provided by torches at regular intervals, far apart which made the whole place very dim. It was exactly as he had expected but it was still very intimidating. He quickly realised that it would be extremely easy to get lost in the labyrinth. Any enemy who managed to penetrate the interior of this castle would not find it a simple job to navigate their way to the central hub where Reynard assumed the throne room would be located.

After what seemed like a long time Festus halted outside a large oak door. He grinned his typical grin and pushed the door open. "Please, make yourselves comfortable," he said, indicating that the group should proceed him into the room. Reynard thanked him and stepped into the room beyond, followed by Evantia and Tanithil.

The reception room was cold and bare. There were none of the usual refreshments laid on as would be typical in these situations. There was not even a chair for any of them to sit on. It was simply a square stone room with no windows and one torch in a corner.

Festus followed the group inside. "Please stay here until you are summoned. My lord Ebon will speak with you presently. I shall go now and make him aware of your arrival." With that the seneschal bowed and left, closing the door behind him.

"This is unpleasant," stated Evantia shivering. "And cold," she added.

"At least he was a friendly fellow," put in Reynard brightly.

"Don't be deceived," replied Tanithil, moving to one side and sitting himself down, cross legged on the floor.

"What do you mean, Tani?" asked Reynard.

"Despite his friendly appearance and ridiculous clothing, he was in a constant state of alertness and was highly suspicious the whole time he was with us," reported the telepath. "His happy demeanour was all a façade."

"Interesting," said Reynard. "Perhaps he acts this way to throw people off balance?"

"Seems highly likely to me," came back Tanithil.

"Well, the sooner we are out of here the better," said Evantia, hugging herself tightly. "I hate this place."

"I don't think it is supposed to be a fun place to visit," replied Tanithil.

"But it's one we need to deal with," stated Reynard. "Now let us wait until the Dark Lord deigns to see us.

The three companions were left in the cold, dimly lit room. Time passed slowly with nothing to do and none of them seemed inclined to chat. Reynard felt angry at the treatment they were being shown by the Dark Lord and his household. He was hungry and his back was beginning to ache from standing still for a long time. The golden Armour of Lucar was light – virtually weightless – but there mere act of being forced to stand for such a long time was beginning to annoy him. He refused to sit down like Tanithil and Evantia had done. Somehow that seemed beneath him.

"This is ridiculous!" stormed Evantia, rising to her feet angrily. "How dare he leave us here, freezing and hungry? We are being treated more like prisoners than as guests! Reynard – you need to do something about this. Demand we are seen now!"

Reynard felt his emotions rise and threaten to engulf him. "What do you expect me to do?" he queried, his anger just in check, his face flushing. "March into the throne room of the Dark Lord and demand an audience? Even if I could find the room in this gods forsaken cesspit, I would never make it past the Dread Guard. Or are you suggesting I battle half our host's personal guard before demanding he listen to me and give me his support? You're being stupid."

"Stupid? How dare can you call me that? I am the representative of the Guild of Master Merchants and Sea Farers! When you talk to me you talk to the Trade Lords. Never forget that!"

"Stop this now." Tanithil's voice was calm, yet full of authority. His command was softly spoken but timed to fit perfectly into the natural break in the argument. "This is exactly what he wants us to be doing. Don't you see? The Dark Lord has us greeted by his pompous 'friendly' seneschal which is not what we would have expected in this fortress. We are then virtually locked up as prisoners and left with no comforts for an entirely unacceptable period of time. He is deliberately upsetting us and putting us off balance. And now we are arguing amongst ourselves. This is exactly what he wants in a group who are about to come before him. He's sown discord and dissent between us and we haven't even met him yet."

Reynard took a deep breath and reflected on his friend's words. "I'm sorry, Tani. You are right, of course. We cannot allow the Dark Lord to manipulate us this way. We have to put all thoughts of discomfort and insult out of our minds. Rather than letting his ill treatment divide us, let us use it to unite us in our cause. We are here to save the empire and have to put the good of the many before the egos of the few. Evantia, I am sorry. You are not being stupid at all and I should never have reacted that way. You have my heartfelt apologies."

Evantia blushed deeply. "No, Reynard, it is I that should apologise. I acted like a spoilt child. And Tanithil is right. We must unite, not divide at this time."

"Right, that's good," declared Reynard. "We will not be deflected from our purpose here, for it is noble and we all believe in it. Yes?"

"Definitely," agreed Evantia, smiling a dazzling white smile.

Tanithil nodded curtly. "Agreed."

Moments later the door opened and Festus appeared.

※

    As Festus lead them through the twisting corridors toward the throne room, Reynard thought ahead to the meeting with the Dark Lord and how it would go. He imagined the throne room would be a huge cavernous affair, with giant banners of the raven in flight covering the walls and a score or more of the infamous Dread Guard protecting the Dark Lord. He imagined a huge throne, constructed of human bones and imagined the Dark Lord as a powerful warrior sat imperiously on that throne, dominating the massive chamber.

    Passing deeper into the dim castle, Reynard smiled to himself as he thought back to their recent hospitality. Mere moments after the group had put their quarrels aside and agreed to use the Dark Lord's terrible treatment to unite them rather than divide them, the door to the waiting room had opened and the seneschal had entered, telling them that the Dark Lord was ready to see them. It was almost as if they had been watched and listened to, and that their hosts had realised that any advantage they had achieved by making their guests wait in the inhospitable surroundings was back firing on them.

    "We are here," came Festus' jolly voice, breaking into Reynard's reverie. Ahead, Reynard was expecting to see giant double doors guarded by members of the Dread Guard. Instead he looked up to see a simple oak door, with no soldiers in sight. Frowning, he made a mental note not to assume anything of the Dark Lord and to stay open minded. Festus pushed open the door and stepped in to the room beyond. Reynard, Evantia and Tanithil followed him.

    The Dark Lord's throne room was the complete opposite of what Reynard had expected. It was small, no bigger than his own bedroom at home in the Iron Fortress. The room was austere, with a plain grey wool rug thrown across the floor to keep the cold out. A simple mahogany table dominated the centre of the room and three plain wooden chairs were arrayed around it. At the back of the room a short standard hung on a pole, the House symbol of the raven in flight prominent, but not overwhelming.

Reynard quickly scanned the room as he entered and was surprised to see just one person present. There were no Dread Guard here as either protection, nor as a show of force. Instead only a single figure sat in one of the simple wooden chairs.

The Dark Lord.

Barrius Ebon was thin – skeletally so. Dressed in simple but elegant matching grey shirt and trousers, the head of the Ebon House had raven black hair, something rare in the Lucarcian Empire. His emaciated face was drawn and pale, showing protruding cheek bones and thin, watery lips. But Reynard's gaze was drawn instantly to the piercing grey eyes at the centre of the bony face.

Immediately any feelings of superiority were gone. Here was a man of immense power. Reynard could feel the aura of supreme confidence and self-belief. It didn't take Tanithil's ability to read emotions to know that the man before him was probably the most dangerous person he had ever met.

Reynard knew he needed to be at his sharpest and most alert if he was to succeed here. He was suddenly very aware that he had just walked into the throne room of the very man who had thrown him into slavery. It was possible his very life was in the balance and that he may well not survive the encounter. But he also knew the existence of the empire itself depended on the next few minutes.

He must not fail.

*

Reynard took a deep breath. He had given it his best shot. He had sat down opposite his mortal enemy and tried to explain to him why he should pitch his lot into the fight against the Writhing Death. In coming here, he had risked his life for the empire he believed in. He was wearing the golden Armour of Lucar and he knew that had the power to sway weak minds, but he was pretty sure that the Ebon lord would not be in any way affected by the influences of his magical armour.

"Poppycock," exclaimed the skeletal figure across the table from him. "Absolute rubbish. You are a deluded little upstart, young buck, and are surely mistaken if you think you are going to convince me of your ridiculous, made up story."

This was not what Reynard had expected. Most people were surprised and shocked to hear about the resurgence of the catastrophic Writhing Death, but none had yet flat out refused to believe his story.

"My lord," came in a soft voice from Reynard's left. "If I may?" Evantia's tone was deferential without being subservient. It got the Dark Lord's attention.

"Of course, my dear," he replied, grey eyes roaming across the beautiful woman's body and finally resting on her pretty face.

"I am the representative of the Trade Lords on this matter. And I am here to tell you that the Trade Lords are also behind this venture. We are raising an army to send to Granita to fight the Writhing Death. I can also tell you that members of the Guild of Merchants and Master Seafarers have seen evidence of the Writhing Death and that the Trade Lords are in no doubt as to the veracity of the story Reynard has just told you, nor of the terrible danger the threat poses to the very fabric of the empire we all serve."

The Dark Lord blinked as if coming out of a dream. "So you are telling me that the Trade Lords believe this tale? What proof do you have?"

Evantia rose elegantly to her feet and from her cleavage pulled a slim silver tube. Lord Barrius' eyes savoured the show. She smiled at him and handed the small tube to the sitting lord. "That is a scroll case, milord. You will see that it is sealed with the seal of the Trade Lords. Open it."

The Dark Lord tore his eyes from Evantia and looked down at the silver tube in his hands. He examined the small seal intently and then cracked open the delicate tube. Tipping it up he gently shook out a very small piece of fine paper which was headed with the crest of the Guild. His eyes scanned the few words written on the page. A look of acceptance came across his face and Reynard assumed that the paper was Evantia's proof and that the Ebon lord had at least accepted her position as envoy to the Trade Lords, if not their story.

Barrius looked across to Reynard and asked, "Who else do you have on board for this little caper?"

"The Dragon," replied Reynard simply, sitting back in his chair to read the expression on the Ebon lord's face.

Barrius laughed. It was an evil sounding cackle and ended up with the Dark Lord having a brief coughing fit. Reynard could not help but notice blood at the corner of the man's mouth when the coughing fit was over. The Dark Lord was clearly not a well man.

"What is so funny?" asked Reynard when the Ebon lord had recovered.

"The Dragon is sending his resources with you to fight against this fairy tale in the east? That is so perfect. I will ravage the lands of Ursum whilst his eye is turned outward. The emperor is dead; the Azure House is crumbling and weak. If the Ruby House chooses this time to take its eye off the game then more fool them." The Dark Lord sat back in his chair and crossed his arms, a look of satisfaction on his face.

"My lord, is there nothing we can say or do to convince you to join us? I fear that without your help our task is doomed and if we fail then all your political advances in the lands of Ursum will be for nothing as the Writhing Death will eventually reach these shores and will surely make your opportunity to enjoy your new power base short lived."

"Nothing you can do or say will make me join the Dragon in any endeavour!" the Dark Lord spat, his face even more venomous than before. Reynard guessed there was something more here than merely the fact that the Ruby and Ebon houses were effectively the two super powers on the island and competing for control of the land.

"Why?" he prompted, simply.

"The Dragon holds my son," the Dark Lord explained, face flushing with anger. "He was taken prisoner by the Ruby House and taken off to Cansae where even now they are torturing him. Nothing you can do will make me join forces with that bastard, even if the empire is in peril," he continued. "Not unless you can somehow bring my son home, will you get any help from me and the Ebon House."

"He already has," said a new voice from behind Reynard.

Turning in his chair Reynard saw a familiar figure step into the room from the corridor beyond. It was Wiktor – the man he had rescued from the Dragon's Pyromancers.

"My son!" exclaimed the Dark Lord, surging to his feet, a look of exultation on his face. "You are home!"

"Yes father," replied the Ebon noble. "All thanks to Reynard, here."

*

"Quite fortuitous I think," said Reynard. The group were back on the *Javelin* that evening, sat in his quarters, discussing the events of the day. "I really did think that we were going to have to do without the help of the Ebon House."

"You were amazing Reynard," replied Evantia. "I'm sure you would have brought him around to our side in the end anyway. You can be very charming when you want to be," she smiled coyly at him. Reynard blushed deeply.

"I'm not convinced," he responded. "I think we were going to have to leave without his help until Wiktor turned up. Just as well we were polite to him when we met him in Cansae I suppose. It just goes to show – you never know how being nice to someone will help you out in the future. I'm very pleased," he declared putting his boots up on the low table, crossing his feet, and taking a long draw from his glass of Pembrose Red.

"You weren't just polite to him – you rescued him from certain death. He had every reason to be grateful," Evantia pointed out.

"Yes, I suppose so," Reynard agreed. Taking another sip he continued, "So, the Dread Guard have been promised to our cause. That is a great coup. They are well renowned as formidable warriors of unswerving courage. They will be a wonderful addition to the force we take to Granita. And Wiktor himself, son of the Dark Lord will lead them in battle."

"Excuse my ignorance," said Evantia, shifting forward in her seat, "but what makes them so 'formidable', as you put it?"

"They have a fearsome reputation," responded Reynard. "I have heard so many tales of their courage and bravery. It is said they never run from battle. They are indomitable. It is almost as if they don't know the meaning of the word fear."

"They don't," interjected Tanithil from this position standing near the book shelf in the corner of the room. Reynard jumped. He had quite forgotten the telepath was there.

"What do you mean?"

"They don't know the meaning of fear, because the dead do not feel afraid of anything."

"What?" asked Evantia, turning to look at Tanithil. "What do you mean, 'dead'?"

"The Dread Guard are not just well-trained soldiers with great courage born of great tradition and leaders. They are the walking dead. They are reanimated skeletons, compelled to serve the forces of the Ebon House with unswerving loyalty. They do not feel fear. They do not need to eat, drink, or sleep. They will never revolt, will never be disloyal, will never be tired, and will never be demoralized. They will obey orders without question or pause, no matter how dangerous.

In short, they are the perfect soldiers."

"That's disgusting," said Evantia, turning pale. "You mean underneath all those suits of armour there are walking skeletons?"

"Exactly. Walking skeletons under the control of the Ebon House nobility."

"How do you know this, Tani?" asked Reynard, finding that as amazing as it was, it all made sense.

"It was something we were taught as a working theory when I was in the Thought Guard years ago. But now I have been to the very centre of the Ebon House's power base I know it to be true."

"Why? What did you sense?"

"Wiktor," Tanithil answered simply.

"What about him?"

"He is one of those responsible for raising the dead and turning them into animated corpses. He is a practitioner of one of the most dangerous and foulest of the dark arts.

He is a Necromancer."

-Chapter Seven-

"Have no fear," assured the shimmering-robed man. "Despite my warning to those mercenaries that I am in a bad mood, I feel far more effervescent than I let on. We are all friends here. Welcome to Hollytree."

Kita bowed her most respectful bow. Here was the great *Wu-jen* of the West, a figure of legend in her homeland. Stories of the magician's evil nature were well known in Honshu, yet her father always maintained that the Archmage Camero was a benign figure. And in her last days with him Kita had learned that her father had ended his life working for the mysterious character. Now she had travelled half way across the known world, risking life and limb to find the mage and tell him that Heremod had been killed, but that they had found out that Camero's worst fears were true – the Writhing Death was back.

"Please, come with me to a more comfortable location," continued the Archmage. "I feel my lobby is not the most appropriate venue for the conversations we need to have. A warm fire and some mulled wine seem much more welcoming than a marble hallway. This way if you please."

The robed figure turned and moved up the marble spiral staircase which seemed to wind its way up the inside of the walls of the tower they had entered. Kita followed swiftly, not wishing to give any offense to the man ahead of her. He may be doing all he could to put them at ease but she had been on the road for too long to be able to relax that quickly, and she wasn't even sure if she could trust this powerful wizard yet.

The Archmage lead the group into the next level of his home. A door, which appeared to be made of solid marble, slid silently sideways into the wall at his approach, revealing a dark room beyond. As the wizard moved into the room it filled with soft light almost as if welcoming the mage in. Kita followed him in and was impressed to find the whole room jammed floor to ceiling with bookshelves, all of which were full of books and tomes of varying types, sizes and colours. Instantly it was clear the owner of this library was an organized type – the rows were all neat and looked orderly and precisely positioned.

Their host passed straight through the library without giving it a second glance and reached the other side of the room where another marble door slid quietly aside at his approach. Passing through the group entered into another room which seemed to spring to soft light as they entered. Kita saw the light in the library dim and go out as they left it, the door sliding into place behind them.

The chamber they had come into was a lounge of some sort. A few leather couches were scattered around the room, all focussed on the fireplace against one curved wall. Soft rugs adorned the floors. A few pictures were hung on the walls and the odd trophy or two. Kita could not help but be impressed by the giant lizard head dominating the wall opposite the fire place. If she did not know better she would almost wonder if it was the head of a dragon. But she was pretty sure dragons didn't exist except in children's tales. But then again, here she was in the Wizard's Tower, so maybe anything was possible.

At a wave of the Archmage's hand the fire burst into flames, the room instantly warmed and made cosy by the blaze. "Do make yourselves comfortable. Sit where you please," he invited as he went and sat in a huge armchair which was next to the lizard head on the wall. Kita, Okoth and Mosi took their seats on various couches arrayed around the room.

"Now, refreshments?" enquired Camero, waving his fingers again. "I have hot spiced wines from your homeland Mosi, *tembo* from Nubia, and of course some of the best *sake* from the Dragon Province to the east. There are also some refreshing local wines from grapes grown on the foothills of the Jagged Peaks just to the north of here. For food there is a selection of sweet meats and small dishes from various parts of the world. Help yourselves." As he said this, silver platters floated into sight from hidden alcoves in the walls. They were heaped with various drinks and food exactly as he had said. Kita had seen nothing like it before. It was only something very simple yet this easy show of power was not lost on the Niten warrior. Here was a man of immense talent. She must make him an ally.

Once the travellers had had a chance to select some snacks and a drink each the Archmage smiled saying, "So, you will excuse me if I bring us straight to business. I am very busy and as much as I would love to sit here before a roaring fire feasting and drinking for a whole evening, there are pressing things I must turn my attention to soon. So, what is it I can do for you, Kita?"

Kita took a deep breath and put down her food tray on a small table beside the couch she was on. Where to begin? At the beginning, she decided.

"You clearly know who we are," she began. The Archmage nodded confirmation. "And so you will probably guess that I am here because of the quest you set before my father. I am sorry to tell you that he lost his life on that quest, but through me he is able to complete the task you set him." It was important to Kita that her father's honour be maintained, and that he not be seen to fail in the assignment he had been given.

The wizard's face grew solemn and it seemed to Kita that the lights in the room dimmed a bit almost in respect. "I know, Kita. You have my sincerest sympathy. Heremod was a great man, but you should know he died doing something which could save the very world in which we live. His sacrifice was not in vain."

"I know. He told me what you sent him to Granita to do. And in his absence I completed the mission you gave him. I have come here to tell you that your fears are justified. The Writhing Death has returned. I have seen it with my own eyes."

For just a moment Kita thought she saw a flicker of uncontrolled emotion pass across the face of the Archmage. She thought she caught the briefest glimpse of shock and fear, then the impression was gone and the gently benevolent smile was back on the wizard's face. Kita was not certain that she had even seen his face change. Perhaps it was just the flickering shadows of the fire.

The Archmage stood and paced to the fire, a look of deep reflection now on his face. "I was afraid this would be so. I wished it was not, but I have prepared for the worst. Now I must tell you a little bit about me and what I do. I will keep it brief as I have little time – less so now with your news.

"I am head of a group of scholars. We call ourselves the Cabal of Callindrill, a fancy title named after the great mage of the past who lived in these parts. Anyway, the name is not important; what is important is that the Cabal has some of the world's greatest minds in its number. We work hard to learn what we can about the threats and risks that imperil this world and then to organise who and what we can to confront those threats and hopefully neutralize them. Much of what we do goes unnoticed by the masses and we prefer it that way. We work in the shadows and behind the scenes. We find that more effective than great shows of strength and power.

"So, when the rumours of the return of the Writhing Death surfaced a year or so ago the Cabal put some actions in motion. One was to send your father to Granita to try and determine the truth of these rumours. Heremod was not a member of the Cabal but sometimes we need people with more than just keen minds to go out into the field and do our work for us. Heremod was one of our best and most trusted operators. Another action was to send one of our greatest minds to research the Writhing Death and find out whatever there was to discover of this creeping menace."

Kita nodded her understanding. It was slightly humbling to think that her father had been part of this elite group, even if only as one of their agents.

"The person we sent was Darian Snow, the son of the Ice King of Manabas. As well as being one of the nobility of the Lucarcian Empire, back where the Writing Death originates, Darian was already the foremost authority on the subject. He has had a great interest in this unnatural infestation all his life. Darian has spent the last year or more doing nothing else than trying to find a way to stop the Writhing Death. If there is a way to stop it, he will know it."

The Archmage picked up a long metal poker and prodded at the fire with it. After a few moments he stopped and looked up at the group. "Do you wish to help us?" he asked them directly.

Kita looked at her friends, already knowing what she would say but hoping to see their agreement. Mosi was stroking his goatee between his thumb and forefinger. He saw Kita looking at him and nodded seriously. Kita acknowledged his accord and looked at Okoth. The big Nubian was clearly a bit overwhelmed by the whole situation. He shrugged and grinned at her.

Kita turned back to the wizard. "We do," she replied simply.

"Excellent," the Archmage responded, smiling. "I believe you will make very competent operatives. In that case," he continued, replacing the poker in its rack by the fire, "I would like you to track down Darian Snow. Tell him what you know and help him in any way you can. The Writhing Death needs to be stopped – and you may be the only people able to do so."

"There is another who is on our side," Kita replied.

"Ah, yes. Reynard Ferrand. As we speak he is endeavouring to unite the disparate factions of the Lucarcian Empire and bind them to our cause. I think he has his work cut out. But I have high hopes for him – he is a resourceful fellow."

"Yes, he is," said Kita, feeling a surge of pride hearing the Archmage speak so about Reynard. "So, where do we find this Darian Snow?" she asked.

"I would start in Stoneheart, the frigid capital city of Manabas, back in Lucarcia. That is Darian's home and they may know where he is."

Kita frowned. "You mean you don't know?" she asked, surprised.

"No, I don't," admitted the Archmage. "We may be knowledgeable, and despite the fact that some of us are able to perform simple acts of prestidigitation to entertain and impress guests on cold autumn nights, we are not all-powerful. Darian left here over a year ago. I have not seen him since. The last word I had was that he had not been seen in Stoneheart for a while, so he may well not be there, but I think his family would be most likely to know where he is, and he is likely to return home at some stage. I think you should start your search for him here."

Kita nodded her consent. "Okay then, Stoneheart it is. The next problem is how we get there. We had quite the adventure getting here from Providentia and that was even with the help of the Church of Light. Getting back to Lucarcia again could take us months."

"There, I can help. I know you have used a Translocator before. Well, I have one in my tower and it just so happens I know the correct incantation to open a portal to the Translocator inside the palace deep in Stoneheart. Be warned though: you are unlikely to get a friendly reception there."

"Don't worry about that," said Kita grimly. "We are getting used to that."

*

Kita blinked rapidly, shaking her head, once more completely disoriented by the act of being Translocated. She had her hand on the hilt of her *katana* but before she could clear her head she felt powerful hands grasp her wrists and move them behind her back. The pain in her shoulders focussed her mind rapidly.

She was in a rough-hewn chamber, carved out of some sort of natural rock. There was no sunlight present, the only illumination coming from a brightly burning torch in a nearby sconce and the still-pulsing violet light of the Translocator's runes, carved into the floor at her feet.

There were a large number of men in the room, all wearing thick furs with white fur cloaks on their backs. It took a moment for her to register that each cloak had a hood made from the skull of a great white bear. The skulls formed sort of helmets for the guards and the cloaks were obviously some sort of uniform, although other than the cloaks, no two guards were dressed the same. One of these men had her arms pinned behind her back. Another man held Mosi in a similar lock and two further cloaked guards held Okoth tight.

Kita breathed out, calming her thoughts, and was surprised to see the air from her lungs misting out in front of her. Then she realised just how cold it was in this room. No wonder the guards were all dressed in furs. Kita shivered involuntarily, thinking that simple Honshu silk robes were entirely unsuitable for the climate here. But her clothing was probably not the most pressing concern at the moment.

"Who are you?" came the gruff voice from one of the guards, his accent hard for Kita to understand. "What you doing here?" he continued.

"I am Kita of Sapporo. These are my friends, Mosi the Haji of Shelech, and Okoth the Champion Gladiator of Nubia. We come here at the behest of the Cabal of Callindrill."

"Never heard of them. Never heard of you," came the brusque reply.

"We seek Darian Snow in a matter of utmost urgency," she tried. The guard's face showed recognition now. At least he knew who Darian was.

"What about?" came the curt question.

"I am afraid I cannot discuss the details with you. My message is for his ears alone."

"Is it?" asked the guard. "Seems like you is going to be keeping it to yourself then. You don't tell me, you don't get to see him."

"You wouldn't be so big mouthed if you didn't have all your lackeys with you," came in Okoth's voice from beside Kita. She closed her eyes – they needed to gain this man's help, not antagonise him. What was Okoth doing?

"What's that?" asked the leader, turning his gaze on Okoth.

"You heard. You're only being unhelpful because there are more of you than us. You're no true warrior."

The bear cloaked guard's face flushed. "Rubbish!" he exclaimed. "I am Yanni, a former First Protector to his majesty the Ice King and the most decorated *Nanuk* in Manabas. I will have it out with anyone who says otherwise."

"I say otherwise," said Okoth, puffing his barrel chest out and rising up to his full height. The guard was tall but Okoth still looked down on him.

"Then we will see who is right and who is crushed. Bring them!" ordered the guard leader.

*

The cavern which the group were led to was immense and bare. The only thing in the room was a large circle, marked out on the floor with a simple hemp rope. Okoth, Kita and Mosi were ushered into the room by the white-cloaked guards. Their grips on the companions had relaxed and they were being led rather than forced. Most of the guards had remained behind at the location of the Translocator but as many as the guard captain had allowed had come along to watch the confrontation.

"Here we find out who is the warrior and who is defeated," said Yanni. "Release the big one, but keep the other two in check," he ordered.

The two men holding Okoth's arms behind his back released him and the giant Nubian rolled his shoulders, loosening his aching muscles. "How does this work?" he asked the guard leader.

"We both step into the ring," the fur cloaked man replied, "and the first one to leave the ring loses. No weapons," he added, as one of the guards took Okoth's spear away. The captain handed his axe to one of his men and nodded to the Nubian.

Suddenly a commotion behind the group caused everyone to turn. A score or more white-cloaks were pouring into the cavern from a side passage. "What is going on?" asked Yanni, his voice full of authority.

"We heard you were going to give an outsider a beating," said one of the new arrivals, a fresh faced youth. "We've come to watch."

"Then you're just in time, friends," smiled Yanni. "It's time."

"More people just means more people to embarrass yourself in front of," said Okoth and Kita smiled in spite of herself. "Let's do this," said the huge Nubian, turning his back on the discussion and walking purposefully into the ring.

Suddenly Yanni rushed into the ring behind Okoth and dipping his shoulder he charged into the back of the giant, sending him sprawling forward towards the edge of the circle. Taken completely by surprise, Okoth was only just able to stop himself plunging forward and over the rope. His huge frame reached the hemp border and he fought to maintain his balance and stop from stepping out of the arena.

Behind him Yanni rushed in again intending to simply push the teetering giant out of the ring. But Okoth regained his balance in the nick of time and ducked gracefully under Yanni's thrust, moving past him and back into the centre of the ring.

"Nice try bear man, but you don't beat the Champion of Nubia that easily. Now, prepare to discover how a real gladiator fights."

The two pugilists clashed time and again, fists beating into each other's faces and torsos. They grappled to the ground on numerous occasions, until one would slip free and both would disengage by unspoken mutual consent and return to their feet and face off against one another again.

Kita watched the fight with great admiration. She had never really seen Okoth fight in this manner before and she marvelled at his skill in the format. He had a built in instinct about the size of the arena. He controlled the space well, always seeming to be in the centre with Yanni on the outside. The guard captain was a brutal fighter though and Okoth was taking a severe beating. But as the fight went on it became clear that there would only be one winner. Okoth was taller, had greater reach and was slightly faster too. And for every sneaky trick Yanni knew and used, Okoth knew and used two. The fight would soon end and Kita knew Okoth would be victorious, unless he lost concentration and made a mistake. Something which was quite possible given how beaten and tired both men looked.

Then Yanni made a mistake. He misjudged his distancing and found himself right inside Okoth's reach, right in the impact zone. Okoth spotted the opening and made it count. A thunderous right hook flew in and landed square on Yanni's left temple. The guard captain sailed backwards through the air and landed in a heap next to the rope, the air rushing out of his lungs with an audible whoosh. Yanni groaned and shook his head. Okoth moved in and gripped the captain by the throat and the thigh, picking him up off the ground.

The Nubian then jerked the captain up high in to the air, lifting the stunned guard above his head in a spectacular demonstration of strength. He was about to throw the groggy guard out of the ring and win the fight, when Yanni let out the most bestial of growls, loud and feral. Okoth stopped in mid throw and looked up to the man held above his head. To his amazement Yanni was no longer wearing the skull of a white bear on his head as part of a cloak. Rather his head had actually turned into that of a white bear! Okoth dropped the body in shock and jumped back.

The giant white bear, which had moments before been the captain of the guard, growled ferociously and got onto all four paws. It threw its head back and bellowed a deafening roar.

"*Nanuk!*" cheered the white-cloaked guards surrounding the arena. "*Nanuk! Nanuk! Nanuk!*" they began to chant. It was clear this transformation was not unexpected to them.

Okoth blinked rapidly and dropped into a deep stance. He wasn't sure if the bear he now faced understood the rules about the ring and he was also deeply aware that whilst he was unarmed, the bear had wicked curved talons and teeth the size of his fingers. This fight had changed and he wasn't sure if it was now still a competition or a real fight to survive. He resolved to be ready for either.

The bear, though savage in appearance, was also badly beaten. Okoth could see numerous welts on the bear's fur where he had struck Yanni earlier. So at least the bear was also tired and injured.

Suddenly the bear rushed forward, rising up on its back legs, towering now even above Okoth. The bear lurched forward, going to hug Okoth and squeeze him between its huge paws. The giant gladiator dropped down onto his back, letting the bear land on top of him.

Kita gasped in horror as Okoth disappeared beneath the vast mass of white fur, muscle, teeth and talons. She didn't see how Okoth could survive. Then suddenly, as quickly as the bear had landed on top of the Nubian, it was flying off him, spinning through the air. Okoth had rolled onto his back and brought his powerful legs up above him. As the bear had landed on him, he had planted his feet into the bear's chest and then pushed with all his might, using his great strength and the bear's enormous momentum to drive it off him and away.

The timing was perfect and the huge bear flew through the air to crash land on the far side of the rope, outside the circle. Okoth had won. But did the bear know that?

The white bear rose up on its back legs. For a moment Kita thought it would charge back into the ring, but instead it shook its coat and seemed almost to blur before their eyes. In moments the bear was gone and the guard captain stood in its place once more.

"It seems I was wrong," Yanni said. "You are a formidable warrior, gladiator. I will escort to the King."

*

Like the majority of the city of Stoneheart that it was part of, the Ice Palace was built entirely underground. Carved directly into the mountainside, this fortified city was perched high in the Stoneheart Mountains and much of it lay beneath the surface. It was known as one of the most impregnable settlements of the world.

Ruled by Lord Agamedes Snow, the Ice King, Stoneheart was home to a few thousand people. It prospered chiefly because of the mines which dotted the mountainside around it. Copper, tin and silver mines were common in the foothills and precious gold was mined in abundance high in the peaks of the Stoneheart Mountains. All that wealth meant that the Ice King was one of the richest men in the empire. House Snow had always sworn fealty to the emperor, and Agamedes had always been a loyal subject to his liege. However the Ice King hardly ever left his mountain fortress and his interests in the politics of the empire had always been close to nothing. House Snow was politically aloof. Their geographical isolation from Ursum, the hub of the empire, meant that they could essentially remain independent and that was how the Ice King liked it.

The throne room of the Ice Palace was, like most of the structure, built of large blocks of quartzite, mortared with sand cement. Rectangular in shape, it was wider than it was long and the roof above was flat and square. Various hangings adorned the walls and a huge tapestry of a rampant ice bear dominated the rear of the room. A single pair of huge doors, large enough for two horse-drawn wagons to ride through side by side, was the only obvious entrance to the chamber. At the far end of the room from these doors a large dais rose, built from dark granite. Upon this podium three sandstone thrones were built, equally spaced across the terrace. The thrones looked cold and uncomfortable, yet the man who sat upon the middle throne looked relaxed on his perch.

Dressed in rich looking furs, made from the hide of the giant, hairy elephants that roamed the high glacial plains adjacent to the city, Lord Agamedes Snow rested his head in one hand, palm open and supporting his bearded chin. His gaze swept out across the cold room beneath him and settled on the three outsiders who were walking into his domain, following the Translocator guard captain, Yanni.

Agamedes' gaze was first drawn to the hulking black-skinned fellow at the back of the group. He was immensely strong and moved with a limp. He looked like he had taken a beating recently. From the blood and bruises covering Yanni's face, and knowing of the *Nanuk's* love of brawling, Agamedes guessed what had happened there.

His scrutiny next passed to the white-robed man who walked slightly ahead of the black man. He looked like a priest of the Light from what the Ice King could see, and a poor one at that. Agamedes had more respect for poorer priests that he ever had for the rich ones. He had always felt that a rich priest was a priest more interested in his own wellbeing than that of the people in his congregation.

Finally his eye was drawn to the woman who led the three visitors to his throne room. There was a warrior. She may not have all the attributes that the warriors of Manabas prized; she was not powerful and tall. Her step was light and perfectly balanced. She moved with a grace seldom seen in these halls. And the red silk of her robe shimmered as she moved into the chamber. Agamedes was entranced. Not a beauty, the woman was yet attractive in her own way. Lithe and somehow sensuous in the way she moved across the room, he found he could not look away.

Lifting his head from his hand, Agamedes straightened up in his throne and subconsciously straightened out his furs. Letting out a breath, which misted in the cold air in front of his face, he wondered what the three newcomers wanted of him.

Especially the woman.

*

Kita was cold. No one had thought to offer her something warm to wear and she was too proud to ask. *Never show pain*, she reminded herself. The cold was not bad enough to cause actual pain, but a Niten warrior never admitted to discomfort either. Following Yanni into the throne room she resolutely put her disquiet aside and concentrated on the matter at hand. She had to find Darian Snow and he was the son of the Ice King, who sat on the throne ahead. She would worry about the cold later.

She followed Yanni's lead. The guard captain walked purposefully up to the base of the dais on which the king sat and stopped. "Visitor's sire," he announced. "I deem them worthy of an audience," he finished formally.

"You mean the black one impressed you enough to agree to let them see me," the king guessed.

"Yes, your majesty. He did," Yanni said simply. "A true warrior. He would make a fine *Nanuk*."

The Ice King nodded, "Thank you Yanni. Return to your post. The Translocator must be guarded well, especially in these dark times."

"At once, sire," bowed the captain. He turned and strolled out, patting Okoth affectionately on the shoulder as he passed.

"Come forward," ordered the monarch. "I would know what brings you to the Ice Palace at this time?"

Kita moved to the edge of the dais and looked up into the pale blue eyes of the man above her. There didn't seem to be any point in being anything other than direct. "We are searching for your son, Darian Snow."

The Ice King laughed a deep and resonant laugh which echoed around the hall. "Well, you have come to the wrong place then, milady. For I have not seen my son in over two years. He fell in with bad folk. Which leads me to wonder what it is you want with him?"

"We need his help," Kita admitted, wondering what approach to take in this conversation. For now she decided that simple truth would do until she could get more of a feel for the man on the throne above her.

"His help, hmmm? In what?"

Kita took a deep breath and dived in. She told the Ice King of the return of the infamous Writhing Death. She told him of their experiences on Granita and of seeing the threat first hand. She told him that her father had been sent to find out the truth of the matter by a group of wise men and that those same men had sent her to find Darian, because he apparently knew more about this threat than any other man alive.

When she was finished the Ice King sat back in his throne and closed his eyes. She was not sure what would come next. Moments later she could hear the soft sounds of a chuckle coming from the throne. Bit by bit that sound grew louder until the King was sat forward; laughing fully and heartily, his booming giggles exploding off the stone walls. Kita stood patiently, saying nothing, her expression neutral as she waited for the king to finish.

At last he drew a deep shuddering breath and opened his eyes. There were tears running down his cheeks. Kita was not sure if they were tears of mirth or of despair.

"My son," the Ice King began, "has always been weak. His mother was struck down by a wasting sickness whilst she was carrying him. The priests said she would not survive but that she was carrying a son, and that they could save my unborn son, but not my beautiful wife. She died giving birth to him. He was tiny then and he has never recovered. He suffers from the same wasting disease that killed his mother. He is a shadow of a man unable to brawl or even pick up an axe.

"But he is my son and I have tried to do right by him. I sent him to the best warriors in the land, the *Nanuk* shaman, but they could do nothing with him and he was sent back to me, a failure. All that he ever wanted to do was to read books. There is precious little need for books in Stoneheart milady. Especially for one whom would one day be king. But I relented and sent out to the far corners of the empire to collect tomes and volumes for my son to consume. And he did.

Then he came across the legend of the collapse of the Rainbow Empire and the Writhing Death. He was captivated. From that moment on that was all we heard from him. His mind was never on the moment. It was never on learning the skills of kinghood. It was on the death of one empire and the foundation of another.

Soon afterwards, *he* came. He arrived through the Translocator though I do not know how he found the key to activate it. My best *Nanuk* guards tried to stop him but he brushed them aside like they were seal pups. He burst unbidden into this very throne room and walked up to me. Without so much as a by-your-leave he told me he was taking Darian away for a year. He said that my son would be cared for, looked after and trained. He told me that it would make Darian a better man and that he would return stronger and more powerful. And so he took my son.

"I hoped and prayed that such a man as him would transform my son, that he would make him into the warrior which my best men had been unable to. I counted the days until he would return. A year passed and as promised my Darian returned. Had he been trained? Certainly. Was he different? Oh yes, immeasurably so. Was he stronger and more powerful? Yes, definitely. Was he the warrior son I had always wished for? No.

"My son could still not wield an axe. He was still weak and suffering from the same wasting disease that had killed his mother. Yet he had somehow learnt things which even now I do not understand. He could do things which were simply unexplainable. It's unnatural. He is unnatural.

"I do not blame him. How could I? He is my son. I blame the one who barged in here and took my son away and returned him a different person. Darian was never the same. But his interest in the Writhing Death had not changed; in fact it was stronger than ever.

"Then, about two years ago now, Darian announced that he was going away again. This time he was leaving of his own accord. I tried to explain to him that he is heir to my throne and that he needs to be here in Stoneheart, but he would not listen. He told me that he was working on something which was far more important than the kingdom of Manabas and the fortunes of House Snow. What on this cold earth could be more important than that?!

"He left the next day, stepping into the Translocator and disappearing to who knows where? Somehow he had learnt to activate the device himself, without the help of the *Nanuk* shaman, and so even they do not know where he went. As I say that was two years ago, and we have not seen him since. So, if you wish to find him I am afraid that as much as I would like to be able to help you, I simply cannot. I have no idea where my son is, or if he is even still alive."

"Sire!" a guard in a white-bear cloak called out from the doorway. "Sorry to interrupt, but there are more outsiders here, your majesty. They have just arrived in the city on horseback. They say they need to talk to you about a threat to the empire. Their leader wears a suit of golden armour and looks like a figure out of the legends of old, sire."

A suit of golden armour. Kita felt a lump form in her throat. Reynard was here.

-Chapter Eight-

"Now, I have pressing business to attend to," said the Ice King dismissively. "You will, of course, be housed, fed and watered whilst here. My guards will show you to your quarters in the east wing of the palace." Agamedes Snow rose to his full height and looked over Kita's head to the back of the chamber where he was clearly waiting for the arrival of his new guests.

Kita bowed curtly and turned on her heel. A guard nodded briefly to his king and turned to Kita, indicating a side door. "This way," he said perfunctorily, heading towards the exit. Kita had no choice but the follow him. She walked as slowly across the chamber floor as she could, her eyes darting often to the main entrance where any moment now Reynard would enter, but the Ice King turned to her and waited for her to leave, obviously wanting one guest gone before he invited the next one in. Kita would be denied the chance to see Reynard – for now.

*

"Captain Reynard Ferrand, Heir to the Iron House of Ursum, at your service," said Reynard, with a courtly bow. The golden armour glinted brightly in the white surrounds of the Ice King's audience chamber, making his face glow. Next to him stood Evantia, in a sky blue dress, made warmer by a fox-fur shawl which was wrapped cosily around her shoulders. Slightly behind the two of them stood Tanithil, in his usual practical green and browns.

The Ice King, still standing in front of his throne, looked down upon the threesome and smiled a huge smile. "Welcome to Stoneheart, Captain," he said. "You have come a long way. What brings you to our mountain home at this time?"

"Grave tidings, your Majesty. Grave tidings indeed," began Reynard. "You will of course be aware of the events of the summer down on Ursum and Granita. Well ..."

Agamemnon held up a gloved hand to interrupt Reynard. "Stop right there, Captain." Reynard paused in mid-flow. "We are a long way away from the capital of the empire here," continued the king. "Events in that far off place have little significance here, and we take, at best, only passing interest in them. Additionally, rare is the messenger who comes here bringing news from the empire. We are almost an independent country here."

"Surely you know of the death of the Emperor?" queried Reynard.

"Of course!" exclaimed the Ice King. "We may be remote but news of that importance does not escape our attention."

"And are you also aware that the other noble houses are taking steps to prepare for the inevitable political confrontation which is brewing in the vacuum left by his death?"

"The politics of the empire do not concern us here. Let the other 'noble' houses plot and scheme. We are simple folk with simple needs. We have our honour and we do not stoop to the levels of the other houses."

"The politics of the empire may not concern you, but the events occurring on the cursed island of Granita will, whether you want them to or not." The Ice King sat down on his throne as Reynard proceeded to describe the events of the summer leading up to his discovery of the Writhing Death and its return.

The Ice King listened to the whole tale from start to finish, without saying a word. From his position behind Reynard, Tanithil could see the king was entranced by the whole story. Reynard had clearly judged the Ice King well and had chosen his words and manner of speech appropriately. He talked of the massive threat to the lands – even here in far-off Manabas – from the Writhing Death. He talked of the need for heroes to rise up and defend the lands and the innocent. He talked of legends being born and legacies being forged. All things which the Ice King clearly found inspiring and rousing. Tanithil could see the stirring of emotion in the king's face and posture. He was hooked.

Reynard came to the end of his tale and finished with, "So, your majesty, as you can see the Empire of Lucarcia faces the biggest threat in its history. The Empire needs you. I need you."

Agamedes Snow stroked his beard and looked down on Reynard and his friends. "Ah, the Writhing Death. Yes, I know of this abomination. I know more about it than I would care to. My son, Darian, is somewhat of a scholar and has been studying this aberration for many years. But he has never found anything useful out about it. However, you have been to stare into the very face of this impending doom and have seen it first-hand. You have travelled here to speak to me face to face about the threat. You have been honourable and brave. For this reason I will send my elite *Nanuk* warriors to aid your cause."

"Thank you, your majesty. You are as wise as the bards' tales proclaim," praised Reynard with another bow.

"It is curious though," stated the Ice King, his gaze sweeping across Reynard, Tani and Evantia, "that you three should turn up here in my throne room only moments after three other strangers had been here talking about the Writhing Death. I assume your visits are related?"

"Three others?" asked Reynard with a grin. "A giant black-skinned fellow, a bearded man wearing a white robe and a dark haired woman in a red silk robe?"

"The very same," nodded the king.

"They are here? Now?"

"Indeed they are. They are being settled into their quarters in the east wing as we speak."

"May we see them?"

"You may. I will summon the *Nanuk* shaman and we will work out the best way to get you the help you have come asking for."

"You have my undying gratitude, great king – and that of the empire".

*

Okoth's face split into its customary white grin as Tanithil, Evantia and Reynard stepped through the door into their quarters. "Well met little man!" he exclaimed in joy. "Tis great to see you again!" He stepped forward and hoisted Reynard into a big bear hug, lifting him off the ground.

"You look well Reynard," said Mosi smiling as Okoth placed him back on the ground. "The Armour of Lucar sits well on your shoulders."

"Thank you, both" replied Reynard with his easy smile. Turning to Kita his face split into a grin. "Hello Kita," he began. "It's been a while."

"It has, Reynard," she replied, coming to her feet and bowing to him, the slightest trace of a smile on her face.

Kita, Okoth and Mosi all then greeted Tanithil in the same way, all clearly pleased to see him again too. Tanithil complained of having the wind crushed out of him by Okoth, and gave Kita a hug which might have made the stoic Niten warrior a little uncomfortable, but if she was she didn't show it.

Then Evantia was by Reynard's side, slipping her arm into his and moving in close beside him. "Are you going to introduce me to your friends, darling?" she purred, smiling up into Reynard's face, her fingers gently stroking the gold of his armoured forearm.

Reynard flushed crimson as all traces of warmth deserted Kita's face, to be replaced by a cold, impassive mask. "Err, yes, of course," he replied. "The big man is Okoth, Champion Gladiator of Nubia." Okoth grinned his usual grin, seemingly oblivious to any discomfort in the room. Turning to the white robed priest, Reynard continued, "This is Mosi, Haji of Shelech." Mosi bowed smoothly. "And this is Kita, Niten Warrior of the Sapporo dojo," he said indicating the woman from Honshu. Kita said nothing.

"Everyone, this is Evantia, representative of the Trade Lords. She has been sent with us to help convince the ruling nobles that they should join our cause."

"Well met Evantia," replied Mosi with a smile. "And how is the recruiting going?" he asked, moving back into the room.

The quarters were bare but comfortable. Nothing here was luxurious, with tables and chairs being made of simple pine, sturdy and functional. Wall sconces held torches which were unlit at this time. There were no wall hangings or carpets. A single door led off the main room, presumably to bedrooms beyond. A table in one corner held a carafe of wine and some goblets, plus a small selection of simple cold meat dishes. A large fireplace was home to a moderate blaze which warmed the room and made it almost cosy.

Reynard untangled himself from Evantia and moved to the carafe, pouring himself a large goblet. Sniffing it, he wrinkled his nose. "Bostwick plonk, if I am not mistaken," he judged expertly. "A cheap alternative to the Pembrose Red. Typical. We travel all this way, to within a hundred miles of the slopes where the Pembrose grape is grown and we get served this rubbish." Shaking his head he took a small sip of the drink and cringed.

"Anyway, we are not here to discuss wine," he continued. "Our recruiting is going extremely well," he reported. "Obviously we managed to get the Trade Lords onside from the start," he said nodding towards Evantia who was standing where Reynard had left her, head titled alluringly to one side, a stunning smile on her pretty face.

"Obviously," commented Kita dryly as she sat herself neatly down on a pine stool by the fire. Evantia's smile faded.

"From there," continued Reynard hurriedly, "we acquired the services of the Dragon's Pyromancers, the Ebon Lord's Dread Guard, and just now, the Ice King's elite *Nanuk* warriors. In short, every noble house we have visited has agreed to come to our aid."

"Great job Reynard!" proclaimed Mosi, clapping his hands together. "You have done exceptionally well!"

"It wasn't just me," offered Reynard dismissively. "Tanithil and Evantia both did their bit too."

"I'm sure they did," said Kita coldly, eying the blonde woman.

"Actually, I didn't really say a thing," came in Tanithil as he took his place on a seat by the pine table in the centre of the room. "It was really all Reynard and Evantia."

Evantia crossed the floor and stood next to Reynard at the refreshment table, selecting a small meat delicacy, "Of course, we still have to visit the Verdant Queen and try and get her agreement," she said, taking Reynard's arm in hers once again. "But I am certain Reynard can convince her. He has a way with women," she finished, smiling up into his face once more.

"The problem there," said Reynard, looking uncomfortable under totally different gazes of Evantia and Kita, "is that we have reason to believe that Lily Jade sponsored Captain Kester's escapades in the summer. We think he may have been her nephew. How is she going to take to us asking for her help?"

"A good question," replied Mosi. "And I suppose one which you can only answer by going there and finding out for yourselves."

Reynard nodded. "That is my plan, yes. Our next stop is the jungles of Ibini. Should make quite the change from the cold up here in the Stoneheart Mountains. Now, how goes your progress, Kita?" Reynard asked, trying to get something more out of the Niten warrior than one word sentences.

"In truth, not well," she said, looking up at Reynard and studiously avoiding catching Evantia's eye. "We managed to get to Camero, the *wu-jen* who my father was working for. He told us we needed to track down Darian Snow, son of the Ice King, to find out more. So we came here to look for him, but with no luck." Standing, Kita continued, "I am tired. I am going to retire to my room and consider my options," she said poignantly, looking from Reynard to Evantia and back. Turning smartly on her heel she moved to the far door and stepped through it, pulling it close behind her.

*

"I'm going to get a breath of fresh air," said Tanithil as Reynard, Evantia and he arrived at their quarters in the north wing of the palace. "You two go on in. I will catch up with you in an hour or so." Moving past the door, Tanithil didn't look back as he walked away.

"That was sweet of him," smiled Evantia as she opened the door to their quarters. "We will have some time to ourselves." Taking Reynard's hands in hers she backed into the room, her eyes on his. "I have just the thing to take our minds off the rigours of politics and danger," she said, dropping his hands and reaching up to the buttons down the side of her figure-hugging blue dress. Deftly she undid the top two. "Are you going to shut the door, or do you like the idea that anyone could pass by at any moment?" she asked, tilting her head and letting her long blonde tresses cascade over her shoulder with a coy smile, as her fingers continued to undo the buttons.

"Stop that, please" replied Reynard stepping into the room and closing the door behind him. "I'm not in the mood."

"What? I've never heard you say that before, Reynard," she replied, looking slightly abashed. A pout appeared on her face then, "but I'm sure I can change your mind," she continued, stepping up to him and putting his hands on her hips. "Will you help me out of this dress? It is most uncomfortable."

Reynard looked into her eyes. Uncontrollably his eyes then moved down across her body, unable to help himself. Finally they tore themselves back to her face. "I'm sorry Evantia, but no. And this has to stop," he said taking his hands from her hips.

"Why? What is wrong?" stepping back, the smile was gone from her face, replaced by an angry frown. "What have I done?"

"Nothing," returned Reynard, moving into their quarters. He spotted a bottle of wine on a table and instinctively crossed to it, poured himself a glass and drained it. Wrinkling his nose at the second glass of plonk he had drunk this day he poured himself another.

"It's her, isn't it? The dark haired girl – Kita? The moment she saw we were an item she changed. She hates me and I have done nothing wrong."

"We are not an *item* Evantia. We have had some fun together, that is all."

"You are in love with her!" Evantia accused him, hands on hips. "I don't believe it. Why would you … do what you did with me, if you are in love with her?"

"I'm not in love with Kita. She and I are good friends. That is all."

"You may say that with your mouth but your actions say otherwise," stormed Evantia. "I suddenly find that Tanithil is not the only one wanting some fresh air," she raved and marched to the door. Wrenching it open she stepped through and slammed it shut behind her.

"I'm not in love with Kita," Reynard repeated to the empty room.

*

"Come in Tanithil, Evantia is not here," shouted Reynard to the door, upon hearing the smart knock. He was in his room, sitting on the bed, nursing his fifth cup of wine. His head was a little fuzzy and he was looking down at the small drips of spilt plonk which spotted on the chest plate of the golden armour. He heard the door to the quarters open and footsteps entering. These were followed by a scraping noise as if someone was dragging something heavy across the floor. Reynard blinked, his mind not really following what was going on. "I'm in my room," called out Reynard. "No one else is here, don't worry."

"That is helpful, I'll admit," answered an unknown voice from outside the door to his room. The door opened and stood in the frame was a tall man dressed in the uniform of the Stoneheart guards, his ice bear hood pulled over his head to hide his features. "It would have been inconvenient had I needed to kill all of you at once."

Reynard's mind came desperately into focus as he rose to his feet. He was extremely conscious of his mild intoxication and knew that he would be at a serious disadvantage if he had to defend himself now. "What are you talking about my good man?" he asked, stalling for time.

"I am sorry I have to do this," replied the guard. "You seem an honourable man and are clearly a companion to the mighty Okoth, but I have my orders. Now, if you would just step into the main room here we can get on with things."

"Orders? What are you saying?" asked Reynard, wondering blurrily who might have ordered his death? The Ice King?

"Yes, I'm afraid so. My patron has decreed that you are to die. And I will succeed where others have failed. But I will allow you to come out here where there is space to wield that sword of yours, and give you a moment to compose yourself."

Reynard moved slowly into the main room as the guard stepped back. Reynard could see that the man had shifted a large, heavy table in front of the door to the apartment – so as to stop Reynard fleeing and to stop any help coming his way. Drawing his sword calmly from its scabbard, he saw that his opponent was unarmed. "Awfully kind of you, sir, but now I seem to have you at a disadvantage. I am armed and you, it seems, are not." Reynard dropped into a defensive stance, hoping that his balance and footwork would hold up after five glasses of strong wine.

"That is where you're wrong, mate," replied the guard and with a bestial growl he dropped onto his hands and knees in front of Reynard. The swordsman shook his head, momentarily confused until, before his very eyes, the guard grew in size, hands and feet turning into giant paws, the ice bear hood he wore transforming into the actual head of a bear. Where, mere seconds before, a guard in a bear's pelt stood before Reynard, now a real-life ice bear was in front of him, roaring a challenge.

Then the bear reared up onto its hind legs and attacked.

Reynard stumbled backwards and tripped over a pine stool, crashing back to the floor. The trip probably saved his life as two giant bear paws clamped into thin air where his head had been a moment before. Rolling quickly to his feet Reynard circled to his left, to the table which held the now-empty bottle of wine, and a pitcher of water. As the bear growled and came at him, Reynard grabbed the pitcher and emptied it over himself. Shaking his head to clear away the water from his eyes he saw the bear begin to rise again, and smelt the foetid breath from its mighty jaws. Reynard brought the empty pitcher down on its muzzle as hard as he could and the ice bear howled in pain as the pitcher smashed and muzzle bone cracked.

Reynard moved quickly into space in the room and brought his rapier up, pointed as best he could, directly at the bear. The adrenalin was kicking in now and he felt his head clearing. But still his reactions were slow and this time the bear's rush was too fast for him to evade. The ice bear bounded into him and knocked him flying backwards. Claws scrabbled to get a hold of him and a pair of bloody jaws clamped down on his shoulder. Luckily for Reynard he was wearing the Armour of Lucar and even if he was not at his best his armour was still doing its job. The bear was unable to get a grip on the polished golden plates and even the immense crushing power of the bear's jaws focussed into the points of the needle sharp fangs could not break the famous amour. The huge weight of the bear did not crush him, as the golden chest plate protected his lungs, enabling him to breathe normally. The bear was on top of him, but it was not hurting him and Reynard was able to use the two seconds it took him to reclaim a strong grip on his rapier's hilt and then to drive the razor sharp blade deep into the bear's side, up through the rib cage and into the heart.

The bear gave out a huge scream of pain and rage and thrashed about madly on top of Reynard. Even when he felt sure the bear must die, its death throws seemed to continue, claws scratching at the sides of his armour. Finally, the ice bear's life force ran out, the thrashing slowing until the giant bear came to a stop on top of Reynard.

As it died the giant creature shimmered and before his eyes the creature transformed back into a guard, the hood of his uniform pulled back to reveal a man's face. Reynard's head slumped back, relief washing through him as he closed his eyes.

Suddenly the door burst open, three armed Stoneheart guards shoving the table aside and rushing in, Tanithil on their tail.

"Yanni!" shouted one in dismay, "He's killed Yanni!"

Tanithil shook his head in disbelief as he looked on at Reynard, wearing the blood-soaked golden Armour of Lucar, lying under the body of a guard, with his rapier thrust into his side. Even when Evantia wasn't around he couldn't leave Reynard alone for a minute.

*

"It was self-defence," repeated Reynard for the third time. Standing with his arms bound behind his back he looked up at the dais and the three thrones which sat atop it. The Ice King leant forward on his seat, staring down at the accused. Next to Reynard stood all five of his companions. Though not bound like he was, they were all surrounded by armed guards.

"So you have said," proclaimed the king, "yet you can offer no reason why Yanni – once my First Protector – would attack you."

Reynard was struggling to decide what to say. Yanni had declared himself sorry for the fact he had to kill Reynard and had said that his patron had ordered him to do so. But who was his patron? Was it the bearded, fur clad king who sat on the sandstone throne before him or some third party? And in either case, why? Figuring that unless he came up with some sort of an answer he was likely to be executed for murder, Reynard decided that honesty was the best option. "He told me that his patron had ordered my death," Reynard declared. "However I do not know who his patron was."

Agamedes' brow furrowed. "His patron," he stated, "was me. But I never ordered your death. Or are you saying that his loyalty was suspect?"

"I am sure it was not you who ordered my death, sire. But he definitely said that his patron had ordered him to kill me. So, yes, I can only assume this means he was no longer loyal to you."

The Ice King looked furious. "This is a grave accusation. Loyalty is valued above nearly every other trait in this land, Captain. And Yanni can do nothing to refute your accusation." His brow furrowed again as he struggled with his next move. "This needs to be looked into properly," he decided. "You will stay here as my guests, but will be confined to quarters until the truth of the matter can be determined."

"Your majesty," said Kita, stepping forward confidently, her hands on her hips. "I ask that I, and those I arrived with, are allowed the freedom to leave." Looking at Reynard and Evantia, she continued, "we are not with Captain Reynard and his friends, but came here separately and for separate reasons. We need to find your son, Darian, or the fate of the whole Empire may be at stake."

"Yes my dear, you did come here looking for my son. And by some twist of fate, just when you come here looking for him, he chooses to pick this time to return to us," he replied. Kita looked shocked. "Yes, he arrived here just this morning after nearly two years of absence. So, I allow you to speak to him, but I repeat: neither Reynard, nor any of the rest of you will leave your quarters until I say otherwise. I will see to it that Darian visits you in the east wing at his earliest convenience, my dear."

*

Darian Snow was thin and emaciated. Having suffered from the wasting disease since he was born, he had never gained any weight or strength no matter the efforts he had gone to. As such he found it all bar impossible to even hold a battle-axe, let alone wield one in combat. As such his worth in the city of Stoneheart was minimal. And his value to his father was less.

Darian had always loved books. At a tender age he had discovered the small library in Stoneheart and had made it his retreat. Whenever things got on top of him, this was where he would run to. This was where he would flee when his father's rage threatened to consume him. This was where he would go when he wanted some peace and solitude.

Here he had first come across the small treatise on the Writhing Death. He had consumed it eagerly, his imagination fired by the creeping doom and the destructive power it took to stop it. From that day forth, though he read and learnt about all manner of things, whenever he could find and study any books mentioning the Writhing Death, no matter how fleetingly, he would do so. He would order books to be shipped from all corners of the empire and beyond to the mountain fortress and slowly his collection grew.

Then one day Camero had arrived and offered him the chance to spend every day with books; to be valued for his intelligence rather than his sword arm, and to learn the ancient secrets of the Cabal of Callindrill. Darian had never looked back.

Now, he found himself back in Stoneheart once more. Before leaving on his last quest, to locate a hidden library deep in the Great Desert on the other side of the world, he had put into place a tiny and almost undetectable enchantment in the throne room of the Ice Palace. This enchantment was designed to alert him if ever the words "Writhing Death" were mentioned in the throne room. The words had not been spoken in nearly two years. Then suddenly they were spoken repeatedly, by more than one different person, over the course of just a few minutes. Darian had decided it was time to return home and see why the Writhing Death had come up in conversation so much in his father's palace.

Stepping into the Translocation portal in the hidden library he had found, he had Translocated back to Stoneheart and reported to his father.

Agamedes Snow was not proud of his son, but he was a son, nonetheless and he always tried to do well by him. He had been absent for two nears but now was back. All in the same day that six strangers had arrived with news of the Writhing Death's return and that Yanni, a trusted and old friend, had been killed by one of the strangers, who claimed it was self-defence. This was an unusual day indeed.

"I believe him, father," reported Darian. Sitting in the king's private quarters Darian was wrapped in furs to keep him warm, even with the huge fire roaring in the hearth. He was sat in a large comfortable chair which, even with the thick layers of furs on, made him appear tiny, like a small child. His thick-set father was sat opposite the fire from him in a similar sized chair which he almost filled, even wearing no furs. The difference was marked.

"Why? What proof do you have? Or is it just because it causes me problems?" asked the Ice King, archly.

"Of course not. I am not so trite as that," the undernourished son replied. "The reason is that it doesn't make sense."

"Explain yourself," demanded the king, settling back into his chair.

"Well, firstly, why would Captain Reynard get drunk if he was going to attack Yanni?"

"Who knows? Probably it was the fact that he was drunk that led him to lose his temper and attack the *Nanuk*," replied the king.

"Possible, I suppose. But why would Reynard invite Yanni to his quarters? If he wanted to kill him, surely a remote place would make more sense? It would be impossible to hide the inevitable confrontation or murder if it took place where it did."

Agamedes shrugged, "if the attack was one of anger then Captain Reynard would not have been planning where or when he waylaid Yanni."

Darian nodded in agreement, "Also true. But why was Yanni there at all? He was supposed to be guarding the Translocator. He was on duty. No reason should have been good enough to make him break that trust. The mere fact he was not where he should have been makes me think the captain's story is true, or at the very least is plausible enough that you cannot execute him for murder."

"That is the part I have to agree with," said the king. "Why was Yanni not at his post? And if the captain is right and Yanni had been ordered to kill him by his patron, then who was that patron, and why did they want Captain Reynard dead?"

"That, I have no answer for, father".

*

"And so, the Archmage sent us to find you, to see what you could tell us. And now we have, so the question becomes: what do we do next?" finished Kita.

Kita and Darian were alone in her quarters, Okoth and Mosi both having retired to their rooms for the night. Sitting upright on a simple pine chair near the fire, Darian considered all the woman from Honshu had told him. It was a lot to take in but he couldn't help but feel a shudder of excitement pass through him as he realised that all his studying was about to pay off. "A fascinating story and one which leaves me breathless," he confided. "I have long dreamed that my interest in the Writhing Death would prove useful, but never in my wildest dreams did I imagine that this could happen. That the gate to the Void would re-open and that the Writhing Death would once more threaten our lands is worrying beyond belief. We must do something to stop it."

"But what? Everything I have heard tells me that this curse is unstoppable. Reynard believes that his flame-wielding *wu-jen* army, his shape-changing warriors and undead soldiers can defeat the Writhing Death, but how? Even if we kill them all, from what I see all that will happen is that more will come through the gate from the Void. How many aberrations exist in the realm beyond? How do we know their numbers are not infinite?" she finished.

"They are infinite," replied Darian gravely. "Which means there is only one solution."

"What?" asked Kita, greatly concerned.

"We need to close the gate," answered Darian.

"Close the gate? Is that even possible?" she returned.

"I believe so," responded the thin lordling, "but there is only one way to find out for certain."

"How?"

"We need to open a Translocation portal into the lost city of Antissa," Darian declared.

"Antissa?"

"Indeed. The old capital of the Rainbow Empire. The city which was at the centre of the ritual earthquake which split the old empire asunder and created the new, destroying the Writhing Death in the process. That city held a University where the High Conclave of Magi convened. Those Magi knew the ritual to close the gate the first time around. I am hoping that details of that ritual survived the cataclysmic destruction of the city."

"So, you want to open a portal into a city which lies deep beneath the Inner Sea, which was the centre of an earthquake so huge it ripped the lands apart some five hundred years ago, in search of a ritual which may, perhaps, be found in the remains of the University there?"

"Yes, exactly"

"Even if that plan was not mad, which it is, how would you possibly be able to open such a portal?

"I have been studying the Writhing Death all my life. During that time I have found accounts of life at the University in Antissa. I have found maps and blueprints of building works there. I have found inventories, and records. I have found diaries and journals. I am fairly confident that I could find my way around the University if I could get there, and find my way to the Great Library, where records say copies of all known rituals were stored.

"And on my recent trip to the Great Desert I found a hidden library which held a book which I have been searching for my whole adult life. I found the key to the Translocation circle in the heart of the University of Antissa. I can now open a portal directly there."

*

"You don't have to do this, Kita," pleaded Reynard.

"I do. It is the only chance we have to stop the Writhing Death, once and for all. And it is what my father would have done."

They were stood in the corridor outside the Translocation chambers deep in the Ice Palace. Mosi and Okoth had already gone inside with Darian. The Ice King had decided that there was no real proof either way in the case of Yanni's death and that Reynard was free to leave, but he had made it clear he wanted all the strangers out of his city as soon as possible. Reynard and the others were glad to comply.

Reynard, looked down at his feet, seeing his reflection in the golden armoured boots he wore, as always, surprised to find he was wearing the armour and not his traditional black boots, so light was it. It was always hard to talk Kita out of anything she had set her mind on. When that included the line *it is what my father would have done*, it was impossible. "I know. But it is so dangerous."

"I am taking Okoth and Mosi with me, and Darian knows more about Antissa and the University than any man alive. We are as well protected as it is possible to be."

Reynard shook his head. "I know I'll never stop you," he conceded. "I just wish I could come with you."

"No, Reynard. Your place is here, in the Empire. You need to take Tanithil and Evantia and go and get the Verdant Queen on your side. Use your charm and win her over. Then you really will have a chance to stop the Writhing Death and keep the Empire from falling apart. I have faith in you."

Reynard nodded. "I will," he said simply.

Kita turned to open the door into the Translocation room. As she pushed it open, he called her name. She turned back to him.

"I'm sorry," he said.

She paused, looking deep into his eyes for a while, then nodded, turned and entered the chamber beyond, shutting the door behind her and leaving Reynard alone in the corridor with his thoughts.

*

The violet runes of the Translocator pulsed with an unearthly light, partly blinding Kita. The *Nanuk* shaman chanted the words to drive the ritual to open the portal and Darian stood nearby, a small leather-bound book in hand. As the ritual progressed, Kita could feel the build-up of arcane energies in the room, standing the hairs on the back of her neck on end. Suddenly, just when it seemed like there was no way to contain the pent-up energy, Darian shouted out a series of staccato syllables, which Kita took to be the special code for the University in Antissa, now located deep beneath the Inner Sea.

Shaking her head at the craziness of it all she focussed on the space inside the Translocator. It shifted from a violet hue to a swirling blue-green, and as it did so the *Nanuk* guards in the chamber hefted their axes in preparation.

Fortunately nothing came through.

"Move!" shouted Darian from his position near the shaman, as he snapped his book shut and started to run forward.

Kita knew she should be the first one through the portal. She knew it was her responsibility to keep Darian safe so he could find the ritual and close the portal to the Void on Granita. But her feet would not obey her. Stepping into that Translocator would mean trusting that the chamber the Translocator was housed in was still somehow intact; that it was somehow stable and that it was somehow full of breathable air. Yet this is what Darian had assured her. She knew she should trust him and even if she did not, she knew her honour demanded that she go first.

But stepping into that portal would mean leaving Reynard behind. And worse still, leaving him behind with *her*. That was hard to stomach.

Then Darian reached the portal and stepped through. With an almost audible pop he was gone. All Kita's deliberations and hesitation were gone in an instant. She drew her *katana* and *wakizashi* and rushed after him. Reaching the portal she stepped into it and felt her body lurch painfully as she disappeared from sight.

Interlude

The Verdant Queen sat in a small wood-panelled office, behind a large mahogany desk. Arrayed across the desk were the latest reports from her spymaster, Karim Moonleaf. They did not make happy reading. A soft knock at the door interrupted her study. "Come in, dear," she called, secure in the knowledge that it would be her daughter who was standing outside.

The door pushed open smoothly and in glided Kululu Jade, auburn hair today falling loose in waves down her back. The assassin pushed the door to behind her until it clicked shut. Moving gracefully forward she stood before the desk, feet shoulder width apart, weight planted naturally on the balls of her feet. Her hands were clasped behind her back.

Lily Jade looked up from her reports. Though there was another chair positioned opposite her next to the desk, she did not bother to invite her daughter to sit. She knew it would be pointless as Kululu rarely ever sat down, saying that it was safer to remain on her feet at all times.

"Good morning, dear one," greeted Lily Jade with a deep smile. Kululu nodded tightly in return. The lack of warmth neither surprised nor annoyed the queen. She was well used to her only daughter's cold heart. It was what made her so good at what she did. "I will get straight to the point," she continued. "I have read the latest reports from the spymaster, and they do not read well. His agents in Providentia and Stoneheart have both made attempts on Captain Reynard and his companions. Even with their considerable resources, influence and power, they have both failed to stop Reynard and friends."

Kululu's face showed no sign of emotion. It was almost as if she had not heard a word that was said. Her mother looked her up and down. Such an automaton. Such an effective operative. Such a cold hearted killer. Perfect.

"And now, Karim tells me, Captain Reynard has set sail for Ibini. He is coming here on his whirlwind tour of the Empire. He is going to walk right into my throne room and ask for my help. We must be wary."

The slightest rise in Kululu's eyebrows told her mother that the young assassin was not sure quite why the need for such caution.

"He may suspect," the queen explained. "It is possible that Captain Reynard has figured out that Nikolai was my nephew. It is possible that he has worked out that I was the sponsor behind the corsair fleet which ravaged the empire in the summer." Kululu nodded almost imperceptibly in response. "Worse still, he may have worked out that it was I who was responsible for re-opening the gate into the Void."

"Actually, no mother," said Kululu, her face remaining impassive. "It was not you. It was I."

The Verdant Queen fixed her daughter with a penetrating stare. "It may have been you who found out how to re-open the gate," she conceded, "but never forget you are my tool. You do everything at my behest and at my command. I am the queen here, you are only a soldier."

Kululu's face remained impassive. Only a tiny quiver in her cheek showed any signs of controlled emotion she might be feeling. The Verdant Queen let her stand for a moment, knowing the silence added weight to her words.

"So," she continued at length, "we cannot kill Reynard here on Ibini – that would be too obvious. So we have to greet him warmly, as if we know nothing of his quest or the issues of the Empire. But we must be wary. We must be prepared for anything."

"I always am, mother," replied Kululu simply. "I always am."

PART TWO

-Chapter Nine-

"The thing is, I don't know exactly where the Verdant Palace is or how to get there," admitted Reynard. He, Tanithil and Evantia were moving down to the waterfront where the *Javelin* was tied up. They had left the citadel of Stoneheart and were about to leave the Island of Manabas to set sail for Ibini and the palace of the Verdant Queen. The only problem was Reynard had no idea how to get there.

"Neither do I," agreed Tanithil, striding alongside him. "Perhaps Birgen or one of the crew will know. What surprises me most is that the capital is in the south. From the maps I've studied, the north of Ibini is open farmland and fertile hills. The south seems to be all steep mountains and impenetrable jungles. So why build your capital in the jungle?"

"The Verdant Queen has never liked visitors," answered Evantia from just behind the two.

Reynard and Tanithil stopped and turned to face her. "What do you know of her?" asked Reynard.

"Not much, to be honest. But I know she is reclusive, at least in terms of foreign visitors. I've heard she is paranoid about assassins," Evantia replied.

"Funny behaviour from someone well known to use assassins," commented Tanithil.

"Quite," agreed Evantia. "The Verdant Palace stands alone in a dell, deep in the southern mountains," she continued. "One trail leads into that valley and it would take a highly skilled tracker, or someone who knows the way, to find it."

Reynard frowned, "And we have neither," he replied, frustrated.

"On the contrary," Evantia responded, "I believe I can find the way."

"You?" returned Tanithil sceptically, "How come? Are you some master hunter in your spare time?" he asked, semi-seriously.

Evantia laughed a gentle laugh, the sound of merry bells twinkling in the morning air. "Of course not, Tani," she answered, putting her hand on his arm and smiling at him. "I have merely been there before, on a trade mission for the Guild. I've a good memory for places and people," she added. "That is how I have achieved this position in the organization. I think I can find my way back."

"That's excellent!" exclaimed Reynard, grinning. "Isn't it, Tani?"

"It is," Tanithil conceded, hoping that Evantia was up to the task and wondering if she might actually bring something useful to their mission apart from just her good looks and position in the Guild. It would be a big improvement if she did.

*

"There!" Evantia shouted above the crashing surf, pointing to a sandy cove which was just coming into view off the port bow. "That's the one – I'm certain of it," she said to Reynard who was standing at her shoulder on the forecastle, arrayed in the full golden Armour of Lucar. The strong easterly gusts were causing his loose blond hair to flow out behind him, out of his eyes. He put his hands to his eyes to shade them from the rising sun off the port side and squinted. Sure enough, as the *Javelin* skipped forward across the swell, the cove grew in size, until it fully revealed itself. It was deep enough for a three-masted carrack like theirs to anchor in, and big enough to form a fairly calm bay in which the ship could safely remain for an extended time. It was definitely suitable, but was it the one Evantia remembered?

"You are positive?" Reynard asked her.

"Definitely," she replied assuredly, as she studied the cove. "I recognise the small stand of acacia trees on the left side as we look. Oh, and tell Birgen to beware – there are rocks on the right side."

Just at that moment a shout went up from the crow's nest above, "Reef! Reef ahead, port side!"

"It seems the lookout has just spotted the rocks you remember," smiled Reynard. "This must be the place. Well done." He leaned in and kissed Evantia lightly on the cheek.

She blushed and looked up into his face. It was the first time he had been at all affectionate towards her since they had met Kita, back in

Stoneheart. She wondered if this meant he had changed his mind towards her.

"Reynard..." she started.

"Not now, Evantia, I'm sorry, but I need to get the ship into that cove," Reynard cut her off. He moved to the rail looking down onto the main deck and shouted, "Birgen!" The boatswain was right across the other side of the ship on the poop deck, hands on the wheel. "That cove off the port side!" Reynard pointed, "That's our destination! Make land there! Oh, and watch out for a submerged reef on the starboard side as we go in!"

"Aye, aye, Capn!" came the shouted reply from the boatswain. Birgen handed the wheel to Florus, and moved to the main deck where he started ordering the crew into position to turn into the cove and make landfall. Under his expert handling the *Javelin* turned gracefully, and slid majestically into the sandy cove, steering clear of the razor sharp reef which Evantia had warned them of. The anchor was dropped and the ship settled into place, rising and falling gently on the small swell which wrapped around the cove's headland and rolled into the bay.

They had made it to Ibini without incident. Now only the infamous jungle and rocky mountains lay between them and the Verdant Queen.

*

Florus hacked at the palm fronds in front of him. His machete was getting blunt and his arm was fatigued. His white shirt was almost see-through it was so drenched and his eyes stung from the sweat pouring off his brow, down his face. But behind him was Captain Reynard and the sailor was not about to let him down. Not on such an important mission.

Florus was proud that his captain had chosen him to accompany his party on this trek. He realized that the silver-haired Tanithil was not cut out to carve a way through the thick, overgrown Ibini jungle, and of course the delicate Lady Evantia would not be expected to perform such menial work. The captain had his hands full organizing the mission and concentrating on the audience with the Verdant Queen – Florus made a sign to ward off evil as he thought of her – so it was obvious that the captain needed someone to help cut a path to the palace. Birgen had wanted to go, but Captain Reynard had explained to him that he was needed to remain with the *Javelin* and keep charge of the ship in his absence. And Florus knew that Birgen was not physically up to this job anyway.

Of course, had the mighty Okoth have still been with the group then he would have been the one cleaving a way through the foliage, but he had escorted Mistress Kita and the priest Mosi on whatever special mission they were off doing. So with Okoth not here and with Birgen not up to the job, Florus had volunteered – and had been delighted when the captain had agreed.

Florus stopped and wiped a wet sleeve across his brow, whilst he took in a huge gulp of air. Even breathing in this close atmosphere was difficult. They had reached the edge of the mountains at the centre of Ibini and Evantia had directed them up an overgrown trail. The track led slowly up into the peaks, following a valley floor which was thick with vegetation. Acacia trees, palms, liana covered mangroves, teak and mountain ebony filled the basin. Shrubs and thick ferns made travel hard. There was no wind and the air felt full of water.

Florus' mind drifted back to Mistress Kita, the Niten master. She had taught him, and many of the crew on the *Javelin*, the ways of unarmed combat and Florus had become her best student. So much so that he had taken over the training of the crew after she left them back in Providentia earlier in the autumn. He dearly wished to see her again as he felt he had progressed as far as he could in his training and needed her expert eye to polish up his skills in places and refine his style. Plus maybe teach him a few new techniques.

"I think it is time to find a camp," the rich, powerful voice of Captain Reynard broke into his reverie. "We are all exhausted and the sun will soon set behind the mountains. I imagine it will grow dark quickly here once it does," he added.

"Aye, aye, capn!" responded Florus, immediately looking around for a suitable spot. "You wait here, sir. I'll seek out a campsite and return presently."

Reynard nodded, smiling gratefully. "Thank you Florus – you are a good man."

The praise made Florus' spirits soar and all fatigue left him in an instant. He hefted his machete once more and began hacking into the undergrowth with renewed vigour.

*

Tanithil slumped to the floor and watched the sailor disappear into the undergrowth in search of a home for them all for the night. He shook his head in wonder, "Incredible," he muttered.

"What is?" asked Reynard from his position standing on the trail next to him.

Tanithil looked up wearily. "The effect of the Armour of Lucar," he answered. "Florus should have dropped from exhaustion by now," he continued. "But one simple word of praise from you and he is off again, slashing his way manfully through the vegetation like he's just woken from a perfect night's sleep in a feather bed. It's unnatural."

"But very handy," grinned Reynard.

"Just be careful, Reynard," Tanithil warned. "You are not replenishing the energy in his body, merely banishing the fatigue from his mind. His body is still suffering from dehydration and weariness; he is simply blocking it out from his mind. Eventually you'll damage him. Maybe even kill him."

Reynard stopped grinning. "Understood Tani," he replied sombrely. "As soon as Florus returns I'll make sure he rests."

Tanithil nodded and closed his eyes. All he had done was to walk along the path which Florus had cut for them, and yet he was still shattered. He could only imagine how the sailor would be feeling now if it wasn't for the effect of Reynard and his enchanted armour. At least Reynard was listening to his warnings and advice.

For now.

The campsite was small and uncomfortable, but none of the travellers cared. An open clearing had been made slightly bigger by Florus' machete and the chopped fronds had been placed on the floor of the clearing to make things a little more homely.

Florus was lying off to one side of the clearing, fast asleep. Reynard had ordered him to eat some rations and then lie down and rest. Once ordered to take it easy by his captain, the sailor was asleep within moments. Tanithil sat with his back to a small jagged rock, tired enough that he didn't care about the discomfort. Reynard was talking to Evantia, apparently still full of energy. Tanithil wondered if the armour was somehow protecting him from the humidity and draining environment.

"I don't get it," Reynard said to Evantia. "This is clearly the route you came when you travelled here last as you keep recognising natural landmarks along the way."

"Indeed it is," she agreed, "but what don't you get?"

"How come the trail is so overgrown? If Lily Jade's men are travelling into the palace regularly, they can't be using this route," he stated.

Evantia smiled at him. "Not many people visit the Verdant Palace, my love. The queen has her advisors – perhaps half a dozen of them the last time I was here – she has a few servants to cook and wait on her, and it is rumoured she has the Jade Assassins in attendance too of course. But other than that she has no one in the palace. No guards, no traders or merchants, no courtiers, no nobles, no stables, no hound master, no squires. The palace is basically empty."

"So how do we get in?" asked Reynard. "When we arrive there I mean."

"We play it by ear I guess," shrugged Evantia. "When I was here last we were expected. We had sent word that we were coming. I'm not sure how the Verdant Queen will react to us turning up uninvited. But I suspect you'll be able to win her over, Reynard," she finished, smiling a dazzling smile at him. "You always do."

Tanithil sat cross legged at the edge of the clearing. He had eaten and moved away from the uncomfortable rock and was preparing to sleep. Reynard was already asleep, still wearing the golden armour. His head was pillowed on a golden sleeve and he looked peaceful and childlike in his slumber. Evantia was curled up next to him, her arm draped across his chest. Tanithil had noticed that she had wriggled nearer to him once he had fallen asleep and that she had cuddled into him before dropping off. He wondered briefly what Reynard would say and think when he woke to find her tangled up with him. The encounter with Kita in Stoneheart had finally made Reynard look beyond Evantia's undoubted stunning looks and realise that Kita was far more suited to him than the pretty blonde. Tanithil was glad of that and hoped that Reynard was not once more won over by Evantia's allure in Kita's absence.

The telepath mentally shook his head and quickly blanked out these distracting thoughts. He was preparing for sleep and needed to get his mind back under control. Taking a deep breath in through his nose, he slowly let it out through his mouth, exhaling steadily and completely. A second breath and his mind found the blackness of the Void. The meditative state was becoming easier and easier to reach these days. Tanithil focussed on nothing and let his subconscious float. A feeling of weightlessness filled him as his mind left his body behind. Spreading his awareness out, he felt the jungle around him. It was teeming with life. From insects and arachnids, too many to count, through the oozing sap of the myriad flora around him, he felt vitality everywhere. In the trees above his body a small family of monkeys were settling down for the night, safe in a tight embrace.

Suddenly Tanithil became aware of a predatory mind. The consciousness was not advanced but it was highly evolved to perform the role of hunter and killer. And the telepath was instantly aware that the killer had its eyes on him. The shock dropped Tanithil out of his meditation and almost made him fall over. He just managed to stop himself from collapsing as he opened his eyes to stare straight into the face of a snake.

The *naja* was a species of snake native to the jungles of Ibini, but well known through the lands of Lucarcia. Travelling circuses sometimes had tame *naja* in baskets which snake charmers would summon by playing on wooden wind instruments. They were famous for their hooded necks which would expand when the snakes were agitated, or about to strike. And the hood of the *naja* facing Tanithil was fully flared. The snake's tongue flicked out, tasting the air. It almost touched Tanithil's face, it was so close. A soft, sibilant hiss escaped the snake's jaws and black, lifeless eyes stared into Tanithil's.

The telepath shut his eyes, instantly recovering his calm and centring his emotions. It looked like the snake was about to strike, but Tanithil was no botanist and didn't really know how to read the movements of the reptile. So he used the one tool he did have at his disposal: his mind.

Tanithil knew he had to act and had to act immediately. The snake seemed ready to strike and he knew enough about the species to know that a bite from such a serpent would be fatal – probably in seconds. In his desperation Tanithil attempted something he had never tried before: he sought to control the snake's mind with his own.

The act of coercive persuasion was something which he had heard advanced members of the Imperial Thought Guard had tried to perfect. And of course he was aware that the golden Armour of Lucar seemed to impart this power to its wearer. But this was something more. The snake's intellect was too primitive to be able to cajole and coerce. It needed to be forced. And Tanithil had a split second to attempt it.

Coiling his mind like a loaded spring, Tanithil gathered his psyche and opened his eyes. Staring right into the black eyes of the reptile before him, he lashed out with the full power of his intellect, seeking out the tiny but deadly mind inside the body before him. He felt the arrogance and self-belief of the predatory thoughts and overwhelmed them with thoughts of doubt and fear. He flooded the synapses of the *naja* with confusion and horror. He overpowered the aggression and voracious instincts of the snake with aversion and trepidation.

The deadly *naja* snake dropped from its striking pose, turned and slithered rapidly off into the undergrowth. Tanithil let out a huge breath of pent up emotion and felt a sob of relief escape his lips. His mind was exhausted but he had done it. He had forced the snake to flee with the power of his mind alone. What were the ramifications of this incredible development? He would have to meditate on that. The telepath lay down on the fronds beneath him and was asleep in seconds, his mind and body utterly spent.

Across the other side of the clearing, behind where Tanithil had been sitting, Florus lay still, with his eyes wide open. Had he just seen what he thought he had just seen? He had never really understood why Captain Reynard put such trust in the silver-haired man. But now, unless he was very much mistaken, he had just witnessed Tanithil stare down a deadly *naja* and somehow had made it turn and flee when it looked about to strike. Was it possible that the thin and weak looking man had just used some sort of mind control power on the snake? It certainly looked that way. Florus could not wait to get back to the ship and tell the crew what he had seen. They would probably never believe him.

*

The small group had hacked and cleaved their way to the site of the palace and were tired and dehydrated. From the edge of the dell they looked up at the towering building ahead. The Verdant Palace was well named. Covered with Verdigris, vines and trailing plants, it was difficult to make out the palace structure beneath the foliage.

The building itself was constructed of white marble, which was now crumbling in places. The creepers and vines were slowly pushing their way into the cracks and literally pulling the palace apart stone by stone. The intense micro-climate of this region didn't help, with the combination of mountains and verdant flora combining to ensure that little moisture escaped the area and that it was permanently wet or raining here.

From the outside it was possible to see that the palace was covered with soaring towers and minarets, and the centre of the whole structure was dominated by a huge glass dome, which once would have looked resplendent but now was tarnished and green, with moss covering its northern side. Exactly as Evantia had predicted there were no guards in sight. In fact there was no sign of anyone. The Verdant Palace looked more like an abandoned ruin than the home of the Queen of Ibini.

"I guess we just wander up and see if we can find a way in," suggested Reynard to the others. He was not particularly feeling the ill effects of the jungle, despite being encased in armour. It was clear that, in the same way as the armour appeared to protect him from the flames of the Pyromancers in Cansae, it was also protecting him from the debilitating effect of the jungle environment.

The others grunted their agreement and Florus once more took up the role of trail beater and started to hack his way forward. The foliage in the dell was far less thick than it had been coming up the trail so his job was nearly done now. Soon the group broke out into the more open ground in front of the palace and from there they could begin to appreciate the size of the edifice before them. The central glass dome must have risen nearly four hundred feet into the jungle skyline and the marble building itself stretched off into the near distance on both sides to be lost in the jungle. It was impossible to say exactly how big the place was.

Ahead, in what appeared to be the centre, Reynard could make out a pair of ornate looking double doors made from the same marble. The doors were carved with swirls and frescos but now looked chipped and tired. A trailing ivy vine climbed up one side of the doors and meandered across the top to disappear up into the canopy overhead.

As they approached, one of the marble doors creaked open and out stepped a fat, bald man, wearing white linen trousers and leather sandals. His chest was bare and he appeared unarmed. Reynard was instantly reminded of Bayo, the obese Ibini drum master from his time as a slave aboard the *Javelin*, before they had taken it over.

"Well met Captain Reynard and friends," smiled the man, clasping his hands together as he spoke. "You are expected. Please, follow me to your quarters where refreshments await you." He turned smoothly and glided back into the building without checking to see if they were following him.

Reynard looked at the others. Tanithil shrugged and Evantia smiled a weak smile. He figured they were all too tired to care. Florus was looking utterly exhausted and Reynard made a mental note to make sure the sailor got plenty of rest here at the palace and once they returned to the ship. "Let's go," he declared and set off after their guide. The others followed along mindlessly.

The interior of the Verdant Palace was much like the exterior. Mostly constructed of white marble, it showed signs of opulence and decay. All the furniture and fittings that they passed were once valuable but now looked tarnished and uncared for. Reynard knew that the palace was constructed back in the time of the Rainbow Empire, over five hundred years ago. He guessed that some of the fittings and furniture were probably as old as the palace itself.

The guide led them along marble corridors and Reynard immediately noticed that it was nice and cool in here. The insulating properties of the marble construction appeared to keep the heat out. They did not see a single other person on their journey through the palace.

"Her majesty sends her greetings, captain," the Ibini said. "She bids you make yourselves comfortable. Baths have been drawn for you and food and drink laid out. Please take a few hours to rest and recover from the arduous journey here and she will summon you at sunset this evening for an audience," the bald man informed them. "Ah, here we are."

Pushing open a stiff white wooden door, the Ibini stepped inside. Their quarters were huge. They moved into a large circular common area. Off to one side a deep alcove branched off and inside that were set out three tin baths, with steam gently rising from them. A wooden screen was propped up near the entrance and could easily be used to separate off the alcove to give the bathers privacy.

There were five large, comfortable looking couches dotted around the room, mostly focussed on a set of low tables in the centre, festooned with snacks and drinks. Carpets dotted the floor in places, making the room appear homely. The carpets and couches, like everything else in the palace, had seen better days and were frayed and worn in places.

The Ibini went to the back of the room where two more white doors stood side by side. "The left door leads into the gentlemen's bedroom, captain," he explained. "There are three beds made up in there for you. The right door leads into milady's chambers," he continued, nodding to Evantia, "and a separate bath has been drawn for you in there, ma'am."

Evantia smiled a dazzling smile, "thank you so much," she beamed. "A bath is just what I need. Excuse me gentlemen," and sweeping across the common room she opened the right hand door and stepped through. "See you in a few hours," she announced shutting the door behind her.

*

"It is a tricky situation, certainly," agreed Tanithil.

Reynard and Tanithil were sat in their quarters. They had both taken a bath and eaten their fill and were now sat comfortably around the low table, picking at a few choice morsels and sipping some exquisite Pembrose Red. Florus had bathed, eaten and, at Reynard's suggestion, gone off to bed. Faint snores could be heard drifting through the door to the bedroom. Evantia had not emerged from her chambers where she had disappeared a few hours earlier.

The two friends were discussing their current predicament. It was, Reynard estimated, about an hour till sunset so they would soon be called to see the Verdant Queen. They had strong reasons to believe that Nikolai Kester, the pirate captain who had plagued the empire in the summer, was Lily Jade's nephew and that she had sponsored his raids. Reynard had killed him in a duel and had broken up the pirate ring, thus smashing the queen's pieces in the power game. Of course, there was no proof of any of this, and there was no way that Reynard was even going to bring it up. The question was: did the Verdant Queen know of Reynard and friends' involvement in the breaking up of the pirate operation, and if she did, what would be her reaction to it?

"And now I have to try and convince her to join with the other noble houses and give her aid to our cause," Reynard continued. "It could be an interesting meeting."

*

The bald Ibini pushed open the double white doors with great ceremony. Striding into the throne room he marched across the open floor to the raised platform which dominated the centre of the chamber. Reynard, Tanithil and Evantia followed in his wake. Tanithil was in his usual subtle green and browns. Evantia was wearing a trim white shirt and black leggings with soft black boots – she had clearly decided not to bother dressing to show off her figure or looks today, but was smart and business-like. Reynard was, of course, dressed in the Armour of Lucar.

"Your majesty, allow me to present Captain Reynard Ferrand, heir to the Iron House of Providentia," he began, sweeping to the side and presenting the group to the lone figure on the throne above them. Reynard, Tanithil and Evantia stepped up. Reynard dropped into his most courtly of bows and deferentially looked up at the woman sat upon the throne.

Lily Jade, the Verdant Queen, was dressed in a pale green formal dress with a stiff high collar. Her auburn hair was streaked with grey in places and cascaded down her back in waves. She was clearly middle aged and looked like she was probably stunningly good looking in her youth. The throne itself was large and uncomfortable looking, made from mountain ebony and carved to look like a giant acacia.

"Captain Reynard, welcome, welcome," greeted the Verdant Queen. "I hope you are suitably refreshed after your arduous journey here?"

"Extremely, thank you, your majesty. Your guest quarters and the refreshments laid on by your staff were wonderful. We are in your debt."

"Nonsense! We don't often get visitors here and it is always a pleasure to have people make the trip to come and see us. So – what brings you to the Verdant Palace? More than just a social visit I assume?"

"Trouble, I am afraid, ma'am. Trouble of the most serious and severe kind," replied Reynard, looking deep into Lily Jade's eyes. The noble then took a deep breath and began.

He explained all about the return of the Writhing Death. He avoided telling anything about the pirate raids of the summer and of his duel with Nikolai Kester. He explained that the gate to the Void had somehow reopened and that the curse of creeping death was once more spreading across the island of Granita. He went on to describe how this time the Writhing Death was headed by a force of aberrations from the Void, and that these creatures appeared to be intelligent and were somehow controlling the swarm of insectoids which formed the bulk of the curse.

Reynard then went on to point out to Lily Jade that the island of Granita lay off the southern edge of Ibini and that only a very short, shallow stretch of sea separated the two. It was not inconceivable that the Writhing Death could cross that gap, even without the guidance of the intelligent creatures at its head. Once Granita was full of the biting, swarming insects, Ibini would definitely be the first place it came. And the Verdant Palace was one of the first places of civilization which would be reached by the swarm. To all intents and purposes, Lily Jade would be one of the first people to be affected if the Writhing Death could not be stopped.

Lily Jade listened intently to Reynard's tale, never once interrupting him and never once taking her eyes from him. Her expression did not really change; there was no sign of shock or fear on her face, just of rapt attention to Reynard. Once the tale was told, she blinked twice as if coming out of a reverie.

"Amazing," she said eventually. "Truly so. And what, may I ask, are we supposed to do about it, this curse of which you speak?"

"Bring the full force of the Empire of Lucarcia to bear against it," replied Reynard immediately. "I have already visited the leaders of the other noble houses," he continued. "The Dragon, the Ebon Lord and the Ice King have all pledged their support to our cause. The Trade Lords too," he added, gesturing to Evantia, who smiled at the queen. "I am here representing the Iron House, vassal to the Azure House, which of course is... in a state of flux presently. Your house is the only one which has yet to dedicate any resources to our pursuit, ma'am."

"Then you shall have them, of course. But we are a small island, captain, of mostly uninhabitable jungle and mountains. There are a few farmers in the north of my country that could raise a militia if I asked them I suppose – but I cannot see what good farmers would do against the Writhing Death."

"If I may be frank, ma'am?"

"Go ahead, captain. We are all friends here," the Verdant Queen replied, smiling.

"The Jade Assassins, your majesty. Everyone knows of them and of their extraordinary reputation. Lend them to the cause, and we will truly have a chance."

Lily Jade's expression turned cold. "The Jade Assassins are a myth, captain – created by drunken storytellers in the waterfront bars and taverns of the more 'civilized' regions of the empire. Reynard looked about to interrupt her, but she held up her hand. "However," she continued, "my daughter Kululu is training some women up to become personal guard for me – even this far away from the centre of the empire it is wise to protect yourself in these troubled times - and at great risk to myself I will command Kululu to join you and to take her fledgling company with her."

Reynard bowed deeply. "You are most gracious, ma'am. I am sure any such company trained by your own daughter will prove extremely helpful to our cause. You have my thanks and the debt of the empire."

"When will you need them ready?" asked Lily Jade.

"Soon," replied Reynard. All four of the noble houses are with us now and the Guild is recruiting mercenaries. I will return to Lucar now to plan our strategy. Once there I will send word."

"We will be ready for your summons," the Verdant Queen promised him.

*

"Well, that went better than I had anticipated," asserted Reynard, drawing deeply from his Pembrose Red. He was sat in his quarters on the *Javelin*, joined as usual by Tanithil and Evantia, who were both also sipping wine. Behind him the Armour of Lucar was back on its customary stand in the corner and Reynard was back into his favourite black outfit, and sat with his boots up on the low table in front of him.

"You were amazing, Reynard," praised Evantia, beaming. Dressed in a loose fitting shirt with the buttons undone slightly more than was proper, and tight fitting trousers, she looked refreshed and recovered from the rigours of the journey into the jungle. She was radiant. Reynard returned her smile and let his eyes enjoy the view.

"It was too easy," cut in Tanithil, sharply. "She didn't seem at all surprised or worried by anything you said, Reynard. I watched her carefully throughout your entire speech and didn't see or sense a single thing to upset her balance. She expected every word you told her."

"Well, I suppose if she was the backer behind Kester and the pirates, then none of that would have been too much of a surprise, no," agreed Reynard, dragging his eyes from Evantia. "But the important thing is she has agreed to support the cause. That's a full house."

"Indeed," admitted Tanithil, "but actually I'm not sure that having Kululu Jade and her 'fledgling company' accompanying us in this quest is a safe thing. I think I would almost rather the Verdant Queen ad refused us."

"You worry too much Tani," Reynard chided him.

*

"You and your Jade Assassins have one simple goal, my dear," said the Verdant Queen to her daughter. "You must ensure that Reynard and his companions do not succeed in stopping the Writhing Death. Now is the time to make the Jade Assassins' reputation grow even beyond its current legendary status. Join Reynard's crew, integrate yourselves into his army, make yourselves trusted; and when the time is right, do what you have been trained to do – kill them all," ordered Lily Jade.

"It shall be done, mother," replied Kululu coldly. "None shall survive to oppose you."

-Chapter Ten-

Light exploded behind Kita's eyes and she blinked in pain. Her stomach lurched and she heaved. Then she was somehow falling sideways and felt herself go underwater. Instinct took over and she stopped breathing instantly. She opened her eyes and tried to figure out where she was and what was happening, but she was too disoriented.

Suddenly a hand grabbed her arm and dragged her physically upwards. She felt herself leaving the water and gulped down a revitalizing and steadying breath of air. It tasted stale and salty. As she came to her senses she saw that Mosi had a hold on her and was pulling her from a large pool of salty-tasting water. Beside the priest, the skinny Darian was trying to pull the hulking figure of Okoth from the same brine. "Be careful, Kita," warned the priest, not letting go of her arm. "The floor here is not level, and is very slippery." Kita blinked again and looked around.

Kita noted that Mosi's sun symbol was hanging outside his robes and was giving off a soft light, which was illuminating the area. The room they were in was almost a cube, perhaps some forty feet across in all dimensions. There was a golden circle of runes engraved in the centre of the floor, which was still glowing softly, and where the image of the Translocation room in far-off Stoneheart was just fading from view. A single wooden door, warped and twisted from centuries of water damage, was set in the middle of one wall. The walls and floor were of worked, grey granite and were covered in wet slime and sludge. On one wall was carved an intricate fresco in the shape of a circle with a seven-pointed star in its middle, and an image at the end of each point. Any furniture which may have once been in this place had rotted away. Very strangely, in one corner of the room a pool of water seemed incomprehensively to slope upwards. This was the pool herself and Okoth had been dragged out of by Mosi and Darian. As her senses began to return to her she realised what Mosi was saying. It took her a moment to comprehend but eventually her brain figured it out – the whole room was on an angle. The pool of water was actually level and everything else was skewed. So everyone had stepped through the Translocator and in the aftermath she had effectively slipped into the pool in the corner of the room and gone underwater. Mosi had dragged her out.

"Everyone okay?" Kita asked her companions. Okoth and she were both drenched from their dunking in the pool but she noted that neither Mosi nor Darian had fallen in. She recalled that Mosi seemed to have a much better ability to deal with Translocation than she did and guessed that Darian must also be the same. Clearly Okoth was no better than her. The group all nodded their confirmation that they were fine so Kita moved carefully across the slippery floor to the fresco on the wall. The others joined her.

"The sigils of the seven noble houses of the Rainbow Empire," explained Darian. "Five of them you'll be familiar with: Azure, Ruby, Ebon, Jade and Snow – these are the houses which have survived to the Lucarcian Empire. The two houses which fell at the collapse of the Rainbow Empire are also here: House Citrine and House Coral."

"That one there," said Mosi, pointing at a sigil of a sunburst, "Which house is that?"

"That is the Citrine House," answered Darian. "The house was based on northern Granita and their sign was the sun. They were wiped out when the Writhing Death swept across that island."

"That symbol is almost an exact match for the holy symbol of the Light – the deity I serve," observed Mosi.

"Indeed," agreed Darian. "Back in the Rainbow Empire the Citrine House was run by a ruling class of priests and the High Priest of the order was the head of the Citrine House. He was known as the Phoenix."

Mosi nodded in understanding. This was of great interest to him, especially as he had been sent to this continent to learn about how the Light was worshipped here. To find out that five hundred years ago an entire ruling house had been run by priests of the Light was fascinating and would no doubt be of great interest to his superiors.

"The seventh house is the Coral house, whose sigil, here," Darian continued, indicating another of the points of the seven-pointed star, "is an Angelfish – a beautiful fish which was abundant in the reefs of the southern end of Granita where the house had its base."

"So, what now?" asked Kita, who, though interested in the history of the Rainbow Empire, was more intent on doing what they had come here to do – find the ritual to close the gate to the Void and stop the Writhing Death pouring through.

"Now, we need to find the Great Library," explained Darian. "That was the place in the University where all the rituals were housed and if there is anything here which explains how we could hope to close the gate; that is where it will be. I know the way – I have studied many maps and floorplans of the University over the years. Unfortunately the direct route is through the sunken door in the corner of the room."

Kita looked at the pool of water, confused. She had not seen a door under the water. But now that the water had settled down after Okoth and she had been pulled out of it, she could just make out the silhouette of a second door in the corner of the room, half hidden under the salt water.

"However, I have another idea," continued Darian. "Clearly there is the other door," he said, indicating the warped door which was not underwater. "Beyond that, if my memory serves me correctly, is a preparation area. That was where the High Magi who controlled the Translocator here would prepare for the ritual of opening a portal. Now, that preparation area was self-contained with no exits, but of course that was before the University was split apart by a massive earthquake. It is my hope that we can find another, drier, passage to the Great Library by going that route. It is just a hope though – I have no reason to believe there will be a route that way."

"Seems sensible to me," responded Kita. "There is nothing to lose in at least taking a look."

"Agreed," said Mosi. Okoth grinned his usual white grin and shrugged to show his accord.

Kita moved carefully to the door, having to watch her footing on the slick, slimy granite. Darian almost fell but was caught by Okoth as they reached the wooden door. The door itself no longer quite fitted the entry and Kita was able to see beyond it easily.

The light from Mosi's holy symbol illuminated a partially collapsed area beyond. Rubble was everywhere, along with the common algae and slime which seemed to adorn all the walls and floors in this place. There were no obvious exits or doors from the chamber beyond, but a few of the walls looked like they might be passable. Kita decided it was worth a look inside and pulled on the wooden door. It fell apart in her hands. Shrugging, she stepped over the collapsed wooden debris and moved into the room ahead. The others followed after.

    The preparation chamber was basically a ruin. The grey granite walls were crumbling in places and the ceiling looked likely to drop in on them at any time. There were signs of rotten wood and fabrics – the ancient furnishings of the area – scattered about the place everywhere. This room was mostly dry at least and the footing was more certain than in the wet room they had just left.

    "Let's check the walls and see if there are any signs of passageways beyond which might have been opened up," suggested Darian as he looked around.

    "Watch your step," cautioned Kita mindfully. "The ceiling looks precarious and any loud noises or shaking could trigger a further collapse."

    The four companions moved deeper into the room, with Darian, Kita and Okoth each moving to a separate wall and beginning to check over the gaps and cracks for any possible exits or openings. Mosi, meanwhile, moved off to an area of rubble and rotten fabric towards one corner. Here he knelt before a large pile of rocks and wreckage. Carefully he picked up a decaying cloth which may have once been white. The material all but disintegrated in his hands as he moved it, but he wasn't interested in the cloth itself. As he displaced the rotten fabric the soft light emanating from his sun-disk illuminated something golden. Beneath the ancient white cloth covering was a small chest made, it appeared, from solid gold and embossed with sigils of a blazing sun.

    "What have you found there, Mosi?" asked Okoth from nearby, a huge grin splitting his face. "That looks beautiful." Everyone turned to see what the priest had uncovered.

    "I'm not sure," admitted Mosi, still kneeling, "but I feel somehow strangely drawn to it, like I knew it was here, hidden under this rubble."

"Then perhaps you should open it," suggested Kita, moving to the priest's side and staring down on the dazzling chest.

Mosi looked up at her and the others, who had all gathered around, as if seeking approval to do as she suggested. Seeing nods and smiles, he turned his attention back to the chest and clicked open the soft metal clasp which held the valuable box shut. Gently he lifted the lid.

Inside, the golden chest was lined with velvet and it contained a single item: a sun-disk, similar in design to the one Mosi wore about his neck, but expertly etched and engraved. It was clearly an ancient holy artefact and as the chest lid fell open it began to slowly glow with a warm internal light as if reacting to the group's presence – or perhaps the presence of Mosi's similar symbol.

"It seems it was calling to you, priest," offered Darian from his position behind Mosi's right shoulder. "It would be a shame to let such a relic as this lie here in the depths of the earth when it could be brought out and used for good."

Mosi shook his head. "I am not sure I agree with you, Darian," he responded. "I have my own sun-disk, which was given to me by my superior when I was ordained. It would seem somehow wrong to replace it with this one, no matter how grand and important it appears to be."

"Well, even if you do not choose to use it yourself, I would imagine an item like this would be of utmost interest to your church, would it not? It would surely count as one of the most significant finds in recent times, I would guess?" replied Darian. Mosi nodded, thoughtfully.

"We have a word for this in my homeland," cut in Kita. "*Shogunai*. It means this was fated to happen, Mosi. You were meant to find this holy symbol and, I believe, to wield it in the name of the Light. You should not shrink away from fate, but embrace it.

Mosi took a deep breath and reached out to grasp the holy symbol, drawing it reverently out from its five hundred year old resting place. As he did so Kita saw him close his eyes for a second or two and watched as his body shuddered almost unperceptively. Then the quiver was gone and his eyes opened once more. Kita looked searchingly into his face, her expression asking if he was okay, and Mosi's countenance responded that he was indeed. "I can feel great power in the disk", Mosi explained. "It is indeed a relic from the Citrine House and, more significantly, I think it was once the personal symbol of the last Phoenix himself. It is a great honour to find and utilize this holy artefact and I shall do so with compassion and care." Saying this he took off his old holy disk and carefully folded the chain around it, putting it safely in one of the many hidden pockets of his old white robes. In its place he respectfully placed the new disk over this head and onto his shoulders. The light spilling from the artefact seemed to intensify as he did so and the room was now bathed in a warm and comforting golden glow. Kita felt the security and protection of the powerful relic wash over her. It was a good feeling. A couple of seconds passed and then Mosi rose from his kneeling position. It was as if a spell had been lifted and Kita felt somewhat back to normal. The relic was still glowing softly but Kita was no longer aware of any strange effect coming from the disk. She shook her head and moved back to looking for gaps in the wall they could pass through.

*

"I will go first. I am the best swimmer. And besides, if I can squirm through any gaps then anyone can," asserted Okoth with a white grin. "If one of you goes you'll probably find a route which will leave me stuck," he added, laughing. The group were back in the Translocator room. Their search of the preparation area had been unsuccessful, at least in terms of finding an alternate route through to the Great Library. So now they had to resort to take the direct route, which unfortunately meant going through the submerged door in the corner of this room.

Darian had explained the route from here to the Great Library itself. It was not far, if you were walking, but who knew if there were any air pockets or dry sections of the University left? In fact, who knew if the route that would have been direct five hundred years ago would even be passable now? The person who tried to make it through would be going into the unknown and would have to swim out as far as they could; searching for another air pocket along the route. They were discussing who that person should be and Okoth was insistent that it should be him.

"I think you are right," agreed Kita smiling back at the grinning Nubian. "But it is a dangerous task. You will need to judge how long you can hold your breath for and return when you reach the half way point of that time."

"I understand that," said Okoth patiently. "As a child I grew up on the south western corner of Nubia," he continued. "My family were hunters, but we would also farm lobster in the deep lagoons of the coast there. I would regularly dive down from my father's fishing boat to where we dropped the lobster traps. I learned how to hold my breath for a long time and how to judge the time I could stay underwater. This will be a breeze – although the water here is a lot colder than back home," he finished.

"Take that into account," advised Darian. "You will not be able to hold your breath for as long in the cold temperatures here as you could at home. Nubia is a long way south of here and the waters there are far more temperate than those of the Inner Sea."

Okoth nodded his understanding. "Wish me luck then," he said, wading out into the pool. He took a deep breath and slowly dropped under the water, disappearing from sight. Kita watched him go and strained to see him as he sunk. She thought she could just make him out swimming down to the submerged door in the corner of the room. He pulled the door open and then the shadowy figure that was her friend was gone.

*

"It's been too long," said Darian apprehensively. "He should have been back by now."

"He should have been back some time ago," corrected Kita, her voice remaining calm though inside she was deeply troubled. Okoth had been gone for a long time. Kita knew that at these moments time passed strangely and a few seconds could seem like hours, but any which way, Okoth had been gone for an extensive duration.

"He is a resourceful fellow," counselled Mosi. "For all we know he has swum out and found an air pocket and recovered his breath and gone on to a second air pocket and even a third. He could at this moment be inside the Great Library, about to return to us and tell us he has been successful."

Kita considered this optimistic angle and had to agree it was entirely possible. But it was still worrying that the big man had not returned yet. If he had not found a way through was it possible that he could still be holding the breath he took in this room all that time ago? "I suppose you are right, Mosi," she began, "and perhaps…"

Kita was cut off as suddenly Okoth's hulking form burst from the pool of water beside them. The black-skinned giant gulped in a huge breath of air and pulled himself to the edge of the water, where he lay gulping down huge lungful's for a few moments.

"You're back then," pointed out Darian unnecessarily.

"Indeed," agreed Okoth, still laying down recovering his breath, his customary grin missing from his face. "Unfortunately," he continued between further gulps of air, "I was unable to find a way through. I tried the route you told me but there was nothing but water. The whole route was totally submerged. I could have pushed on and hoped that there was an air pocket ahead but I knew that if there hadn't been one…" Okoth didn't have to add that he would have drowned if he had swum on and failed to find a place to regain his breath.

Darian's face fell. "No!" he cried out. "It's not possible." The scholar's head dropped into his hands and he half collapsed to the floor. "This can't be," he said, shaking his head disconsolately, his skeletal body shaking uncontrollably. Kita could see tears forming in the man's eyes.

"Let me regain my breath and I'll try again," Okoth offered. Perhaps now I know where I'm going I'll be able to make it a bit further."

"You may be able to," agreed Kita, "but the rest of us cannot hope to hold our breaths for as long as you. If there was no air pocket in the distance you covered then I fear there is no way we can continue. We will either have to come up with another solution, or abandon our attempt and return to the surface."

Darian was sobbing openly now. "We can't fail – not after coming so close," he moaned. "We have made it to the lost city of Antissa and down into the University of the High Magi; a building thought destroyed five hundred years ago. The Great Library is literally a stone's throw away. We can't give up now." He looked around, clearly seeking agreement from the others, but all he saw was sympathy. His head fell into his hands again.

"I may be able to help," came the soft voice of Mosi from the back of the room. Darian looked up with faint hope in his eyes to see the white-robed priest stroking his goatee between his thumb and forefinger. "The sun-disk we found," Mosi expanded, "I think I may be able to use it to perform an enchantment. It is something which the priests of the Citrine House used to do as part of their rituals. The enchantment will allow someone to hold their breath for an extended period. The trouble is I'm not quite sure for how long it will last. Though my gut feeling is it might allow you to swim for maybe twice as long as without the aid of this incantation."

Okoth dragged himself out of the pool where he was still laying half submerged, stood up and grinned at the priest. "Let's do it," he said enthusiastically.

"You realise that if I am wrong and you swim too far and the charm fails, you may not be able to get back?" pointed out Mosi seriously, his dark brown eyes looking deeply into the giant's.

"I know," acknowledged Okoth, "but I will try. For Darian's sake and for the sake of the people whose lives are at risk from the Writhing Death. It is the least I can do."

"You are a noble man, Okoth," praised Mosi earnestly. "It is an honour to call you friend."

"Thank you! Thank you so much!" cried Darian, smiling appreciatively at the Nubian.

Kita gave the giant a deep bow and held it for a long time. "You have my sincerest thanks too," she told him.

Okoth blushed, "And for the memory of your father," he added. "For this was his quest."

Mosi took hold of his holy symbol, shut his eyes and muttered some arcane words under his breath. Everyone saw the golden symbol glow brighter and then the priest held out his hand and touched Okoth's barrel chest. The giant man felt a warmth enter his body and suddenly it was as if he was able to take in a massive breath. His lungs felt like they could hold huge amounts of air. Smiling at the priest, Okoth turned back to the water. Taking another deep breath he waved a farewell and dipped under the water once more.

*

"Well done, well done!" congratulated Darian, patting Okoth enthusiastically on the back. "You've done it, you've done it!" Clearly excited, he was beaming like a child on their name day.

"It was Mosi's doing," Okoth replied, climbing out of the pool. "With his magic I felt like I could swim for miles without needing a new breath. It was amazing. I could have made a fortune lobster fishing with that power back when I was a child," he added grinning brightly.

Okoth had just returned from his second exploration and had reported that he had been able to swim all the way through to the other side. In fact, a little further on than he had originally ventured he had discovered a small air pocket. In the top corner of a chamber there was just enough space to lift your head out of the water and gulp down a few breaths of life giving air, ready to continue on. He'd actually not really felt the need to do so but had done so just in case. And then, a little further on through the sunken structure, he had come to a staircase down. Incongruently this staircase led down to a chamber which had managed to stay free from water, even though the structures above it were totally submerged. And according to Darian that chamber was one of the seven entrance halls to the Great Library.

"There is something, I don't know – strange – about the room I came to though," added Okoth as he wrung the water out of his trousers.

"Strange?" asked Darian, curiously. "What do you mean?"

"I'm not sure. Something magical was going on in there. I've no idea what it was or what it meant. That's not my area of expertise, so I decided to swim back here and let you guys deal with it," he added, indicating Mosi and Darian. "You're the clever ones," he finished with a grin.

"I suppose we'll have to swim through there to see it for ourselves then," stated Darian. "Can you help us Mosi? Can your charm be worked on all of us?"

"I don't see why not," replied Mosi. "It should be pretty easy."

"I am mightily impressed with your new found powers, priest", reported Darian. "Without them we would not have succeeded here."

"Though I agree with your comments about Mosi's new abilities, let's not get carried away," cautioned Kita. "We've not succeeded yet. We haven't even reached the library."

"True – but thanks to Mosi's enchantment, we soon will be able to," responded Darian happily.

"Let us hope so," said Kita.

Mosi used his holy symbol to apply the incantation to each of them in turn and they agreed to follow Okoth's lead. They would swim through to the air pocket and take it in turns to gather a fresh breath and then would swim on to the lower chamber; the entrance hall to the Great Library. There, Okoth told them, there was enough space for them all to get out of the water and move around, much like in this room. When all were ready Okoth dived into the water once more and ducked through the door into the sunken passage beyond.

Swimming swiftly, but checking back often to make sure he was not leaving the rest behind, Okoth pushed on confidently. He knew the route now and knew that he had enough air to make it through easily, although he did feel like somehow his lungs were not quite as expansive as they had been last time. Still, he was sure that was of no great consequence. Presently he reached the room where the small air pocket lay in the top corner. He was starting to feel a little bit concerned now as somehow he felt like he would need to take a breath very soon. He didn't really understand but he was certainly not feeling as strong as the last time he came here.

Looking back he saw Kita and Mosi swimming along behind him. Both looked to be moving fairly easily through the water, but as they got nearer he saw that both had extremely uncomfortable expressions on their faces. It seemed that both of them were also in dire need of a breath. Realizing that his capacity was certainly the biggest, he signalled for Kita to go up and take a breath. Ever honourable and courageous she shook her head, indicating that Mosi should go first. The priest, looking desperate for air did not argue and swam for the surface and the life-giving air pocket. He reached it and took in three or four huge gulps before dipping back down under the water and letting Kita surface. Okoth was starting to feel fire in his lungs now.

It was then that Okoth realised Darian was nowhere to be seen. The skeletal man had obviously not had the strength to keep up with the speed Okoth had swum at and had got left behind somewhere. Okoth quickly pushed for the surface as Kita ducked away, leaving him space. He took just one huge lungful of air and dived once more, swimming powerfully back the way he had come. Kita and Mosi remained in the room, staying near the air pocket.

Okoth drove on and as he passed into the corridor beyond he saw Darian struggling weakly along. The man's face looked in agony as he fought to hold onto the last morsels of oxygen in his lungs. Okoth made two powerful stokes and reached the man just as Darian's air ran out and he was forced to open his mouth to breath. Okoth planted his mouth over the other's and breathed out. Darian was able to take in a breath of air. Okoth grabbed the pitiful man by the arm, turned and swam powerfully back for the air pocket. It was excruciating – he had hardly any oxygen left in his system and was dragging a half-unconscious person with him. Just as he felt his lungs would burst his head broke the water and he took in air. Quickly he ducked down again and pushed Darian into the space above, letting the nearly incapacitated man recover his breath.

The four explorers stayed in the area around the air pocket for a long time, taking it in turns to recover their breaths and prepare for the next stage. At least, Okoth knew, the next section was shorter than the first and they should have no problems reaching it. He just didn't understand why they had all struggled with breath this time.

*

"I suppose the charm was shared between all four of us and so was not as powerful as it was when just used on Okoth," mused Mosi.

"That would explain why we all could swim a little bit further than usual, but not as far as Okoth was able to when he went on his own."

"It would make sense," agreed Kita, "But then again I know next to nothing of these matters. What do you think Darian?" she queried.

Darian was sat on the floor, still recovering. His face was ashen where he had come close to drowning. Flickering flashes of blue occasionally illuminated his face in the half dark room – flashes from the next obstacle they had to face.

They were in an entrance hall to the Great Library. According to Darian there were seven of these chambers, with seven entrances to the central seat of learning for the whole of the Rainbow Empire – one for each noble house. The hall was long and thin, made from the same grey granite as most of the rest of the structure. The staircase they had swum down was at one end of the hallway and an opening was at the other. There were no other visible exits to this room. Like most of the rest of the University they had seen so far, this corridor area was in ruins. Rubble lay everywhere and if there had once been any wall hangings or furniture of any description they had long since rotted away to nothing.

The opening at the far end of the hallway from where they had come in led on into the Great Library itself. They could almost make out the vaulted ceiling of the huge chamber they had come here to find beyond the arched doorway. But filling that opening was the magical anomaly which Okoth had seen and been unable to understand.

Blue sparks arched across the opening and it was filled with crackling electricity like a mini lightning storm, rooted in the doorway. The lightning did not seem to want to travel anywhere from the entrance way, but anyone wishing to pass into the Great Library would have to pass directly through that fizzling wall of electrical energy.

"Darian?" Kita prompted again.

"What?" asked the thin man, looking up at her from the floor, as if he had only just noticed she was there.

"The charm? Mosi's theory? Did that make sense to you?" she repeated.

"I'm sorry," he replied. "I have no idea what you are talking about. I wasn't listening. Anyway, it doesn't matter now. We are thwarted at the last step," he finished disconsolately.

"What do you mean?" asked Okoth.

"The lightning field," Darian pointed to the crackling energy wall blocking the doorway into the Great Library. "It is a powerful ward, put there by the High Magi some five hundred years ago. There are seven entrances into the Great Library, each one a hall like this. We cannot reach any of the others from this location so this is the only way in. And it is still warded. I never expected this. I never imaged that a warding spell could survive the great quake that split the Rainbow Empire and created the Inner Sea, and furthermore that it could persist for five hundred years after that event. I never planned for this. And I have no idea how to bypass or deactivate such a ward. I have failed."

"It is too early to give up," replied Kita, moving forward and running her fingers gently along the dusty leftmost wall of the hallway. "There are some sort of runes here – maybe ancient letters. I can't read them. Can you, Darian?"

The skeletal man rose unsteadily to his feet. He was clearly still suffering from his ordeal on the swim here. He came to join Kita and looked at the letters she was indicating. "You are right," he replied. "They are the runic alphabet of the High Magi from five hundred years ago. The language is ancient too, but I am versed in it."

"What do they say?" the Niten warrior asked.

"Let me see," said Darian, studying the runes carefully. "*Factim ist unti custodian oppositan virtis*. Roughly translated that means something like, 'Passing here uses the opposing power' – which actually makes some sort of sense. You see each noble house of the Rainbow Empire had an energy type which they specialized in. For example the Ruby House specialized in summoning and controlling fire. Electricity was the energy of the ruling Azure House. But if we need to find the opposite energy to electricity in order to pass through this ward, what is that?" he questioned.

Kita shook her head, unable to offer an answer. Okoth merely shrugged, clearly also being in the dark. This sort of stuff passed way over his head. Kita turned to Mosi to see if he had any ideas. The priest seemed to be far away, looking off into the distance, eyes almost slightly unfocussed, and apparently not listening to the conversation at all. Suddenly the white-robed man blinked twice and his eyes came back into focus. He looked at Darian. "Back in the Translocator room," he started, "you pointed out that the houses were arranged in a seven-pointed star formation, with each house's sigil on the end of a different point of the star."

"That is correct," agreed Darian.

"On a seven-pointed star, or heptagram, every vertex has two opposite vertices. When this polygon is used to represent the houses in the Rainbow Empire, this means that every noble house has two notionally opposite houses. So perhaps what we should try is the energy of one of the houses in opposition to the Azure house on the seven-pointed star. Happily, the two houses in opposition to the Azure House were the Coral and Citrine Houses and of course I have a relic of the Citrine House here in my hands."

Whilst the others took a moment to try and understand what Mosi had just told them, the priest took up the golden sun-disk in both hands and muttered a single word of power. A short, sharp burst of golden sunlight jumped out of the centre of the disk and into the lightning field. The arching electrical ward instantly fizzled and died, leaving the way into the Great Library clear for them to enter.

A few seconds of stunned silence followed and then Darian let out a loud cheer as he realised that his dream to enter the place where the ancient Writhing Death had been stopped had come true. "Congratulations, Mosi! That was an amazing piece of insight! I am deeply impressed, and forever in your debt."

"Good work," praised Kita. "Truly inspired thinking." She gave him a curt bow. Okoth merely stepped up and clapped him heartily on the back, almost making Mosi stumble.

Darian led the way and he, Kita and Okoth moved carefully into the Great Library. Behind them Mosi's eyes went unfocussed once more.

You have my congratulations too, Haji. You listen well when I share my knowledge with you and when I offer some small advice, and you act on it in a resourceful and intelligent way. I can already see that together we can become a great power for good in the world, acting in the name of the Light. I am delighted it was you that found my phylactery and that together we can advance the cause of our deity, our two spirits in tandem. Now, I think we should move on and follow your friends or they will start to ask difficult questions.

Mosi blinked again and his eyes refocussed. He stepped into the Great Library behind the others.

-Chapter Eleven-

"A *naja*? A proper wild *naja*?" asked Reynard in amazement as he pulled his long blond hair back into a pony tail to keep it out of his eyes. He and Tanithil were standing at the front rail of the poop deck watching down on the crew of the *Javelin* as they went about their business. The ship was skipping westward into the sunset on a stiff following breeze and Birgen had the men at their usual, efficient best. The fact that Reynard watched them, wearing the enchanted Armour of Lucar didn't hurt either. The crew wanted to impress. They were two days out of Selkie, crossing the Inner Sea on their way to the capital of Lucar and a meeting of all the noble houses of the empire.

"Yes, indeed. I think the fact that I was staring the snake in the eye may have helped. It certainly focussed my mind," Tanithil smiled, gripping the rail as the ship dove over a crest and dropped rapidly down the far side of the swell. Of all the ex-slaves who now commanded the ship, Tanithil had adapted worst to the life of a sailor and still struggled to find his sea legs.

Reynard slapped the slim man on the shoulder with a big warm smile. "Well I never," he responded. "Tanithil the real life snake charmer!" A calculating look came into his eyes and he stared at Tanithil. "Do you think you could use it on a person, Tani?" he enquired.

"I'm not sure", admitted Tanithil. "As you've seen with the armour you wear, the ability to influence the mind of another human being is complex and not at all a precise science. Some are easier than others. And a human mind is far, far more complicated than that of a simple beast like a snake. I know some of the senior members of the Thought Guard, those who were the personal bodyguards to the Emperor himself, were rumoured to be able to do it. But even in the Guard no one ever confirmed or denied it. I think the power of the rumours in dissuading potential assassins was enough that they let it persist, even if there was no truth in it. I don't know," he admitted.

"Well don't go using it on me!" Reynard laughed easily at his friend.

Tanithil smiled back. "Never Reynard, you know that. Now, onto more serious business," Tanithil changed the topic suddenly. "Do you know what will happen when we reach Lucar?" he asked Reynard.

"Honestly? No. Not a clue."

Tanithil shook his head slightly. "Really, Reynard, you need to pay more attention. The fate of the entire empire is at stake here. Not just the short term future but the long term composition of the ruling houses as well."

"Okay, Tani. Tell you what – let's get out of this cold breeze and drop down into my lounge below. You can outline it all again over a glass of Pembrose Red," Reynard suggested.

"Okay, but not too much wine. I need your mind focussed and concentrating," Tani replied, his eyes staring hard into the taller man's.

Reynard blinked. "Did you just use mind-control on me?" he asked his companion; then suddenly he burst into a grin. "Only joking! Yes of course, just a couple whilst we go through the political stuff. I'll focus, I promise."

*

"So, with Emperor Jovius II dead, the Azure house has no ruler and no heir. If we ignore the fact that he was the Emperor and concentrate on the fact that he was also head of one of the five ruling houses, this means we have an unusual situation," began Tanithil. He and Reynard were below, sat in the captain's lounge and, as promised, Reynard had cracked open a bottle of Pembrose Red. The swordsman had also removed his armour and was dressed in his more traditional black shirt and trousers. His black knee-length boots were crossed over at the ankle and up on the low table in the middle of the room – a table which Tani fancied spent more time being a foot stool for Reynard than it did being an actual table.

"In what way?" queried Reynard as he sipped on his glass.

"Well, tradition holds that the ruling houses must continue," explained Tanithil. "In the ancient past when any of the lines of the ruling houses has ended, as the Azure House's has now, then one of that ruling house's vassal houses rises up to become the replacement ruling house. This way the empire always maintains the same number of ruling houses."

Reynard nodded, but his eyes narrowed as he struggled with a thought. Tanithil spotted that his friend was still confused. "What have I not explained properly?" he asked.

"The end of the Rainbow Empire," Reynard began. "That entailed two houses – I can't recall their names, the ones on Granita – getting wiped out by the Writhing Death. Why did those two houses not get replaced by vassal houses?"

"Excellent question, Reynard! It shows me you are listening and understanding. I'm pleased. The reason is simple: both houses – the Coral and Citrine houses – were wiped out to a man. But so were all their vassal houses. All those houses were located in the region which became the island of Granita when the empire was sundered five hundred years ago. None of them survived the Writhing Death. With their destruction there was no house to replace the ruling houses and so the number dropped from seven to five."

"Okay, so now one of the vassal houses to the Azure house has to rise and take its place. So that there are still five ruling houses," summed up Reynard,

"Correct. And the two most powerful vassals to the Azure house would be?" prompted Tanithil.

"The Sickle House and the Iron House," answered Reynard.

Tanithil nodded in agreement. "So, the rulers of the four remaining ruling houses will vote which of those two houses will rise to become a ruling house in its own right."

"What happens if there is a tie?" asked Reynard.

"Well, I believe that the casting vote at times such as that would have gone to the Emperor. With him being dead, that kind of takes that option away. To be candid I don't know what happens then. I guess that the Imperial Chancellor will tell us. His is the highest office of law in the Empire. If anyone knows how this works, it will be him."

Reynard pulled deeply from his glass, draining it to the bottom in one smooth motion. Reaching forward to the bottle on the table, and pouring himself a second, he asked Tanithil, "So, once we have five ruling houses once more, what happens next?"

"Okay, so in order to get the Lucarcian Empire to go to war, ancient law says you need a unanimous vote from the heads of all of the ruling houses. If any refuses then a state of war cannot be declared," replied Tanithil, still sipping reservedly from his first glass of wine.

"Why do we need to declare a state of war?" asked Reynard, leaning comfortably back into his chair again and resting his topped-up glass on his stomach.

"Again this is ancient statute," explained Tanithil, putting down his glass on the low table and rising to his feet. He walked over to one of the bookshelves in the lounge. As he reached it the ship lurched as it slid over a big wave and Tanithil had to stretch out to grasp the bookshelf and steady himself.

Reynard laughed a friendly laugh at his companion's plight. "Still struggling to get used to the ship, aren't you?" he commented.

Tanithil looked momentarily annoyed but then it was gone. "Yes, I'm still not comfortable out here at sea. I admit – I'll be happy once we get home again."

"Of course – Lucar is your home city, I almost forgot," replied Reynard. "Looking forward to returning?"

"In a manner of speaking, yes. But that is not the point. I was about to explain about the law," responded Tanithil patiently.

"Of course, sorry. Do continue," prompted Reynard.

"So, ancient legislation states that without the unanimous agreement of all the ruling houses we can't go to war. And unless we are in a state of war, ancient law also says that no sizable group of armed men from any noble house may enter the territory of one of the ruling houses. The law was set up in the ancient past to protect the ruling houses from the other houses, and from each other.

"The result of which," continued Tanithil, "means that without the agreement of all the ruling houses we cannot actually gather the mercenaries of the Trade Lords, the Pyromancers of the Ruby house, the Dread Guard of the Ebon house, the *Nanuk* of house Snow and the 'fledgling company' of Kululu Jade all into one place in the empire."

"So we need a unanimous vote of the four remaining rulers," agreed Reynard. "But that is okay. We've just spent the winter travelling the empire, visiting every noble leader and getting their agreement to bring their aid to the cause. We will get our vote."

"Not so. We have four leaders, yes. But we do not yet have the vote of the leader of the fifth ruling house – whichever one it is which gets promoted from the Sickle or Iron houses. Now," he continued, "I would assume that your father, the Earl of Providentia and head of the Iron house, will vote in our favour if your house is the one which is promoted."

Reynard nodded in agreement, "I would assume so, yes," he concurred.

"So the only problem is, what happens if the Sickle house gets promoted?" asked Tanithil. "We've not visited their head and enlisted his help."

"I don't even know who he is," admitted Reynard.

Tanithil shook his head once more. "It's a shame you never paid more attention to politics when you were at home," he chided.

Reynard could only stare into the depths of his glass of red.

*

Three days later the *Javelin* was guided neatly into its berthing spot in the deep-water eastern harbour of Lucar. The stiff breeze had held and sped their journey to the capital; a journey which had been safe and uneventful. Reynard and Tanithil had spent a lot of time going over and over the politics of the situation – as best Tanithil understood it – and the thin man was pleased to feel that Reynard was on top of things now.

Reynard and Evantia had spent many hours in Reynard's quarters in the evenings, but Tanithil had seen the beautiful woman leave the quarters each evening and return to her own cabin for the night. He was unsure what this meant for their relationship. He understood it was complex but hoped for Reynard's sake that the fickle man had made up his mind one way or the other. Reynard needed to choose between Evantia and Kita and he needed to decide soon. This issue could not afford to be clouding his mind when the time came to head to the cursed island of Granita to attempt to close the portal to the Void – all assuming that Kita and Okoth were successful in their attempts to find the ritual to close it of course. Tanithil hoped the two of them would already be waiting for them here in the capital, having retuned safely from their dangerous quest to the lost city of Antissa.

Tanithil stood at the rail, watching as a stevedore tied up the ship and then as Birgen lowered the gangplank to the dock. Behind him he heard the door to the captain's quarters open and he turned to see Reynard, clad head to foot in golden armour once more, striding confidently onto the deck like a demigod. The late afternoon sun glinted off the perfectly polished surface of the armour and dazzled the onlookers. Reynard strode up the gangplank and called out, "Birgen, you have the ship!"

"Aye, aye captain," came the response from the boatswain.

"Tanithil, Evantia: you're with me," commanded Reynard and Tanithil felt an immediate need to obey. Closing his eyes quickly Tanithil erected a quick and simple haven for his mind, using an old Thought Guard trick. He felt the compulsion to obey Reynard dissipate and was himself once more.

Opening his eyes again he saw Evantia was with them. She had arrived from her cabin below decks. She was dressed in a sky-blue dress, one which hugged her figure in all the right places and left little to the imagination. Her blonde hair was tied up on one side in a skewed pony tail and hung down over her shoulder in waves. Her lips glistened a sumptuous red and her ice-blue eyes were vibrant. She looked at Reynard in adoration.

Tanithil sensed that Reynard was centred this afternoon. His aura oozed determination and conviction. His eyes were as focussed as Tanithil could ever remember them being. Somehow this sense of purpose was being magnified by the Armour of Lucar and Reynard was simply radiating power and charisma. It would be a very self-assured and self-aware person who was not influenced by his aura today. Tanithil was pleased that Reynard was bringing everything he could to the party. He had a feeling they were going to need it.

Marching smartly down the gangplank, Reynard got to the wharf and strode off in the direction of the northern staircase – cut right into the cliff side, this one led right up to the Azure Palace, their destination this day. Tanithil hurried after him, needing to almost jog to keep up with the tall Lucarcian's purposeful stride. All activity on the wharf stopped as the stevedores, sailors, whores and other denizens of the waterfront stopped what they were doing to stare at the golden figure which looked like something out of a legend. With the sun shining on him, even Tanithil could have been convinced he was following a deity along the quay. It was time for Reynard and his armour to be put to the test.

*

"Father, it is wonderful to see you again," greeted Reynard warmly as he stepped forward to embrace the Earl of Providentia.

"You too, my son. You are looking well – very, very well indeed. I must say, that armour becomes you," replied his father, standing back and holding onto Reynard's arms and looking him up and down, nodding in appreciation.

The two were in Reynard's quarters in the Azure Palace. The quarters were large and luxurious. The walls and floors were all of a shining white marble, run through with subtle flecks of blue and green. Gold and silver were everywhere, from candelabras to drinking tankards and cutlery. The room was exquisitely decorated, showing great wealth and yet balanced with great taste. Reynard felt right at home here.

"Please, can I offer you a glass of Pembrose Red?" asked Reynard, moving to a sideboard and picking up a bottle.

"No, thank you, son. And I suggest you lay off the wine too, Reynard. For tomorrow we go to the Royal Court to decide the fate of the Empire," responded the Earl.

"True, but I actually have little to do, if truth be told, father. I do not get to vote. I'm not even sure I will be allowed to speak at the congress. I am only the son of the head of one of the minor houses," replied Reynard uncorking the bottle and pouring himself a glass.

"Well, we may be a minor house now, but tomorrow a vote will be put in place which may elevate this house to the position of a ruling house," replied Lord Caer, taking a seat on one of the comfortable couches arrayed around the room.

"Yes, I know the politics father, Tani explained it all to me," replied Reynard. "Though I confess I do not know the head of the Sickle house, nor much of their reputation."

"House Sickle are farmers," explained the Earl. "Do not think them weak or insignificant though," he warned. "That house controls the vast majority of the agriculture across the Spine of Ursum and as such is responsible for the food which gets put onto the tables of the majority of the noble houses in this region and beyond. They may lack the reputation of the Ebon House but they are not to be underestimated," he finished.

Reynard nodded in understanding. "And we are the Iron House," he mused. "With a reputation for some of the best smiths in the empire and ... not much more," he concluded.

"That was probably true a year ago son. But much has changed in the last year." The Earl reached across to a small table nearby and fumbled for a grape cluster. His hands shook and Reynard moved quickly across to aid him. The young man was struck by just how old his father looked. "Thank you," Lord Caer said as he began to pick the grapes from the cluster and pop them into his mouth. "Now, take a seat Reynard and listen to what I have to say," he asked.

Reynard moved to a nearby couch and sat, still marvelling at how the golden armour felt as light and unencumbering as Honshu silk. "What is it, father?"

"I am old, Reynard. Now, I've looked old for some years I know, but have never felt it. But this last year or so, since your brother..." The old Earl trailed off, clearly unable to find words to describe what had happened when Reynard's brother had sold him into slavery at the behest of the Dark Lord.

"I understand," responded Reynard kindly. "Carry on," he invited.

"Well, for the last year or so I have felt the weight of my age. I have been a long time waiting for an heir to make himself apparent and of course last year I finally named you." Lord Caer had named Reynard heir after he had proved himself worthy the summer before. "And now I think it is time I left the future of this house in the hands of the one best positioned to advance it." Popping another grape into his mouth Lord Caer chewed thoughtfully. "In the last year you have more than proved your worth Reynard. You are now one of the most famous people in the empire. Everyone knows of the dashing ship's captain in the golden armour. Many people – the important people in the Empire – know that you are of the Iron House, that you are my son, that you are Reynard Ferrand. And those people also know what you are doing for this empire, Reynard. They know that you are working tirelessly to save it."

Reynard looked carefully at his father, wondering where this was leading.

"I have made a decision, Reynard. Tomorrow at the meeting of all the ruling houses I will stand up and I will abdicate my position as Earl of Providentia and Lord of the Iron House. I will formally hand over my lands and title to you and you will become Lord Reynard Ferrand, Earl of Providentia. I just ask that you allow me to keep my quarters in the Iron Fortress," he finished with a smile.

*

The Royal Courtrooms were spectacular. Unlike most of the rest of the palace these rooms were not constructed of white marble; but rather were of deep, almost translucent azure, like the colour of a perfect sea. It was widely held that no rocks occurred naturally of this colour and that Emperor Lucar had the rock magically altered by the High Magi who built the palace, in one of their final ever acts before the practice of the arcane arts was banned at the start of the new Empire. However it was created, it was a master piece.

A giant throne dominated the whole area, set upon a raised dais at one end of the rectangular chambers. The walls rose, crystal clear and glistening, to a height of about forty feet above the floor where they curved in arched buttresses to join in a peaked roof about sixty feet overhead. Large windows set high into the walls ensured the whole place was perfectly illuminated. Even on a dark, dreary day such as this, with the rain lashing down outside and a gale blowing in off the Inner Sea, the Courtrooms were bright and airy.

Reynard looked around him at the assembled throng. A few obvious people stood out. The Ice King, Agamedes Snow, was conspicuous due to his height and imposing figure, all wrapped up in his woolly furs and attended by a three equally giant men that Reynard assumed were *Nanuk*. The beautiful Kululu Jade was very evident, dressed in a high-collared green dress with her auburn tresses plaited up in a top-knot and held in place by two shining hair pins. She was in quiet conversation with another woman, who Reynard took to be one of the Jade Assassins. The red-robed Pyromancer, Catulus Ruby was stood across the far side of the chamber, talking with a small group of like-dressed men.

In the far corner from Reynard, he spotted a group of men who looked out of place here in the trappings of the Royal Courtrooms. Dressed in homespuns and none of the finery of the rest of the assembled nobles, they looked as unhappy to be here as many of the nobles seemed at having them in the room. "The representatives of House Sickle," commented Lord Caer from his position at Reynard's side. "The short one is Fortiscue – their head."

Reynard saw a short, swarthy fellow in their midst, with unkempt hair and a scraggly beard. Yet even from this distance Reynard could see the intelligence in the eyes and noted the way the man took in all that was going on around him. His father was right – this was one to watch.

As he looked around, Reynard saw a dark figure enter the back of the room. Wiktor Ebon was utterly alone as he entered the Courtrooms. Reynard guessed that someone had told him that he would not be allowed to bring any members of the Dread Guard into this place – given that they were essentially undead abominations, if Tanithil was correct. Wiktor caught Reynard looking at him, smiled, nodded and headed over.

"Well met Reynard," he greeted warmly, offering a hand. Reynard took it and shook it assuredly.

"You too, Wiktor. It's good to see you again," Reynard replied smiling. "What brings you to this humble gathering?"

"Oh you know. Nothing important – just the future of the whole Empire. It seems I didn't have anything else in my calendar for the day and with the weather being so awful the Royal Courtrooms seemed like a more cosy place to spend the day than out and about in the storm. You?"

"Yes, much the same," Reynard grinned. He found himself warming to the genial dark-haired man again.

Suddenly the assembled company quietened down and Reynard turned to look towards the throne and raised dais. A tall, thin figure was striding purposefully towards the dais. Dressed from head to foot in a many-hued ceremonial robe which dated back to the time of the Rainbow Empire, the Imperial Chancellor was a striking figure. Obviously full of self-assurance in his position, he strode confidently to the front of the room full of the most powerful people in the continent. Hitching up his robes, to avoid tripping and embarrassing himself, he took his position beside the empty throne. It was clear to everyone below that, though they might be the ruling figures of the Lucarcian Empire, in this room and in this matter, he was in charge.

"My Lords, my ladies, welcome to Lucar and the Azure Palace!" he began, his voice booming out and being amplified by the astounding acoustics of the room. "Today we come together to decide the future of the ruling houses of the Empire." The Chancellor continued to lay out the statute which governed the decisions which needed to be made today and the laws by which those decisions were governed. Reynard was thankful for his repeated lessons with Tanithil as he understood it all and was able to keep on top of the legal jargon.

"So, my lords and ladies," continued the Chancellor, "the time comes where we must elect a replacement ruling house, for the noble Azure House is no more. Who proposes?" he asked formally.

Suddenly Lord Caer stepped forward. "My lord!" he called out, interrupting the process. "There is one matter which I would wish to see dealt with before this vote is cast."

"My Lord Ferrand. We are at your service," responded the Imperial Chancellor, bowing low. If he felt any annoyance at the disruption he was too smooth and professional to show it.

"Thank you, my lord," responded the Earl. Turning to the gathered host he continued. "My lords and ladies, I will be brief. I hereby formally abdicate my position as Earl of Providentia. I hand over my title, my lands and my property to my son and heir, Lord Reynard Ferrand, the new Earl of Providentia."

A quiet mummer ran through the throng and Wiktor turned to Reynard, clapping him on the shoulder, saying, "Congratulations, my lord. May I be the first to offer you your dues. Well deserved too I would say," he smiled.

"Thank you, Lord Ferrand, for your announcement," responded the Chancellor, in command of the room once more. "May we take this opportunity to wish you a long and relaxing retirement," he said. Turning to Reynard he continued, "And to you Lord Ferrand, congratulations on your new position as Earl." Reynard bowed low and said nothing. The Chancellor's eyes scanned the crowd again, drawing everyone to him. "So, assuming we have no more interruptions, I say again: who proposes?"

From across the room Reynard heard a clear voice call out. "I do." The crowd parted to give the speaker space and Reynard saw Kululu Jade step forward. "In the name of Queen Lily Jade, I propose the Iron House of Providentia to rise up to the position of ruling house and take its place in the history of the Empire. All here gathered know the work that Reynard ... sorry, *Lord* Reynard, has put into trying to save the empire in these dark times and it is fitting his house should be recognized and rewarded."

Reynard was shocked. As far as he knew, Lily Jade had sponsored the corsairs who ravaged the empire last year – the corsairs who Reynard and company had defeated in battle and whose leader Reynard had personally slain. That leader, he believed, had been the nephew of Lily Jade and cousin to Kululu, who was now proposing that his house be raised up to the rank of ruling house. It didn't make sense.

"Congrats again, old boy," commended Wiktor from Reynard's side. "Looks like you and your house are on the rise," he said.

"Noted, my lady," commented the Imperial Chancellor from his lofty position on the dais ahead. "The Iron House have long been vassals to the Azure House, so they are a suitable candidate, and your comments about Lord Ferrand are also heard. Does anyone else propose?"

The room was silent and still. Reynard waited for the announcement to come – someone would surely propose the Sickle House in opposition to him and his house. Although he had expected that opposition to come from Kululu but she had already proposed him, and he didn't think she was allowed to propose two houses.

Just when it seemed the matter would be closed and that the Iron House would be the only house proposed Reynard felt Wiktor step away from him and into a space nearby. "I do," announced the Dark Lord's son, for all to hear. "In the name of Lord Barrius Ebon, I propose the Sickle House. The oldest vassal house to the Azure, they have long been the unsung strength of the Empire, the men and women who plough our fields and bring bread to the tables of noble and commoner alike. The Ebon House believes it is time that they were recognized for this, and also that the ruling houses were supplemented with a house perhaps more in touch with the common folk which we purport to rule over," he finished.

This time Reynard felt more disappointment than shock. He had felt a burgeoning friendship with Wiktor and yet here he was proposing the Sickle House to go into direct opposition to the Iron House and force a vote. He noticed Wiktor exchange a look with Fortiscue across the room, and saw the head of House Sickle nod. Wiktor then turned back to look at Reynard and smiled a conciliatory smile and shrugged his shoulders apologetically.

"So, lords and ladies, we have two houses proposed," announced the Chancellor, breaking into Reynard's thoughts. "Are there any others?" A few seconds passed and it was clear that there would be no further proposals. "Thank you all," he continued. "Now I invite the heads of the four remaining ruling houses to come to the dais to cast their votes. Please come forward and collect your voting tokens. The white token represents the Iron House and the black token represents the Sickle. You will each move to the area behind the screen to my left and cast your vote. Drop the token representing the house you wish to be elected into the golden chalice on the table. Drop the token you wish to discard into the coal bucket on the floor. Please proceed."

Agamedes Snow, Kululu Jade, Catulus Ruby and Wiktor Ebon all headed forward from their respective places around the hall. Each stepped up to an aide and took a small white and a small black pebble from him. They then proceeded to the screened off area, one at a time. Reynard could clearly hear the sounds of pebbles being dropped into their voting containers, as each of the heads of the ruling houses made their choice.

Presently the voting was complete and the four rulers were all back in the main hall again. An aide collected the golden chalice from the table behind the screen and presented it to the Chancellor, who peered inside. He looked up at the assembled group. "My lords and ladies. We have a result."

*

Tanithil was impressed with the speed of the political machine which was at the centre of the Empire. Only yesterday Reynard had been the second son of a minor noble house, and yet this evening he was Lord Reynard Ferrand, Earl of Providentia, head of the fifth ruling house of the Empire of Lucarcia and also the official head of the rapidly deployed War Cabinet.

As he strolled through the dark, quiet corridors of the Azure Palace, on his way back to his quarters he mused on the day's events. The vote to pick the replacement ruling house had been passed – a simple 3 to 1 majority in favour of Reynard and his house. Reynard had then proceeded to the dais and in a bold move had stepped up on top of it so that all could see him in his famous golden armour. He had delivered a stunning speech, imploring the assembled lords and ladies to agree to bring the combined might of the Empire of Lucarcia and to wield it against the impending threat of the Writhing Death. He had radiated power and authority and it was no surprise at all to Tanithil that the vote to go to war had been carried unanimously. Neither was it a great surprise when Reynard had been voted to lead the assembled parties in the upcoming struggle. It felt only right after all – Reynard and his companions had discovered the threat in the first place and Reynard was the only one of all the nobles who had done anything to gather the forces of the Empire into one cohesive unit. He deserved to lead.

Tanithil stopped for a moment, confused as to where he was. The limitless corridors of the palace were easy to get lost in at the best of times, and now in the middle of the night, with only a few lanterns lit along the way, he had got momentarily turned around. Was it left or right at this intersection? He was just about to turn back for Reynard's apartment, where the group had been celebrating their success, when he heard footsteps coming from one of the side corridors. At least here was someone he could ask for directions. Only a guard or a servant would likely be around at this time of the night. What came around the corner surprised him, however.

A stocky Lucarcian man with a long blond beard strode quickly into view. Wearing simple street clothes he looked out of place in the confines of the royal palace. As did the wicked looking dagger in his hand. He spotted Tanithil and immediately called over his shoulder, "He's here! I've found him!" Wondering what was going on Tanithil froze in place for a second until two more street thugs appeared to follow the first, daggers in their hands too. Behind them came a figure in the blue uniform of the Thought Guard. Chainmail armour was supplemented by a blue cloak and in the guard's hand was a drawn shortsword. The sword was incongruous as Tanithil knew the standard issue for such a guard was a longer, broader blade. But a shortsword was a good weapon for close-in fighting – if you knew you would be wielding it in a dark corridor for example.

Suddenly Tanithil recognized the guard from his days long ago in the service, and was about to call out for help against the three street thugs who were advancing on him menacingly, when he realized that the guard was not chasing the thugs – he was commanding them.

"Finish this, quickly," ordered the soldier and the three rowdies spread out to encircle Tanithil. Unused to fighting Tanithil found himself quickly surrounded and cut off from his route back to Reynard's quarters or on to his own. He was trapped.

"Hold!" came a commanding voice from down the corridor behind him and Tanithil let out a sigh of relief as he recognised Reynard's voice. "What goes on here?" he demanded.

"Nothing for you to concern yourself with, friend," responded the Thought Guard in anything but a friendly tone. "I advise you to return the way you came."

Tanithil risked a quick glance behind him and saw that Reynard was as had he left him, not dressed in the Armour of Lucar but wearing just his usual black attire. He also knew that Reynard had been drinking and that he was far from sober. He was, at least, pleased to see the noble had his trusty rapier at his side.

"And I advise you to think again," retorted Reynard, drawing his rapier slowly from its scabbard and dropping into a natural stance. "You appear to have found my lost friend – for which you have my thanks – now if you would be so kind as to order your flunkies to let him pass, we will then be on our way."

The Thought Guard did not hesitate. "Kill him!" he ordered the three thugs.

Reynard had given Tanithil a few moments to compose himself, so he was prepared for the command. He had slowed his breathing and closed off all focus on everything other than the thugs in front of him and their leader behind. He had zeroed in on the spirits surrounding him and isolated each one, pin-pointing their exact positions. He had quickly probed each one for any surface emotions, looking for fear and uncertainty. When the order came, he was ready. Letting out all the pent up adrenalin and emotion he had bottled up over the last few minutes he assaulted the three ruffians' psyches with an overload of mental stimulus. Taking all the fear he felt at their presence and at his current situation he flung it back in their faces, using his mind to focus it tightly on the bullies surrounding him.

The three men stepped away from the telepath like he was a ferocious beast before them. One dropped his dagger and fled down the corridor into the darkness. The others cowered back momentarily and Tanithil took the opportunity to slip past them and get behind Reynard.

The young noble wasn't one to let an opportunity pass him by and, given that the Thought Guard had ordered these bandits to kill his friend, decided that lethal force was entirely appropriate. From his position in a relaxed defensive stance, Reynard lunged forward, the point of his razor sharp blade slipping into the exposed rib cage of the first man, who dropped to the floor, blood fountaining out of his mouth to splash all over the marble walls.

This was enough to shock the last rowdy, the stocky one with the blond beard, into action. He lashed at Reynard with his dagger, but the fencer easily parried the blow and with a slash opened the man's guts. He dropped his dagger and tried in vain to hold his life inside him as it worked to escape him and slide onto the floor. He fell to the marble ground and lay still. The Thought Guard stepped over the dead bodies, holding his shortsword at his side. Fully encased in chainmail, and highly trained he would be a different matter to defeat, Reynard knew.

Dropping back into his customary defensive stance, Reynard retreated a little, keeping Tanithil safely behind him. The Thought Guard came on. He appeared in no mood to rush and studied Reynard intently as he advanced. Reynard felt the beginnings of doubt enter his mind. This man was a highly trained warrior, in full armour. He was one of the elite unit that had guarded the Emperor himself. Reynard was not in his usual enchanted armour, and he'd partaken of an excess of wine that evening too. How could he expect to prevail against these odds? It was likely he was going to die here.

"Ignore your doubts, Reynard," came a voice from behind him. "He is trying to undermine your confidence. It is an old Thought Guard trick. Rise above it. Believe in yourself. You are Lord Reynard Ferrand, Earl of Providentia. He is merely a traitor and a coward. You are a hero of the Empire," Tanithil prompted, and as the words cut into Reynard's thoughts, so they pushed out the doubts and disbelief which had been creeping in. Reynard was a hero, and heroes do not die in dark corridors on the end of the blades of traitors.

Suddenly Reynard thrust forward, weight transferring from his back leg to his front with blistering speed. The Thought Guard, whose attention had been focussed on dominating the mind in front of him, was not fast enough to react. The needle sharp point of Reynard's rapier split one of the chainmail rings over the guard's heart and pushed straight through. The blade dug deep into the flesh and the guard crumpled forward as a groan of air rushed out of his lungs. He dropped his shortsword and grasped the blade of the rapier in both his hands. By sheer force of will he pulled himself forward towards Reynard, along the blade, forcing it deeper into his body with every inch, staring Reynard directly in the eye the whole time. He managed to reach right up next to the young noble. Grasping Reynard by the face he pulled him close and with his dying breath whispered into his ear, "I'm sorry."

*

"This is getting to be a bit of a habit," commented Reynard dryly as he rapidly downed another glass of red. Leaning forward he picked up the bottle and was disappointed to discover it was empty. As he reached for another, full bottle, a restraining hand stopped him.

"Enough, Reynard. You will need a clear head in the morning," counselled his father.

Reynard stopped for a moment, nodded and went and slumped down in one of the soft couches, exhausted. "I meant the attacks, by the way," he clarified, "not the wine. That's the second time armed men have tried to kill one of us and then apologised to us upon their failure."

"Renatus, the Thought Guard, was a good man, at least he was when I knew him," reported Tanithil. "I can't believe he would have done this without good reason."

"Or without a lot of leverage being put upon him," added Lord Caer. "It seems you have ruffled a few feathers, gentlemen. Someone out there in the Empire – someone with great reach and influence – is trying to thwart you."

"But the question is: who, and why?" asked Reynard.

"There are two obvious candidates," replied Tanithil.

"Indeed," agreed Reynard, nodding. "We believe the Verdant Queen was responsible for the corsair activity of the summer and if Captain Kester was indeed her nephew she would have great reason to want to see us dead in revenge. And we know that Lord Barrius Ebon contrived to put both of us into slavery, Tani. Although his motives are more difficult to ascertain, but then long has the Dark Lord appeared to undertake villainous activities without any obvious reason."

"So what will you do next?" asked Lord Caer of the pair.

"Next we wait for Kita and Okoth to return," answered Reynard. "Hopefully they will have acquired the knowledge to close the portal to the Void on Granita. Then we summon the armies and march on the Writhing Death," declared Reynard.

"And watch our backs for treachery," finished Tanithil.

-Chapter Twelve-

The Great Library of the University of Antissa was in ruins. Tilting at an unlikely angle, much of the loose content of the room had, over the centuries, slid into the bottom corner which was under water. The remaining furniture, constructed from a wood which was hard to identify, was mostly just rotten and collapsed. Books, paper, scrolls and tomes were scattered everywhere. Most were on the floor, but some remained on the few shelves and desks which had survived. One wall had completely fallen in on itself, spilling rubble everywhere across a portion of the floor. Yet despite all this, it remained intact and somehow only partially flooded, meaning that the explorers could walk around without fear of drowning.

Kita stepped across the threshold and entered the library. Moving carefully on the angled floor she glided into the centre of the area, eyes alert for any signs of danger or threat. Behind her came Okoth, the big man moving with surprising grace for one so huge. He had his spear in hand and was looking wary. Darian followed next, a look of rapture on his face – obviously delighted and a bit awestruck to be walking into this place of great history. Finally came Mosi. Should one of the group have taken particular note of his face at this time they might have spotted that he seemed somehow distant and preoccupied.

"What are we looking for, specifically?" enquired Kita, keeping her wits about her and her eyes on the room. Her hands were on the hilts of her blades but she had not drawn them.

"According to all the records I have read, there was a central location where the most important, powerful and dangerous rituals were located. That is where I would expect them to have kept the copy of the ritual to close the portal to the Void. From the descriptions I've read, I think it was a granite work area with many shelves above it – on which would have been stored the rituals. They themselves would have been written in books, on parchment or papyrus scrolls, on clay tablets and other media – all depending on the ritual itself and the era in which it had been developed or discovered."

"Something like this?" called Okoth from a little distance away. Turning to the voice Kita saw that the black-skinned giant was stood over a cracked work surface, which had toppled over onto its side. Above the work surface was the remainder of the shelves which Darian had predicted would be there.

"Yes!" called Darian. "Now, whatever you do don't..." The thin man's warning was cut off mid-sentence as a loud chime rang out across the whole chamber. "... touch it," he finished lamely. Okoth looked up guiltily, with an ancient leather bound book in his hand.

"Oh dear," moaned Darian.

"What was that chime?" asked Kita, instantly on alert.

"I believe we have just triggered the intruder alarm," replied Darian.

"The what?" she asked, clearly not understanding.

"The most powerful and dangerous rituals were protected to stop access from unwanted individuals," explained Darian. "Spells of warding and abjuration were placed upon them and the location in which they were stored. I think Okoth has just activated the defences."

"What defences?" asked Kita scanning the room. As she did so a loud grinding noise could be heard coming from the far corner, underneath the water. It sounded like rock moving against rock, slowly and unstoppably, as if a hidden door was sliding open. She focussed her attention on the water when slowly a dark shape broke the still surface. Something grey and metallic rose inexorably up from the depths. As it did it became clear that the thing rising out of the water was huge – a twelve-foot tall bipedal beast, which was decked out from head to toe in dull metal armour. It rose up to its full height, flexed its long arm-like appendages and with a sudden flick, four long, serrated and razor-sharp claws snapped out of the end of each arm. The head of the thing was also metal, with a vaguely human visage. As they watched it the two eyes started to glow a deep yellow and as they strengthened in brightness the head seemed to become aware of the people in the room. It turned to focus on each in turn.

"A golem!" exclaimed Darian. "I never would have believed the creation of such a creature possible," he marvelled. "Well, I think calling it a creature is an exaggeration. Truly it is an automaton, a magical creation, typically used to guard areas or carry out menial tasks. I've heard of small ones before, but this one is huge," he observed.

"I can see that," commented Kita dryly. "The big question is – what will it do?" She had her hands on her hilts but was reticent to draw her blades in case the action antagonized the huge machine – which at this stage appeared to be studying the room and the people in it, but didn't appear overtly hostile.

"I suggest you put the book back, Okoth," proposed Darian.

"Yes, good idea," agreed Kita. "Put it back – gently."

Okoth carefully placed the dusty old tome back into the shelf from which he had pulled it. As the book touched the granite structure once more the golem's head twitched and rotated to face Okoth.

Then it charged.

The thing moved across the angled floor with extraordinary speed, its two long legs covering the ground rapidly. Okoth only just had time to grasp his spear in two hands and prepare to receive the charge of the monstrosity. The big warrior drove the butt end of the weapon into the ground, finding a gap between two broken flag stones to wedge it securely. From there it was all about timing. Kita had a moment to marvel at how small Okoth appeared as the huge automaton towered over him and then the two collided.

Okoth had been raised with spear in hand and had learnt the art of preparing the weapon to receive a charge many years ago. That skill probably saved his life. The golem crashed full on into the pointed end of the spear, seemingly intent on ripping Okoth's head from his body and with very little concern for its own hide. The spear drove right into the golem's metallic midriff but it didn't penetrate the skin. Fortunately for Okoth the exterior of the machine was embossed and uneven and although the point did not dig into the golem, it did catch in place.

Okoth held on as the spear bent under the huge momentum. Thankfully the spear was of great quality and rather than snapping – which would have left the golem right on top of him – it bent almost in two. In doing so it absorbed the momentum of the charge and slowed the creature down to a stop. As it reached a point right next to the giant man it swiped two long claws at Okoth's head. The Champion Gladiator was fast though, and easily ducked under the attacks. Then, the full momentum of the charge spent, the spear began to repel its adversary. Rapidly returning to its natural state, the spear straightened and in doing so it pushed the golem back, and away from Okoth. Kita saw that as an opportunity and rushed in.

Moving swiftly up into a position behind it, Kita finally drew her blades. The well cared for edges glistened in the soft light of Mosi's holy symbol. She stepped into range and brought both weapons slashing into the machine simultaneously, one from each side. The blades clanged into the metallic hide with a loud ringing noise and Kita almost dropped them as the vibrations ripped into her arms. It was like striking solid stone.

Dropping back she studied the golem as it slowly turned its head around to face backwards, appeared to focus on her, and then swivelled on the spot alarmingly quickly, to face her. She was dismayed to find that even with both her blades striking the golem's sides cleanly with all her speed and power, the skin was not even dented. And there was nothing more than a scratch mark where Okoth's spear had embedded itself in the midriff – a blow which would have skewered any natural creature she had faced or heard of.

The golem advanced on her and swung its lethal looking claws at her, one across at head height and another lower down. She was able to evade the attacks with quick footwork and by using her long *katana* to partially deflect the attack at her head. It seemed that the golem's blows were not as fast as its feet, but she knew that to get hit by one of those claws was to die. The power of the swings was more than any human could match.

"How do we defeat it?" she called out. "Neither Okoth nor I have even dented it with our weapons." Moving surefootedly backwards she ducked easily beneath another swipe from a metallic claw.

"I have no idea," replied Okoth, "he's a tough thing alright."

Suddenly Mosi cut in. "The eyes are the power source," he told them. "You need to take out the eyes to stop it."

Kita didn't have time to stop and ask how Mosi knew this but she trusted the priest implicitly. The trouble was in order to get to the eyes, which were ten or more feet off the floor, she would need to get inside the reach of those fearsome metallic claws. To do so would be to invite death. But she was a Niten warrior and the prospect of death did not faze her. "Okoth – I need you to distract it. You have to get its attention," she called to the giant who was now behind it.

Okoth roared a bestial challenge, rushed in and drove the point of his spear into the seam between the head and the shoulders – where the neck would be on a normal person. Although this did nothing to damage the armour of the golem, it did cause it to stagger forward a little and seemed to achieve what Kita had hoped it would – the golem spun in place and was facing Okoth.

Kita knew her plan was risky, but she could see no other approach. Assuming Mosi was right and that the key to this victory was to strike at the golem's eyes, she realized that she would need to get up close and personal. With the practiced ease of a master swordsman she sheathed her *katana*, and flipped her short *wakizashi* into her right hand. Taking a quick but steadying breath, she ran forward and leapt as high as she could. Landing up on the golem's hard metallic back she scrabbled for a hold. Her left arm grabbed a hold of a ridge on the side and her legs tightened around the monster.

Okoth stabbed and stabbed again at the automaton, not really trying to do any meaningful damage but trying to keep its attention focussed on him. As far as he could work out the golem was only using its eyes to detect enemies so he figured that maybe it didn't know Kita was on its back. So far at least it had made no efforts to dislodge her. The golem stepped forward and swung a powerful arm at the warrior's head, which he ducked underneath. Stabbing out a riposte Okoth tried to go for a low target to keep the golem's attention downwards, but the creature blocked his jab with its other arm, and the power of the parry was such that the spear was ripped from his hands. It flew across the floor and landed in some rubble nearby. Okoth knew he was in trouble.

Kita saw what had happened from her position on the golem's back and knew she had to act quickly. She would have wanted more time to climb into a favourable position, but taking that time would put Okoth's life in serious jeopardy. She would not do that. Scrambling rapidly up the golem's back she reached its neck. Throwing her left arm around the neck to hold on and steady herself, she reached out forward with the *wakizashi* in her right arm and plunged it into one of the eye-holes of the golem.

The golem shuddered, and Kita thought it was going to stop or maybe topple over. She was about to leap free when, faster than she could react, a huge metallic arm grabbed her by the collar and pulled her over the golem's head. For a second she dangled there, grasped in the golem's wicked claw and then the other claw came up and slashed at her head. With nowhere to go she could not escape the terrible blow. At the very last second she turned her head aside which stopped it being pulled from her shoulders, but the serrated claws dug deep into the skin of her face, tearing her nose clean off and ripping four deep channels into the tissue. She stifled a scream at the intense pain and blinked the blood from her eyes.

The golem still had a hold of her. She was dangling in front of it, right before its monstrous metallic face. As she looked through bloodshot eyes she saw that the golem's right eye was dark. That must have been the one which the *wakizashi* had gone into. The left eye was still glowing with a strong yellow light. She felt more than saw the automaton's arm rise again and knew it would not miss her this time. The arm would slash down once more and it would mean her death. But through the pain and blood she had never let go of her short sword, and now she was in reach of the golem's face. Quick as a flash she thrust the sharpened blade deep into the second eye socket, driving it right up to the hilt.

The golem shuddered again. The light from the eye faded. The arcane power driving the machine failed and the death blow never fell.

*

You did well once more, priest. Thanks to you the Guardian was defeated. It was my knowledge and your advice which enabled the young woman to overcome the golem. Well done.

Mosi shook his head to clear the echoes of the voice and tried to concentrate. The wound on Kita's face was horrific. The scratches were deep, having penetrated far into the flesh and, he believed, having sliced into the bone. The nose was destroyed, basically gone. He had no idea what he could do about it. Kita sat on the floor in front of him, stoic and still, showing no signs of the intense agony she must be feeling. Mosi could only shake his head further in admiration for her spirit and self-control. Now he must do what he could to help her.

He put his hand to her face, being careful not to touch it, less he cause her more pain, and began to chant the Holy Scripture. He called on the power of the Light's healing. The symbol around his neck began to pulse and the soft light grew in intensity. The light transferred from the symbol to the palm of his hand and from there spread slowly out across her face. He could see her visibly relax as the healing power took control. He watched as the nose began to rebuild itself, the lost tissue somehow knitting itself back together. He had never witnessed such healing power before.

Presently the light faded and Mosi examined Kita's face. The nose was virtually returned to its old self but was crooked and seemed to have a small chunk out of it. But that was a minor thing. The thing which struck Mosi the most were the four jagged scars which stretched across from her left jaw to her right temple. The scars were grey and old looking – like they had been caused years ago and had healed as much as they ever would, but none the less, her once pretty face was now irrevocably disfigured.

The golem was created by the High Magi of my era. Such powerful magic as that cannot be easily healed. Consider yourself lucky as only my healing would have had any chance of restoring her face. Without my help she would have looked far, far worse. In fact, she was quite lucky. The claw missed both her eyes.

Mosi wondered if that would be any consolation to Kita. Looking more carefully, he saw that the voice was right – the scars ran perilously close to both eyes without actually touching either. In that respect he supposed she had been lucky.

"Thank you Mosi the pain is all gone now," Kita said, standing up. "I am, as ever in your debt." Bowing from the waist she held her show of respect for many seconds.

"It was nothing," he replied humbly. "The power comes mostly from the Phoenix," he responded.

"The Phoenix?" she asked.

"The Phoenix's holy symbol I mean, of course," responded Mosi quickly.

"Well, it's not as if the Phoenix told you how to defeat the golem, is it, Mosi?" asked Okoth, clapping the white-robed priest on the back. "That was genius. How did you know?"

"It just came to me, I suppose," answered Mosi evasively. He wasn't sure quite what to make of the holy symbol and the fact that it appeared to be a phylactery – an arcane container capable of keeping a soul alive long after the host body had died. And that the phylactery appeared to contain the soul of the last Phoenix. For now he decided to keep the knowledge to himself and pray on it.

Mosi looked around the room and found what he was looking for. Crossing quickly to a pile of rubble he picked up a shiny piece of glass-like stone. He quickly cleaned it off on his sleeve and returned to Kita. "There is something, Kita," he started. "The wounds were really deep and my healing was unable to completely fix them. You've been left with a scar."

Mosi passed the reflective bit of stone to the woman. Kita held it up in front of her face. If there was any reaction inside, then nothing of her feelings were evident in her face or her bearing. She simply took a good look, then nodded and handed the stone back to Mosi.

*

Darian Snow was as excited as he could ever remember being. He was stood inside the Great Library of the University of Antissa and directly in front of him was the storage for all the most important rituals of the Rainbow Empire. He could only imagine how jealous the other members of the Cabal of Callindrill would be when he recounted this story to them.

Looking down at the destruction in front of him, he pondered his next move. Should he try and collect as many of these books and scrolls as he could and return them all home to the Cabal? Their value in terms of knowledge would be incalculable. It seemed to make sense. There was little point in leaving all this incredible information and power here in the depths of the sea where eventually it would be washed away. Yes, he would rescue what he could.

Closing his eyes he muttered a simple incantation, opening a tiny but controlled portal into the Void. From there he summoned the arcane energy necessary to feel out the presence of other magical energies. He expected to find that the rituals were protected by ancient wardings, but what he felt surprised him. There was a warding there, but the age of it was wrong. It was recent – perhaps only a year or so old. How could that be?

He sent out his senses again, carefully, suspecting this was some sort of clever trap, but no – he could sense nothing especially powerful, nothing especially clever in the ward. It was rudimentary, and plain. And definitely new.

Focussing the arcane energy he had collected from the Void he twisted it and pushed it in one go at the ward and felt the simple protection dissipate, negated by the energy he had gathered. The two spells had cancelled each other out and he knew the rituals were no longer protected. He would be able to search through the books and scrolls safely now with no risk.

The situation with the wards worried him greatly though. Finding the ancient abjurations which would have been placed on this area gone was no big surprise in itself. They were five hundred years old and had gone through an earthquake. It was quite possible that they would not have lasted till now. But finding a new ward which had clearly been placed here within the last year or so – that meant only one thing.

Someone had been here before them.

*

"Here!" Darian exclaimed finally, "I've found it! I've actually found it!"

Kita was sat alone, deep in thought when the cry broke her from her day dreams. Getting to her feet she moved across the sloping floor to the location in which Darian had been studying for the last few hours. He had a big pile of books stacked up nearby and many scrolls and papers scattered about his position. In his hands he held a sheet of what looked like ancient papyrus. Kita could see strange runes and pictographs drawn all across it. None of them made any sense to her, but she would trust the mystic's judgement. He was a *wu jen* and she knew better than to question their knowledge of these things. All that she knew was that the discovery of this scroll took her one step closer to defeating the Writhing Death and bringing honour to her father's name. "Excellent work, Darian. Do you think you could use it to close the portal?" she enquired hopefully.

"Certainly," he said. "There is only one snag really," he added quietly.

"Which is?"

"I need to get right up close to the gate to do it," he answered.

"How close?" asked Mosi from nearby.

"I'm not exactly sure, maybe a few hundred feet. Maybe a lot closer. I'll know when I get there."

"That could be quite hard with a multitude of crawling, biting, stinging, devouring insects pouring through the gate every second," noted Kita.

"Then you had best make sure you keep me alive and safe," responded Darian gravely.

"I intend to," she finished.

*

Kita's head swam. No matter how many times she used a Translocator she always found them extremely disorienting at best and downright painful at worst. She reflected that this time it was more of the former so perhaps she was getting used to it. Shaking her head to clear the dizziness she looked around her as a blurry silhouette came into focus.

It was a man wearing chainmail and a deep blue cloak. In his hand was a longsword and as it came into focus she saw it was pointing right at her chest. It took a few seconds to register and then she realised she was staring at a member of the Thought Guard. So at least they had arrived in Lucar safely.

"Don't move," he advised her simply. She tended to agree.

"I am Darian Snow, first born of Agamedes Snow, the Ice King. These are my companions. We have urgent business with whoever is in charge here these days," introduced Darian from beside her. As usual he seemed to have recovered from the passage through the teleport portal much faster than her.

The guards seemed to consider this. Then their captain nodded and the soldiers placed their swords back into their scabbards. "You'll be wanting to meet with the Warlord then," he suggested.

"Warlord? Since when has Lucar had a Warlord?" asked the thin man, confused.

"Since we declared war, milord. The heads of the five ruling houses voted and it was unanimous. We're going to war against the Writhing Death," reported the captain, appearing pleased to be up to speed with the latest politics.

"Five ruling houses? But the Azure House has come to an end. There was no heir. What happened?"

"A new house was promoted, milord. The Iron House is now the fifth ruling house. And their head, the Earl of Providentia, has been appointed Warlord – the head of the War Cabinet," the captain explained.

"Old Lord Caer? Why on earth would they elect him to be a Warlord?" pondered Darian out loud.

"Beggin' yer pardon, milord, but not him. He retired. No, the new Warlord is his son, and the new Earl of Providentia: Lord Reynard Ferrand."

*

A soft knock at the door disturbed the silence.

Reynard was alone in his luxurious quarters, and was enjoying some solitude. Wearing his usual black outfit and a pair of soft ankle-high boots, he was sat in a large and comfortable chair, staring into a crackling fire. A soft sheepskin rug was laid out in front of the hearth and a small black cat was curled up on it. He had no idea where the cat had come from or who owned it but it seemed to have adopted his quarters and his fireplace especially. Somehow the cat made him feel peaceful and relaxed and so he let it stay. He had even dispensed with his usual glass of Pembrose Red, such was the calming effect of the feline.

Reynard guessed the visitor would be Evantia. She had spent a lot of time with him recently and he knew she was trying to win him over. And it was taking all his self-control to stop her. She was stunningly good looking, she had a gorgeous figure and she knew how to use it. And when they were alone she would indulge his every desire.

She was intelligent too – he had grown to appreciate that under the beautiful exterior was a shrewd and cunning mind. It was clear why she had been chosen as the Trade Lords' envoy for she was excellent at it. No doubt her beauty caused many men to underestimate her – Reynard knew he had been guilty of that in the past.

But with all that there was something missing. He didn't know what it was, but it was definitely there. Or at least not there. Well, he just wasn't sure. She left him a bit confused, for certain. He knew he wanted her, but that was not enough. He knew he didn't love her.

Perhaps now was the time to tell her? Yes, now was the time he would finally make it plain to her. He would ask her in and sit her down and tell her straight that, as much as he liked her, and had enjoyed all their time together, this was it. They would never be together properly, and he didn't want to continue any sort of liaisons with her. Yes, that was what he would say.

Rising to his feet, he crossed to the oaken door. Straightening out his black waistcoat of Honshu silk he opened it to find Kita standing there.

"Well met Lord Reynard," she greeted him formally, with a short curt bow. "I trust you are well?"

Reynard stood there for a moment and then realized his mouth was open. He shut it. He opened it again to say something and couldn't think what to say, so he shut it again.

"Are you going to invite me in, or stand there doing carp impressions all evening?" she asked, the faintest trace of a smile on her face. A face which Reynard was just registering had been terribly scarred.

"Errrr..." he managed.

The smile dropped from Kita's face to be replaced by a neutral mask. "Yes, I know, the scars are unpleasant to look at. I apologise. I won't take up more of your time than necessary, milord, but there is something I need to tell you and I would rather not do it here in the corridor of the Imperial Palace."

"Yes, sorry, of course," Reynard finally recovered. "Come in, come in." He stepped aside and gestured for the Niten warrior to enter. He noticed she was wearing the old silk kimono from the day he had first met her on board the *Javelin*. It had been repaired and sewn up many times since then but it brought back a flood of memories and emotions in the young noble.

Reynard stood holding the door open and watched as Kita walked to the low table near the fire. He marvelled at the grace and economy of movement and at the incredible balance and dexterity demonstrated in just that simple walk. It was captivating. Kita sat and crossed her legs and looked over at him. He realised he was still standing at the door, holding it open. He closed it and joined her, sitting back in the big armchair he had been in earlier.

"It's wonderful to see you again Kita. So good. I can't begin to tell you," he started.

She held up her hand to stop him. "I will save you the platitudes, Reynard. I am here to make things easy for you. I have had a lot of time to think over the last few weeks and months. And, especially with my recent ... change in appearance, I want to tell you that you are free to be with Evantia. She is a beautiful woman, and I will not stand in your way. I know I cannot compete with her. Perhaps before ... this," she said indicating her face, "but certainly not now. I do not wish to make this awkward or embarrassing for either of us, so I will leave it there. I wish you all the luck in the world, Reynard and I sincerely hope you are happy." So saying she rose to her feet, gave a quick simple bow and moved off towards the door.

Reynard watched her go and before she was half way to the door he made his decision. Leaping to his feet he rushed across the room, grasped her by the wrist and spun her to face him. Holding her by the arms he looked down into her face for a few seconds, then leaned in and kissed her deeply.

"But what about Evantia?" she asked him when they split apart.

"She is nothing to me," he told her, still holding her in his arms. "Time apart from you made me realise something: You are the one I am doing all this for. All this stuff: the wandering around the Empire, all the politics, all the risk, all the struggle. I'm doing it all for you, Kita. Not for the Empire, not for my reputation, or the fame or glory, but for you. Because ultimately I know this is what you want to do in order to honour your father's memory. And I would do anything for you, Kita. Anything."

"But what about my face?" she questioned softly, looking up in this his handsome features. "Evantia is gorgeous, and I am ... disfigured," she finished quietly.

"It's simple, Kita," he answered gently. "I love you for what is on the inside, not the outside. I love you for your spirit, for your bravery, for your compassion, for your wisdom and for your capacity to love others. And anyway, you *are* beautiful. The scars just add to your foreign mystery," he grinned.

For the first time in months Kita felt truly happy.

*

The reunion of the five ex-slaves was a joyous one. Reynard managed to organize it so that all five could be together in his quarters alone and without any interruptions. It was as they all wanted it. Reynard stood by the fire, holding a glass of Pembrose Red in his hand and looking at his friends. He came to realise that these four people were the best friends he had in the world. And he was about to take them into

Hell. Still, he mused, there was no one else he would rather go into Hell alongside.

Okoth was recounting a tale about the battle he and Kita had fought inside the Great Library with some magical guardian. He was surprisingly good at telling stories, Reynard realised, complete with actions and sound effects. It seemed he had just got to the part where Kita was struck by the great abomination and the big man stopped, unsure what to say.

"Carry on, Okoth," encouraged Kita. "We are all friends here and I am not shamed by my scars," she said, glancing at Reynard. "And you are telling a wonderful tale," she smiled. Reynard could not help but smile in response. It was fantastic to see Kita looking so merry. Okoth continued his story and brought it to a gripping conclusion, doing a fair impression of Kita with her short sword. The group all cheered as he mimed the final blow to the automaton.

Reynard looked again and noticed that in fact Mosi had not cheered. He had been present at the battle of course, so it was not like it was a new story to him. But as Reynard watched him he realised that Mosi's smile was almost fixed and that he hardly seemed to be listening to what the group were saying. Crossing to the priest, he put his hand on the robed man's shoulder. "Something bothering you, Mosi?"

The priest almost jumped and looked up suddenly. "Sorry, sorry, I was miles away," he apologised.

"What is it?" asked Reynard carefully. It was unlike Mosi to be distracted. He was always so centred and mindful.

"Oh nothing, nothing," responded the Hishanite evasively.

"Come on Mosi – what is it? Look around you. Are these not the best friends a man could hope to have? If you can't share your worries and concerns with us, then who can you?"

Mosi looked up and realised the whole group was looking at him expectantly. He decided now was the time to tell them about the phylactery. First he crossed to a nearby table, and picked up a wine bottle and poured himself a large glass of Pembrose Red which he proceeded to half drain. The group looked at one another – Mosi hardly ever drunk.

"I have something to tell you all," he began.

Sometime later Mosi had finished his tale. The friends all stood there looking at him, in wonder.

"So let me get this right. You have a vessel of some sort in that medallion you're wearing, and inside it is the soul or spirit or something of one of the most powerful priests who has ever lived, and he is helping you and guiding you, by speaking into your mind?" summed up Reynard.

"I suppose that is about the size of it, yes," agreed Mosi, finishing the last part of his glass.

Reynard paused. "Amazing," he said eventually. "That has to be incredible, I would think, isn't it?"

"It is a little strange," admitted Mosi.

"So what sort of things has he told you then?" asked Okoth.

"Remember when I worked out the way to break the magical barrier stopping us getting into the Great Library?" asked Mosi. Okoth nodded. "That was his idea. And the golem – the power in the eyes – that was him too," Mosi explained.

"Truly exceptional," remarked Tanithil. "I have heard of things like this before but never come across them. I wonder if it would be possible to learn anything about the ability to telepathically speak to you from studying it," he mused.

"It is possible, I suppose," agreed Mosi. "I would be more than happy for you to try, assuming the Phoenix is happy with that idea," he added.

"Of course", agreed Tanithil. "What else has he helped you with?"

"Oh, there is one more thing of significance," added Mosi. "The Phoenix reported something to me and I asked Darian about it and he confirmed it, so I definitely think it's true. I'm not sure how important it is but it definitely bears reporting."

"What is that?" queried Reynard.

"The Great Library," Mosi responded. "Someone had been there before us."

-Chapter Thirteen-

Kululu Jade was restless. Her quarters were cramped and she had never enjoyed sea voyages. She had been allocated a small cabin in the aft of the *Javelin*, below decks, and it stank of stale sweat. She had no idea which of Lord Reynard's crew she had displaced but whoever it was could do with some lessons in personal hygiene.

She was lying in the hammock which was stretched across the cabin from corner to corner. She'd spent plenty of nights sleeping in hammocks in the jungles of Ibini – it was often safer to sleep off the ground than on the jungle floor in her homeland – so the sleeping arrangements were fine by her, though she had needed to spray some perfume onto the hammock cloth to cover up the stench. She counted herself as fairly resilient and capable of dealing with most of what her role in life threw at her – which was often unpleasant – but somehow cleanliness had always been a compulsion with her. She had never been able to work out why.

Neatness made sense – it was important to be organized and structured to be as efficient as possible. So she was always that. But cleanliness didn't actually seem to serve any real function in terms of making her more competent at her role. Yet it was, for some reason, massively important to her.

A soft knock at the door broke into her reverie. "Beggin yer pardon milady, but the cap'n has asked for your presence in his quarters," came a voice from the other side of the door. "When yer ready, ma'am, of course," it added respectfully. Kululu Jade didn't deign to reply, but rolled acrobatically out of the hammock and landed lightly on her feet, her body instantly in sync with the gentle swaying of the ship at anchor. She may not like sea voyages, but she was swift to adapt to them.

Straightening out her emerald green dress, she quickly pulled the two long hairpins from her top knot. Her auburn hair, set free from control, cascaded down her back in waves. She inspected the diamond tips of the needle-sharp pins and quickly checked that the poison-injecting mechanism looked free and in working order. A small jade gem in the wide end of each hairpin worked as a button to release the *naja* poison, which was usually lethal in seconds. Satisfied her weapons were primed and in good order she twirled her hair back up into its top knot and slid the two hairpins into place.

She was ready.

*

The Captain's lounge was overcrowded. Kululu Jade estimated this room would probably have been comfortable for four, perhaps five people to share. Now there were eleven of them squeezed in. Before setting sail from Lucar, Reynard had removed the comfortable couches and the low-lying table from this room, and had replaced them with a large pine table and a dozen chairs: enough to seat every one of the people on his War Council.

The Jade Princess looked around the table. She knew most of those present and could guess at who the others were. Reynard and his band of ex-slaves were obvious. Everyone knew them and she had studied them in depth as part of her preparation for this mission. Reynard sat at the head of the table and his four companions all sat to his left. Next to them, at the far end from Reynard, sat the blonde woman Evantia. She was with the Guild of Master Merchants and Sea Farers and in this council she was here to represent the Trade Lords and the large band of mercenaries they had brought to the assault. Kululu knew her to be shrewd, but of no threat martially. Opposite Reynard's companions and Evantia sat Kululu herself and the other members of this council. Beside her was the diminutive Darian Snow. A brilliant mind, and known to be a member of the Cabal. Kululu Jade knew more about him than she would have wished to. Next was Wiktor Ebon – son of the Dark Lord and a necromancer. Himself of no threat, his Dread Guard were formidable. Lifeless zombies or skeletons, they would never stop fighting. Alongside Wiktor was Catulus, his political enemy. Dressed in his ever-present red robes, the Pyromancer was one to be wary of – as were his followers. The last man she did not know. He was obviously a *Nanuk* from his size and furs, but she could not place him, which annoyed her. The final chair, at the foot of the pine table, was empty.

"Ladies and gentlemen, your attention, please," commanded Reynard, rising from his seat at the head of the table. Wearing the Armour of Lucar he dominated the room, both physically and mentally. Everyone stopped talking and looked to see what he would say. Kululu was well prepared and self-aware enough to be able to resist the feelings of adoration which were gently lapping at her subconscious. She knew it was the armour and had trained hard to repel it.

"I wish to lay out my battle plan," began Reynard.

Kululu listened up. As much as she needed to make sure she didn't let Reynard's armour influence her plans, she needed to be prepared – and that meant knowing his.

"I'm not sure exactly how much each of you knows, so I will cover it all. Forgive me if any of you are hearing things you already know," he continued. "The main threat we will face on Granita will be the bulk of the Writhing Death. These insects are impossible to count. They will crawl over everything, biting, stinging and eventually consuming whatever they come into contact with. Do not underestimate them. Clearly they cannot be fought with sword or axe, so Catulus and his Pyromancers will deal with them. How many men do you have?" he asked turning to the Dragon's son.

"Seventy two," replied the red-robed man simply.

Reynard nodded. "Now, the Pyromancers must focus on the insect threat – they are the only ones who can counter it. But there are more than just insects to be dealt with. A large number of aberrations have passed through the gate from the Void. These things are as varied and multifarious as you can imagine. They are powerful and dangerous, but they can be killed with sword and axe."

"We hope," cut in Wiktor with a grin.

"Yes, quite," agreed Reynard, smiling back, seemingly unfazed at having been interrupted. "So, as we do not know what these... creatures will do, I am assigning Kululu's company to protect the Pyromancers. They will follow the red wizards and keep any of the larger monsters from troubling them."

"How many have you brought?" asked Catulus from his position to Kululu's right.

"Enough," she replied shortly.

"Numbers would be helpful, milady," prompted Reynard diplomatically.

"There are twenty four in my company, myself included" she answered.

"Twenty four?" queried Catulus. "Can that few of the infamous Jade Assassins really keep my men safe? Remember we will be fully focussed on destroying the Writhing Death – we will have no time for fighting."

"There is no such thing as a Jade Assassin, drake," responded Kululu icily. "That is nothing more than a story put together by milkmaids to frighten little children. However, my girls are a well-trained unit of warriors and will protect your spell-weavers, fear not." Kululu was used to having to deny the existence of her assassins, and almost wondered if it was really worth it as everyone seemed to want to believe they existed. Of course after this mission the world would know the truth.

"Good, good," came in Reynard. "So, that leaves the rest of you. The *Nanuk* and the Dread Guard will form the vanguard of the force which will storm the gate itself. They will lead the forces of mercenaries which the Guild have gathered. The *Nanuk* are the bravest mortals in the Empire and the Dread Guard are without any fear. I believe we will need that, for I worry that many of the mercenaries will die trying to reach the gate. Sadly I see no other option. Wiktor and Jared," Reynard indicated the *Nanuk* at the end of the table, "will lead the van."

"Won't that be a lot of fun," commented the Ebon noble dryly.

"The *Nanuk* will do their part," replied Jared.

"How many men do you each bring?" asked Reynard.

"I bring forty *Nanuk*," answered the hulking northerner. "All battle hardened and impatient to begin."

"And I bring fifty six of the Dread Guard," answered Wiktor. "They won't let you down," he promised. Kululu thought she saw a flicker of doubt cross Reynard's face but if it was there it was gone in an instant.

"And though you didn't ask me, Reynard," offered Evantia suddenly, "the Guild brings four hundred and twenty mercenaries from across the Empire and beyond."

"*Lord* Reynard," corrected Kita quietly from her position at Reynard's left hand. Evantia blushed deeply but did not respond. Kululu didn't need to have been paying attention to that exchange to realize there was bad blood there. This was information which was worth storing away.

"Excellent Evantia – thank you," responded Reynard, clearly trying to smooth things over. "So finally that leaves us," he continued, indicating his friends on his left hand side. "We will comprise the command group who will try to get Darian close enough to the gate so that he can cast the ritual to close it. We plan to use stealth to get in close – hopefully Wiktor and Jared will keep the aberrations busy enough that they will not notice us. The five of us will keep Darian safe from anything which comes near whilst he does his work."

"Five?" asked Evantia.

"Yes. Myself, Kita, Okoth, Mosi and Tani will go with Darian," responded Reynard.

"But I thought I would be going in your group," stated Evantia, her blush spreading to her neck. Kululu settled in to see how this exchange was going to go.

"You can't," came the expected reply, but not from Reynard. Instead it was Kita who was speaking. "You are not a warrior. You are not battle trained. You would be a hindrance, not a help. We have to protect Darian at all costs whilst he performs the ritual. We can't afford to be babysitting you at the same time."

Kululu had to work had to supress a laugh as Evantia rose to her feet. "A hindrance!?" she vented. "If it wasn't for me half this group would not be assembled here. I've been from one end of the Empire to the other for this cause. I've brought over four hundred men to this force. How dare you accuse me of being a hindrance?"

"Evantia, please sit down," commanded Reynard from his position at the head of the table. He was still standing, and his tone of voice was powerfully assertive. Kululu guessed that the armour was adding weight to his demand, and Evantia plonked herself straight down. "Now," Reynard continued in a more natural tone, "I'm afraid Kita is right, my dear. It would be too dangerous for you."

"But not too dangerous for her," Evantia replied almost under her breath.

Kita obviously heard, and her response was calm, measured and short, "That is because you are not a Niten warrior." Even Kululu Jade was not sure if the words were meant as a threat or not.

"Besides," cut in Reynard smoothly, "we need you to go with Wiktor and Jared, Evantia – the mercenaries are here because of the Guild and you are their representative. They will want to see you with the army, not skulking off into the wilds as we will be doing."

The words seemed to placate the blonde woman and she nodded slowly, but Kululu didn't miss the evil glare she gave to the woman from Honshu. She wondered if there was anything she could do with this information.

*

The trip from Lucar to the shores of Granita had been uneventful. The weather had held fair and there had been no incidents on route. Kululu stood at the rail of the *Javelin* and looked out across the fleet. Less than a score of ships had set out from Lucar and she pondered the fact that only six hundred men were being sent to stop an invading army which comprised countless millions. She wondered how many High Magi had made the trip – which would have been across land then – to the plains of Granita five hundred years ago, to stop the first invasion of the Writhing Death.

Of course that time the gate to the Void had been opened by accident. High Magi from the Coral house had researched a new way to draw power from the Void – a way which their research said would increase their power tenfold. Unfortunately the experiment had gone wrong and the resulting portal had been a hundred thousand times the size of that which was intended. And the portal they had opened had been large enough to be self-sustaining, drawing power from the Void to keep itself open – which left a passage open for the Writhing Death to enter this world.

Kululu knew this because she had read it in a journal which she had recovered from the Great Library in the University of Antissa. At the same time she had managed to recover the ritual which had been used to open the gate to the Void, stored in a secure area in the library. She had disturbed some ancient arcane guardian but had managed to escape and return home with the ritual. Many months had then been spent studying it. She had received basic training in the arcane arts in clandestine lessons deep in the Verdant Palace from an aesthetic her mother had hired. With that knowledge she had been able to unravel the secrets of the ritual.

A little over a year ago she had travelled to Granita, back to the site of the original gate and had stood and read the words to reopen the portal. On her mother's instructions Kululu Jade had enabled the biggest threat the Empire had ever known to return to its lands. She had brought back the Writhing Death.

Her mother had never fully shared her intentions on this venture. Kululu Jade knew it had been many years in the planning, and knew she had played a big part in much of the project. She had been the one who had liaised with her cousin, Nikolai Kester, and delivered her mother's instructions to him to build his corsair fleet and attack the interests of the Guild and the other noble houses. She had been involved in numerous assassinations over the last couple of years; never striking at the heads of the noble houses, but taking out significant members of their household staff, or high ranking military officers in their small armies. All enough to keep the noble houses unbalanced and on the back foot without ever letting too much suspicion fall on the Jade House.

Now she was travelling with the task force which was designated to get to the portal and close it, stopping the Writhing Death from entering the world. But unknown to them, her role was to stop *them*. She knew her chances of surviving the upcoming encounter would be slim. The moment her Jade Assassins sprung their trap she would be exposed. Even she could not hope to withstand the combined might of Reynard and his companions, plus the elite units of the Empire which would be arrayed against her. But she had an ace up her sleeve: another ritual she had recovered from the Great Library, and one she intended to use when the time was right.

*

The deep water cove of Coruba was much as Reynard remembered it. The circle of white cliffs sheltered the wooden jetties and buildings which had been built a year before by the corsairs who had used it as their base. This place had been the site of the battle in which they had finally caught up with and defeated Captain Kester – and recovered the Armour of Lucar.

It was also the place where Kita's father had been killed and the memory of that made him look across at her. She was stood at the rail, looking out across the sea to the port, her face a mask. Reynard knew her culture and her training would not allow her to betray her feelings, but he knew deep inside she would be feeling a great swell of emotions right now. Probably sorrow and grief, but also anger and rage at the aberration, Baku, who had slain her father.

The *Javelin* slid easily into the cove and under Birgen's expert control gently bumped up against the wharf. Three crew men, who were hanging over the side on ropes, dropped nimbly onto the deck and rushed to tie the ship up. Aside the *Javelin*, three more ships were docking. Behind them the remainder of the score or so of ships in the fleet waited to take their turns to dock and unload their passengers.

As the ships set about the complex dance of dock, unload and undock, Reynard and his four friends climbed the single path which wound up the cliffs to the plateau above the cove. As they reached the top a great flash of purple and orange light lit up the skyline to the east. All five of them knew that was the light of the gate as it spewed forth more aberrations from the Void. They also knew it had been doing so, uninterrupted, for nearly half a year since they had last been here.

Within a few hours the score of ships had unloaded their six hundred passengers and the docks below the cliffs were packed to over flowing with men. Reynard held a final War Council with the ten people who had crammed into the *Javelin's* lounge. This time they were in the spacious hall which Captain Kester had used as his base a year ago. Reynard knew that this place would be hard for Kita as it was the very building in which her father had died, but it was the only sensible place to hold such a meeting.

"We rest here overnight," Reynard told the council. "There isn't space for everyone down here in the village, so the Dread Guard will move up to the cliff tops and serve as watchmen. I'm not expecting to see anything or anyone here, but it pays to be careful." He did not mention that the Dread Guard did not need to sleep, not sure who in the council really understood the fact that they were living dead and not sure now was the time to have that conversation.

"Agreed," commented Wiktor. "I'll go and move them up there now," he added, rising to his feet. "No sense in crowding things more than necessary." He bowed to the assembled group and strode out of the wooden building.

"Tomorrow at first light we set out east. We have a long hard trek ahead of us to reach the site of the gate. I would expect it to take us two days to move the army that distance. I don't want to push on too fast – we need to arrive ready to fight. And make no mistake everyone – this will be the fight of our lives.

"We are not going to be facing men out there, but creatures of nightmare and terror; aberrations from the deepest realms of the Void. And they are ruthless killers, led by a creature with intelligence as well as power. We must not underestimate the difficulty of the task ahead.

"Now – go to your men and prepare. Tomorrow, we go to war."

*

The army had marched for nearly two days. The last time Reynard had been here the lands had been hot and acrid with terrible dust storms raging across them. This time the temperatures were colder and they had mercifully avoided any serious storms. A few tiny tornadoes, more dust devils than anything else, had hastened across their path, but these had been more like diversions and fascinating phenomena than any true risk to the army.

Now Reynard knew they had reached the end. He knew that beyond the crest ahead lay the vast plain in which the gate was located, and where he supposed the Writhing Death was still forming, growing ever larger day by day, hour by hour. He had called his command team together.

"The five of us will climb the crest and do a quick reconnaissance," he told them. Fully into the mould of commander here on the field, he had gotten into the habit of simply deciding what to do and giving instructions, rather than discussing options with the others as he had done in the past. If any of his friends cared or even noticed, they did not say anything, seeming content to let him lead.

"Ready?" he asked them all. Nods all round indicated that they were. Reynard set off up the only obvious route he could see. He seemed to remember climbing this very trail a year ago, though at the time he could not see where he was going as they were in the middle of a ferocious dust storm. The going was tough but the last year or so had hardened Reynard to the point where he was as fit as he had ever been. He strode to the top of the hill easily, soon reaching the deep cave in which the group had sheltered all that time ago.

Moving slowly forward from here, he dropped to his belly and began to inch along, knowing that the crest was only feet ahead. Moments later he had moved forward far enough to enable him to take in the whole valley below him. The sight took his breath away.

The valley was a carpet of moving black, as far as the eye could see in all directions – the Writhing Death. It had grown beyond all imagining in the time they had been away. The sheer size of the menace was almost enough to cause Reynard to lose hope. Dotted in among the crawling mass of insects could be seen larger creatures. Mostly about man sized, a few a little bigger, these aberrations were almost randomly put together with limbs seemingly stuck on in irregular and indiscriminate places. It appeared that they were somehow organizing the creeping doom which surrounded them.

Beyond the crawling mass of destruction, a brilliant pink light flashed and lit up the sky. Reynard's eye was drawn to the twisting, spiralling, almost blurred space in the sky there – the gate to the Void. It looked much as it had done last time he had been here: unnatural, perverse and somehow almost angry. In front of the gate, creating a sort of protective wall around it, was a small legion of huge aberrations. These were the captains of the Writhing Death. And behind them, the last thing between Reynard and the gate itself stood a lone figure.

Baku.

*

"The plan remains," declared Reynard. Back with the main force, he had gathered the leaders of the small army to him for a final debrief. "That is to say, Wiktor and Jared will lead the Dread Guard and *Nanuk* past the bulk of the Writhing Death and strike at the gate itself. Evantia will go with them, and her mercenaries will add their numbers to that charge. Your job is to distract the captains – the large aberrations who guard the gate itself. You are to try and kill as many as possible, of course, but your real goal is to stop them noticing us," with that Reynard indicated Darian and his four friends, "who will be trying to sneak close enough to use the ritual to close the gate," he explained.

"Meanwhile," he continued, "Catulus and his Pyromancers will advance on the main bulk of the Writhing Death. They will use their fire-magic to obliterate their threat once and for all. Kululu Jade and her company will protect the Pyromancers from any of the bigger aberrations who get close enough to disturb their work," he told them.

"Are we all in accord?" he finished, looking around.

"Aye," responded Jared. Nods and words of accession greeted Reynard's question.

"Good. Then let's go. And may the Empire of Lucarcia long remember this day!"

The army moved as one up the slope to the crest of the hill, then, as they neared the summit they split up into two large groups and a tiny one. The Dread Guard, *Nanuk* and mercenaries split off to the right, looking to skirt the main mass of the Writhing Death to fall upon the aberration host at the gate. The Pyromancers and Kululu Jade's company continued straight ahead, directly at the full body of crawling, all consuming insects. And slinking off to the left was the group comprising Reynard, Kita, Okoth, Mosi, Tanithil and Darian. They tried to maintain their cover as they endeavoured to manoeuvre close enough to the gate for Darian to work his ritual and shut it down.

Reynard darted from the cover of a small outcrop to the entrance of a deep gully. The gully looked like it ran nicely along for a few hundred yards, pretty much in the direction they needed to go. This would mean they could cover good ground whilst remaining hidden. As he crossed the short gap to the gully start he saw the first explosion off to his right. Catulus or one of his men had just launched a huge ball of fire into the midst of the first ranks of the Writhing Death. Thousands upon thousands of insects were crisped to nothing in the blast. But it hardly made a dent in their numbers.

Suddenly that first blast was joined by scores more as the full force of the Pyromancers' arcane arts were unleashed. Reynard had to stop and stare, so incredible was the incendiary display. The skies were lit up with fire and he could feel the heat from the inferno even from this long distance away. It was an incredible sight.

He felt someone touch his arm and looked back to see Kita next to him. Her hand was on his forearm and she smiled briefly, and then nodded at the gully, indicating he should set off. He nodded in quick understanding – this was not the time to be gawping at the Pyromancers' arts but using the distraction to good effect and making some distance towards their target. He stepped into the gully and pushed on towards the gate and their final goal on this long adventure.

*

Catulus spoke the final word of his incantation and spread his fingers out in a fan. He felt the surge of power as he drew energy from the Void and forged it into raw flames. The fire burst from each of his fingertips in a great arc and he moved his arms slowly sideways to spread the cover of his conflagration. Multitudes of the Writhing Death crisped before his magic. But so many multitudes more remained. Ahead he could see three large figures surging towards him. Two were almost apelike in appearance and the third was like a bipedal dolphin, or at least that was the best way his mind could categorize them. The dolphin-man screamed in pain as an exploding fireball caught it and a myriad of insects in its blast. But the two apes were almost upon him. Catulus wondered if he might need to attempt to engulf the two in a spell, in order to protect himself. Doing so would use up valuable time and energy – which was supposed to be being spent on destroying the Writhing Death.

Then suddenly rising up from behind a tiny crag which seemed too small to hide anything, a young dark-haired woman appeared with a short blade in hand. She struck the first ape-creature between where its shoulder blades might have been had it had them. The creature shuddered and let out a piercing howl. It spun around to face its attacker, then shuddered again and collapsed. Catulus was impressed that the girl had somehow known how to find its weak spot, considering how alien it was. The second ape-like thing advanced upon the girl and Catulus considered sending forth a burst of fire to help her, but decided to concentrate on the task of wiping out as many of the Writhing Death as he could – his allotted task. The girl would have to cope alone against the creature.

He called forth another torrent of energy from the Void, twisting it with arcane words and gestures until it was raw fire at his control. Pointing at a thick clump of the creeping doom he called out the final word of power and a huge column of fire blazed down from the sky to obliterate a great swath of the insects. As he did so he saw the dark-haired girl stab the ape-thing with her short sword, and duck under a powerful blow. Again the ape-man shuddered and let out an agonized scream, then fell twitching to the ground. Catulus did a double take. There was no way that simple stab could have caused the aberration so much pain. No way unless the girl had been using more than just a simple blade. Suddenly it made sense. The rumour of the Jade Assassins was true. The girl was using a poisoned blade – from the looks of it an exceptionally potent form which was lethal – or at least lethal to the aberrations they were fighting.

In this instance Catulus decided it was a good thing to have poison-wielding assassins on their side. He decided he could leave the girl to deal with any of the larger aberrations nearby and concentrate on the mass of insects which needed to be annihilated.

He would soon come to regret that decision.

*

Wiktor Ebon took a deep breath and steadied his mind. He was not a coward but the sight of the scores of huge aberrations arrayed before him was almost enough to unman him. Taking a second steadying breath he reminded himself that he had in excess of fifty undead warriors to stand in front of him and do the fighting for him. All he had to do was remain focussed enough to be able to control all fifty in the heat of the battle, whilst maintaining his awareness of what was going on and keeping calm enough to employ good tactics. It was not as if it mattered if any of the undead were destroyed – they were easily enough replaced given time to perform the rituals, but it mattered a lot if he was left with no personal protection. He was no warrior and would not last a minute on this field without his guard. Still, he was determined to do his utmost to help Reynard with this endeavour. He was proud to be a part of this task force and to be doing his bit to save the Empire.

Wiktor looked to his left and saw Jared striding forward. As he watched the hulking man seemed to shimmer and blur as he let out a battle cry, "*Nanuk!*" Behind him the scores of his men took up the cry: "*Nanuk! Nanuk! Nanuk!*" Suddenly where before there had been forty fur-clad men in the skins of the ice bears of Manabas, now there were forty actual ice bears. The *Nanuk* force roared with bestial vigour and rushed forward.

Wiktor took that as his cue and willed his Dread Guards forward. He opened his senses to the necrotic energies they were giving off and with rapid thought and precision began to direct his forces. He had never controlled this many of the undead in a combat situation before. He knew he would be tested to his limits.

Behind the scores of enraged ice bears and undead warriors which were pouring into the assembled ranks of the captains of the Writhing Death, the mercenaries of the Guild of Master Merchants and Sea Farers hesitated. No one seemed to be directly telling them what to do. The *Nanuk* leader had changed shape and was gone into battle. The Dark Lord's son appeared distracted in the extreme. The sight of the towering aberrations which were ahead of them was not something to invite an attack, so they began to waver.

Suddenly a call went up. "Men of the Guild! To arms! For the Empire! For freedom! For Reynard!" All eyes turned to see a beautiful woman in a sky-blue dress with blonde hair cascading across her back. She was stood upon a small rock which elevated her above the host and meant every man could see her. "Reynard!" she repeated, punching her hand in the air.

"Reynard!" went up the cry from the four hundred mercenaries, echoing out across the dusty valley. "Reynard!"

As one they charged into the captains of the Writhing Death.

*

Reynard and his strike team had reached the end of the gully when they heard the battle cry of his name from the melee before the gate. "Seems you are being used as a rallying cry, little man," observed Okoth grinning a white grin at Reynard.

Reynard nodded grimly, all too aware that scores of men would die due to that call. Okoth saw the serious look and the grin fell from his face. He hefted his spear and said, "I'm ready."

Reynard turned to Darian, "Are we close enough?" he asked. "Can you perform the ritual here?"

Darian looked at the gate and then closed his eyes for a moment. Opening them again he blinked. "No, sorry. We need to get closer," he answered.

Reynard peered out across the dusty valley floor. The gate was still a few hundred yards away. Most of the captains were engaged in a huge battle with the mercenaries, *Nanuk* and Dread Guard, off to his right, but a number had been kept back. And alongside those reserves was the general, Baku. He didn't see how they could get any closer.

"Maybe I can help," offered Tanithil.

"What can you do, Tani?" asked Reynard, still studying the battleground ahead.

"If we take a route as far away from the majority of the creatures as possible – maybe that low ridge over there on the left – then I could perhaps help to keep us hidden. I know a mind trick which was developed to help the Thought Guard pass guard dogs and the like without them noticing. It is very hard to use on humans, but assuming the majority of these creatures have lesser, animal-like intellect, then it might work."

Reynard pondered something. "Did you use this trick on that waiter, back in the Palace Inn, in Lucar that night we hid behind a plant?" he asked, screwing his face up in remembrance.

"I did, yes. That was just one man, in a quiet place where he was not expecting to see people. A lot of creatures will be hard to effect, especially in a battle and when they are likely to be on alert. But it might work."

"And if it doesn't then we end up fighting them – which seems to be the only other option," pointed out Kita from alongside Reynard.

"Good point," conceded Reynard. "Okay Tani, let's try it. Lead on."

"Actually I need someone to hold my hand and lead me. I'll be concentrating on my mind trick – and won't be fully aware of my immediate surroundings."

"I'll do it," offered Mosi, taking Tanithil's hand. "I'll be your eyes whilst you are keeping us safe, friend," he added.

"Where do we need to get to?" Reynard asked Darian.

"I'd say that craggy bluff over there would be close enough," responded Darian, pointing ahead.

"Let's go," declared Reynard, setting off carefully towards the low rise to his left.

Moving forward quickly he spotted two large aberrations almost directly in the path they would take. Drawing his rapier slowly and quietly he advanced towards them. As he approached, prepared to have to fight the giant monstrosities, both of them turned as one to look away from him. Glancing at Kita he shrugged and she nodded in the direction behind them. Moving carefully onwards Reynard skirted around the two creatures and travelled on into the shelter of a small cliff where the team regrouped. They had got past the first hurdle.

"Still a little further needed," informed Darian before Reynard could ask. The young noble nodded in understanding and peered around the cliff. There was precious little cover to use from here and not far away he could see the unmistakable figure of Baku with three savage monsters beside him.

"I don't think we can use your skills any further Tani. From here it looks like it's going to be down to our martial skills to get Darian a bit nearer and hold off the creatures whilst he does his thing. Is everyone ready?" Seeing that everyone was, Reynard stepped out from behind the cover.

Moving forward with no pretence at stealth or guile he strode across the dusty landscape in the direction of Baku and the huge swirling gate the aberration stood in front of. Behind him his friends followed, naturally fanning out to form a semi-circle around Darian.

"Here will do," called out the thin man after they had covered a short distance. "Now you just need to keep them off me," he added, unrolling the fragile papyrus ritual.

"How long for?" asked Kita drawing both her blades in one smooth motion.

"I'm afraid I have no idea," answered Darian as the bull-headed Baku finally spotted them and ordered his three lieutenants to attack.

*

Catulus was almost enjoying this. His Pyromancers had trained for years to learn and master these arts – arts which had been banned in the Empire for five centuries and which had been lost until recently when he had rediscovered them. Now they were destroying swaths of the Writhing Death – the greatest threat the Empire had ever suffered – with relative ease. He had seen a couple of his followers struck down by the larger aberrations, but this was war and casualties were inevitable. He had never expected to get through this day without losing some of his men. And today would long be remembered as the day when the Pyromancers had destroyed the Writhing Death. After today he would petition the ruling nobles to rescind the law banning the arcane arts and his Pyromancers would be hailed as heroes of the war.

He intertwined his fingers, calling upon the powers of the Void to summon yet more fire. Opening his arms in an expansive gesture he launched a spread of flames in front of him, searing the ground and engulfing yet multitudes more insects. As he did so a large aberration came into view on his right side. It was a short distance away but would be upon him soon enough if not stopped.

Briefly he wondered where the dark-haired girl had gone. She seemed to have taken it upon herself to be his personal guard and he was sure she would soon pop up behind the aberration and slide her poisoned blade into its back.

Suddenly his side exploded in pain. It felt as if he were on fire from the inside out. Momentarily confused he thought that maybe something had gone wrong with his spell, or that he had been accidentally caught in a blaze by one of his followers. Then he twitched uncontrollably as the nerves in his body reacted to the *naja* poison coursing through his veins and he fell forward. Trying in vain to control his convulsing body he managed to roll over onto his back, to see the dark-haired girl standing over him, her short sword in her hand, his blood on its blade.

"The Verdant Queen sends her regards," she said as another excruciating spasm rocked Catulus's body.

The last thing he saw before darkness took him were other Pyromancers nearby twitching in agony as Jade Assassins stood over them.

-Chapter Fourteen-

An agonized scream rent the air. It was loud enough to carry to Wiktor across the battlefield and draw his attention from the fight in front of him. Spinning on his heel he looked across to there the main mass of the Writhing Death was being fought. The sight there took a moment to process as it was not what he had expected to see.

The Pyromancers of the Ruby House were being slaughtered. Their concentration was focussed on destroying the millions of crawling, biting insects which comprised the Writhing Death and, seemingly from nowhere, suddenly the Jade Assassins, who had previously appeared to have been protecting and defending them, were sticking poisoned blades into them.

Wiktor didn't hesitate for a second. The Ruby House were mortal enemies of his house. The destruction of their Pyromancers would be a great boon to his house. If he came back home to Selkie and was able to tell his father that he had witnessed the end of their number his father would be ecstatic. It would probably mean the Ebon House being able to stretch its influence deep into the Spine of Ursum from their powerbase in the Tail. It could even mean them being able to control the whole of the island of Ursum from head to tip.

But the Pyromancers of the Ruby House were all that stood between the Writhing Death and the crumbling Empire that Reynard was trying to save. Wiktor believed in the young lord, and believed in what he was trying to achieve. He would not see it fail because of the treacherous actions of the Jade Assassins. The *Nanuk* and mercenary armies of the Guild were slowly overcoming the small force of giant aberrations they had come to call the captains of the Writhing Death. They would have to manage without his Dread Guard for a while.

Wiktor closed his eyes and sent his mind out to the surrounding battlefield. He felt the necrotic energies binding the bodies of his undead army together. He sent out a mental command and the Dread Guard simply stopped what they were doing, turned towards where the

Pyromancers and Jade Assassins were locked in mortal combat, and marched forward as one.

Wiktor followed on the heels of his undead host, keeping a half dozen of the more powerful zombies behind him as a rear guard, should the captains try to follow him. From his position surrounded by undead he studied the fight ahead. The Pyromancers had now stopped trying to destroy the Writhing Death and were focussed on trying to survive the attack from the Jade Assassins. The Pyromancers had outnumbered the assassins by three to one, but the treacherous women of Ibini had surprise on their side. A good score of the Pyromancers had fallen before they even knew what had happened. Wiktor scanned the battlefield but could see no sign of Catulus; he assumed the Pyromancer leader was already dead.

As he watched Wiktor realized that the assassins were killing Pyromancers all too easily. And every time a red-robed wizard fell to the floor they seemed to be screaming and twitching in agony. Of course – the assassins were keeping true to the traditions of their homeland – they were using poison on their blades. Well, if the Jade Assassins wanted to play that game, he would counter it. The Dread Guard would not succumb to this vile trick so easily. After all, the undead were kept standing and functioning by the force of necrotic magic and the willpower of their controller. They did not feel any pain when poison was in their bodies. They did not need blood running through their veins to function. They were, to all intents and purposes, completely immune to the effects of the lethal *naja* poison being used by the treacherous Jade Assassins. It was time to put things right.

The Dread Guard hit the fight between the Jade Assassins and the Ruby Pyromancers like a black flood. The assassins quickly realized what was going on but a score of lightly armoured warriors who relied on stealth, surprise and the lethal potency of their poisoned blades simply stood no chance against the heavily armoured, organized and poison-immune undead who outnumbered them two to one. Noiselessly the Dread Guard cut down the Jade Assassins until the beaten warrior-women of Ibini tried to flee the battlefield. Wiktor showed them no mercy, commanding his Dread Guard to chase and cut down every last one.

Finally the fight was over. The Jade Assassins were all dead; not a single one had escaped as far as Wiktor could see. The Dread Guard of the Ebon House had saved the Pyromancers of the Ruby House. The assassins had taken a terrible toll and only a score or so of the red-robed mages survived. Wiktor realised that this would be perilously few to try and finish off the Writhing Death, but it would have to do. Then he looked around him and saw the remaining Pyromancers readying to defend themselves against their ancient enemy; the Ebon House. They knew they were at Wiktor's mercy now. There was no way they could survive against the large number of Dread Guard who now surrounded them.

    Wiktor's mind flipped back, unbidden, to his time as a prisoner of the Ruby House. He recalled his personal guard and other minor nobles of the Ebon House who had been captured with him. He remembered the smell of burning flesh as the Pyromancers experimented and honed their skills on the living. On him and his men. A lump rose in his throat as he fought to control the urge to send his undead warriors into the red-robed men before him, to see them wreak havoc and take his revenge on the fire-mages of the Ruby House. But he knew that for the Writhing Death to be defeated, for Reynard's plan to succeed, there was only one option: the Pyromancers had to destroy the multitudes of insects before them. No one else could.

    "You are safe!" Wiktor called out to the assembled Pyromancers. "The treacherous Jade Assassins are no more. My loyal Dread Guard will now protect you from the aberrations. You must resume your role – destroy the creeping doom of the Writhing Death! Only you and your fire magic can do this! The fate of the Empire is in your hand, Pyromancers! Do your part and save the Empire!"

    The Pyromancers took a moment to absorb this unlikely information, but looking around they saw the Dread Guards had slain all the Jade Assassins and now were making a circle, facing outwards away from the huddled Pyromancers, looking at the few larger aberrations which continued to move in towards the humans. One of the Pyromancers made a decision and a burning fist-sized ball of fire shot between two Dread Guards and exploded in the air above the Writhing

Death, crisping thousands more to dust. Others took up the challenge and once more fire rained down on the creeping doom.

Wiktor looked around him. There were perhaps twenty Pyromancers left alive. The Writhing Death had been sorely diminished by the fire mages before they had been struck by the Jade Assassins, but even as the surviving Pyromancers were destroying thousands of those remaining, still more of the biting, creeping creatures were pouring through the open gate from the Void. If the gate was not shut soon, the Pyromancers would be overwhelmed, and there would be nothing he and his Dread Guard could do. Reynard and his friends really needed to get that gate closed – and they needed to do it soon.

Wiktor quickly counted the bodies of the Jade Assassins around the area. Twenty three. That was one less than Kululu Jade had said were part of the task force. One Jade Assassin was missing and unaccounted for. Wiktor knew the missing assassin would be their leader, the Verdant Princess herself, the most dangerous assassin in the entire Empire. But where was she and what was she planning next? Wiktor resigned himself to keeping alert and making sure she did not succeed in thwarting the work of the Pyromancers that she had been sent to protect. He would not fail Reynard. But still he worried: where would she turn up next?

*

Kululu Jade peered out of the deep gully and looked across the broken ground to where Reynard and his companions were fighting. From here she could clearly see that the group had made a defensive wall around Darian Snow, who was deeply involved in reading something from a papyrus sheet – obviously the ritual to close the gate. Reynard, Okoth and Mosi were stood side by side battling two huge aberrations, the three of them utterly absorbed with simply surviving. Slightly to the side Kita stood alone, fighting the remaining aberration single-handed. Behind her was Tanithil and even from this distance Kululu Jade could see he was fully concentrating on the fight with Kita. Kululu knew enough about Tanithil to know what he was likely trying to aid Kita in her fight by trying to mess with the mind of her opponent – if the giant aberration had a mind which Tanithil could reach and influence, that was.

There was no simple way to get to Darian and stop him with his ritual. She could get close enough to throw her poison-tipped dagger but it would be a risky shot, trying to thread it in between the mass melee which was going off around him. And Kululu Jade knew she would likely only have one chance. Studying the fighting for a moment more she saw that Kita was involved in a defensive strategy. She was not pushing the creature she was facing but was letting it come to her. And the creature itself was not as aggressive as she might have expected, often just seeming to take its time before launching another attack. Perhaps that was due to the telepath's influence. Either way, this meant that there were times when the Niten Warrior was static and would be a fairly easy target with a thrown dagger. And if she could take out the woman from Honshu then the aberration facing her would have it easy, ploughing through the unarmed telepath to reach Darian. Then the ritual would be stopped in a glorious and bloody way.

The Verdant Princess moved out of the gully, and skirted the long way around the battlefield, moving into position alongside Kita, some distance away but close enough for a well-thrown dagger strike. She found a suitable outcrop and hunkered down behind it, dagger in hand. Waiting a few precious moments as the battle raged around her she concentrated all her focus on the scarlet-robed young woman, watching her movements and anticipating her next steps. Soon enough the expected moment came where Kita dropped back into her favoured stance, weight shifted to the back leg, twin blades of her *daisho* extended above her head, ready for the next attack from the aberration ahead of her. In one smooth motion Kululu Jade rose to her full height and let the dagger fly. It flew true, spinning end over end directly at the back of the unaware warrior.

Suddenly a flash of sky-blue rushed in from Kululu's right. Before the Jade Assassin knew what had happened the figure was between her and her target. She watched in annoyance as her perfectly judged dagger, which was headed right for Kita's back, plunged blade first into the stomach of the newcomer. The newcomer screamed and fell to the floor, twitching. Kululu Jade knew that the *naja* poison which was earmarked for Kita was now coursing through the body of Evantia.

With extremely unfortunate timing this was the moment that Reynard, Okoth and Mosi chose to defeat the last of the two giant aberrations they had been facing. They turned and saw what had happened and Kululu Jade knew she was in trouble. It was time to turn to her last resort. She reached into the folds of her emerald-green dress and drew out an ancient parchment that she had recovered from the Great Library of Antissa. It was time to try out the powerful ritual she had taken. Closing her mind off from Reynard and his companions she began to chant.

*

Reynard drove his rapier deep into the belly of the giant aberration in front of him. As he did so he saw Okoth's spear pierce the side of the creature and bury itself almost a foot inside the creature's torso. At the same time a blast of holy light from Mosi's symbol struck the creature full on in the face. It seemed to cause the monster terrible pain as if something in the light itself was abhorrent to it. The aberration, green gore dripping from a hundred wounds, shuddered, staggered, and fell to the wasteland floor, dead. Alongside it laid the body of the first aberration they had slain. Turning quickly to survey the area Reynard saw a patch of sky-blue on the floor nearby where previously there had been only dust and dirt. Confused, his eyes went out of focus for a second and then focussed in again.

Evantia. Lying in the dust. With a dagger in her stomach.

All thoughts of the current situation fled his mind as Reynard rushed to her side. He knelt quickly beside her and took her hand. Her wavy blonde hair was across her face and he brushed it aside. Her whole body convulsed and her face contorted in agony. Her eyes met his and she screwed her face up with the effort to fix them on him.

"Reynard," she began weakly.

"Don't talk ," he told her softly. "Save your strength. Mosi can fix you," he promised, looking up for the priest. He spotted Mosi a short distance away. The robed holy man had moved next to Darian and was looking at the nearby figure of Kululu Jade.

"There's no time, Reynard," she responded feebly. "It was all for you," she whispered. Reynard was forced to move his head close to her mouth to hear her speak. "I had to save her," she continued. "Save Kita... I followed Kululu... When I saw her aim the dagger, I knew. You would never be truly happy without her. I always wanted you... Need you to be happy," she breathed. "Need you to live... and love. It was always you, Reyna..."

Evantia's eyes closed and her body gave a final twitch as a shuddering breath escaped her. Then she lay still.

*

Okoth looked around him unsure what to do. Nearby Kita had just finished off the monstrosity she had faced singlehanded. That left her free and Okoth expected her to drop back to guard Darian, as they had all agreed. But the Niten warrior instead was advancing with purposeful stride, her eyes focussed on one thing only.

Baku.

Okoth knew that the monstrous bull-headed aberration had killed her father and that she desired revenge. But he did not think even she could take on the general of the Writhing Death singlehanded. He needed to go to her. The three aberration captains had all been slain so Baku was the only monstrous creature of significance remaining in the area.

But, not far away stood the treacherous assassin, Kululu Jade. She had just tried to kill Kita with a dagger and perhaps would have done had the woman, Evantia, not got in the way. Quite what had happened there Okoth was unsure but he saw that Reynard had rushed to the fallen woman's side and was not fighting anymore.

Kululu Jade had a parchment in her hand and was reading from it. Okoth could hear the words though they made no sense to him. As he looked he became quickly aware of something extremely worrying: the huge swarm of insects which were still pouring through the gate appeared to be coming this way. Before the fight with the captains the insects had moved off the other way, away from Baku and his followers. But now it seemed something had changed. Then Kululu Jade pointed in the direction of Darian, who was still trying to complete the ritual to shut the gate. Incredibly the swarm of insects nearby all began to move in the direction Kululu Jade was pointing. Slowly they flowed around her position, never coming too close to her, and headed towards Darian. Okoth realised something: she was controlling the Writhing Death.

As the insects neared the group Mosi took a hold of his holy symbol. Calling on the power of the Light he held it aloft, chanting loudly in a language the black-skinned Okoth had never heard before. The symbol began to glow with an intense light which bathed the immediate area around Mosi, Tanithil and Darian. The creatures of the Writhing Death reached the holy aura and were somehow repelled. It was as if they could not push forward into the holy emanation. But they soon surrounded the trio and as Kululu Jade continued to read from her parchment and point at Darian, slowly the Writhing Death encroached on the holy aura. It was only a matter of time before the creeping doom reached the group and they were engulfed.

Okoth looked quickly back to Reynard. He was still on the floor, kneeling over the prostrate Evantia and did not look about to intervene. A quick glance at Kita and Okoth saw the diminutive woman giving a slow, controlled bow to Baku as she stood near him, her blades in hand, but down by her sides. Incongruously the bull-headed aberration bowed respectfully back. Okoth knew he should go to her aid but could not let Mosi, Tanithil and Darian be swarmed. They had come here to close the gate and that was what he must try to help achieve.

Okoth hefted his spear into his right hand. Drawing a careful aim, he pulled the arm slowly back and with a ferocious growl he let it fly with all his might. The weapon flew straight and true but at the last split-second the target turned slightly – just enough to mean that the spear pierced her in the shoulder, not the heart.

Kululu Jade screamed in pain as the spear tip ripped into her shoulder and burst out of the other side. Somehow she managed to remain on her feet, but the parchment slipped from her fingers. It floated gently to the floor at her feet and settled in the dust. The incantation was broken and her control over the creeping mass of insects was broken. Almost immediately the Writhing Death stopped trying to break through the holy aura being given off by Mosi's symbol and moved back away from the priest. Back towards their previous controller. Back towards Kululu Jade.

The Jade Assassin had nowhere to run. She was surrounded on all sides by creeping, crawling, biting insects. They moved inexorably towards her as she fumbled for the paper at her feet. But her blood-soaked fingers would not obey her and the parchment slipped from her hand again. A gentle breeze then took it away from her, agonizingly out of her reach. The Verdant Princess looked up at Okoth as the insects reached her. A resigned look came over her face. He could almost fancy that she smiled, and then the Writhing Death engulfed her. Okoth would never forget the screams as Kululu Jade was eaten alive.

Okoth ripped his gaze away from the slowly shrinking mound of insects which was once the Verdant Queen's daughter and looked around. A short distance away Kita was facing the hulking Baku. He wished desperately to go to her aid but firstly his spear had just been consumed by the creeping insects and secondly the way to Kita was cut off by more of the Writhing Death. They seemed to be keeping a respectful distance around Baku as if their general was controlling them and using them to stop any aid getting to Kita – which maybe he was.

The only other option was to try and get to Mosi and Tanithil. Looking their way he saw Reynard dragging Evantia's body across the dirt to the priest and Mosi moved forward to meet him, the insects somehow scuttling back out of the light, unwilling or unable to remain inside its holy and cleansing environment. Okoth moved quickly that way too and was able to join the others as Mosi moved back to where Darian was chanting.

The group were safe from the insects of the Writhing Death for now, but the gate was still open and more were pouring through. Even more worrying though, across the way and isolated from their help was Kita, and she was facing the leader of the aberrations in single combat. As they watched Baku lowered his head, horns pointing directly at their friend, and charged.

*

    Kita dropped into her favoured stance, weight mostly on the back leg, back foot pointed directly to the side, front foot pointed at her enemy. This was a counter attacking stance and allowed her more space and time to react to any attack the opponent might make. In this instance she knew she would need every moment she could get.

    As expected, the attack soon came. Baku dropped his head and charged. Kita could see the needle sharp tips of his huge horns rushing in to skewer her. The width of the bull's head was such that she could not easily dodge to the side, but his imposing height meant that he had to lean over a long way to get down to her level. There was no way she could hope to parry the creature's charge. She knew first-hand the prodigious strength of this monstrous aberration. She knew she could not even expect to deflect a blow from this creature. She had to avoid him totally if she was to survive this encounter.

    Kita knew her timing had to be impeccable. Move too early and Baku would simply adjust his angle and gore her as she shifted. Move too late and she would be impaled where she stood. The timing had to be split-second accurate or she would die here.

    Her timing was perfect.

    Kita waited until the last possible second and moved sideways and forward, ducking under the point of Baku's horn whilst letting the razor-sharp edge of her *katana* trail beside her, her grip tight and sure on the hilt. The blade slashed open a deep gash in Baku's midriff and green gore spurted out. Moving in a quick circle she took a deep breath and dropped into her favoured stance again. Baku stopped his charge, stood up tall and shook his huge bull's head. He turned slowly to face her once more and his eyes narrowed. If the wound in his side was bothering him, he was not showing it. Kita had drawn first-blood but the aberration didn't even seem to notice.

*

Wiktor willed two of his Dread Guards to close in on the large aberration which was approaching his position. All around him the conflagration raged and the heat of it threatened to overwhelm him. His concentration wavered for a moment and the Dread Guards stopped in their tracks. The aberration brushed one aside with a hulking claw and stepped past it, moving towards the human that it somehow sensed controlled these death-dealing undead. Wiktor blinked a drop of sweat from his eyes and swiftly refocussed. He felt the strands of necrotic energy binding him to the undead warriors and pulled on them. The Dread Guards spun around, raised their swords and as one cut the aberration into three pieces.

"I really could do with a cold drink," he muttered to himself. He wiped the sweat from his forehead with a black-shirted sleeve and looked around. Everywhere he could see the Pyromancers obliterating the Writhing Death by the thousands. Fires raged across the desolate countryside. Pockets of Guild mercenaries, fighting alongside hulking *Nanuk*, were engaged in a running melee with the large aberrations which dotted the landscape. And here his Dread Guard were making a stand, trying to protect the fire mages who were endeavouring to destroy the insects which would devour all in their path. But it was all in vain.

Across the dusty landscape he could still make out the giant pulsing and shimmering gate to the Void; the gate which even now allowed the Writhing Death to come into this world; the gate which they had come from all ends of the Empire to close. It was still open. And on came the Writhing Death. He did not see how they could ever win.

*

Kita knew her time was running out. Baku had made four charges now. Each time she had dodged the deadly span of his horns. Just. Each time she had dealt him a fresh wound. But she knew she was not going to be able to continue like this. Sooner or later her timing would let her down. She knew she only had to be a fraction of a second out and she would get caught. And getting caught by those ferocious horns would mean death. Maybe not instantly, but even a glancing blow from the aberration's huge spikes would be enough to incapacitate her and allow him to kill her at his leisure. She needed to be perfectly accurate and she knew she could not hope to do that indefinitely.

Combat was, her teachers always told her, a simple thing: Understand your opponent. Determine his weakness. Exploit it. Win. If you could do that before he did the same to you, then victory was yours. The trouble was, with Baku she could sense no weakness. He was an aberration of the Void. She had inflicted four terrible wounds across his stomach, side and back. They each oozed green sludge like a trickling waterfall of slime. She assumed the sludge was Baku's equivalent of blood but she had no idea how much he would need to lose to affect him, or if losing it was even significant to the monster. Certainly the aberration was showing no signs of fatigue or slowing down.

Risking a quick glance to where her friends were stood a little way away, Kita saw them all watching her intently. Mosi was chanting gently and his holy symbol was glowing, keeping the insects away from them all. Darian was still reading the ancient papyrus and trying to close the gate. She had no idea how long it would take him. Next to them stood the giant Okoth and the smaller Tanithil. Besides them all was Reynard. She could see the young noble had tears in his eyes. She also knew that at his feet was the body of Evantia; a woman who had given her life to save Kita's. She shook her head at the improbable events of the day. People would never fail to amaze and astound her.

Kita brought her mind back into focus and looked back at Baku. As she did so she noticed the slight flicker of an expression cross the bull-creature's face. It was gone as quickly as it was there and she was not certain she had read it right. After all Baku was an aberration and not human. But if she was right she had just seen an emotion cross the face of the general of the Writhing Death; an emotion that the code of the Niten Warrior taught never to show: fear.

Baku grunted and lowered his head once more. Kita was not sure but she felt like this time the horns had dipped a little further than the previous four charges. Was Baku struggling to keep his head up? Was he starting to feel fatigue? A surge of hope flooded into the Niten warrior and her own feelings of weariness left her instantly. With renewed concentration she prepared to receive his next attack.

The last two times she had moved left and down. The two times before that she had moved right. Did Baku expect her to move left or right this time? He was likely to anticipate her movement this time as she had dodged every charge so far. If he guessed right, she would be impaled regardless. So she had to try something new.

The charge came. Baku's head was definitely a fraction lower than the previous attacks. Kita waited, waited and waited. Time seemed to freeze as she watched the needle sharp horns approach. Then at the very last possible moment Kita took a risk. Rather than repeating her actions of previous attacks and dodging to the side, she leapt upwards into the air. With incredible dexterity and agility Kita landed one foot on the head of the charging bull-man. Spinning in place as she jumped she came down on Baku's back, her legs astride the creature as it charged, bent double. Dropping her short *wakizashi* to the floor, she took the long *katana* in two hands and slashed it with all her might across the back of the neck of the hulking creature.

It cut deep, but not deep enough.

Baku howled in pain and reared upwards. Kita was thrown off his back but flipped nimbly and landed on her feet with the acrobatics of a cat. Raising her *katana* over her head in a two-handed grip she dropped into her comfortable back-stance and waited. The next move was the aberration's to make.

*

It had been nearly eighteen months since Baku had felt the rift from this world opening into the Void. He had been on this world for only a short time as he counted it and he liked it here. There was much to feed on and the potential to slowly devour the whole planet was huge. But now he was in pain.

He knew that this human was more than a match for him. If he stayed here and continued this fight, she would likely kill him. She was only a puny thing, tiny, delicate and weak. Yet she moved with such speed, skill and finesse that he could not catch her. And now he was tired and hurting. He could not last much longer without proper rest.

He knew that if he returned to the Void his wounds would quickly heal. Back in his own domain, these minor cuts would rapidly knit together and mend. His strength would return to him in moments and he could return here to finish the annoying human off. Yes, this plan made sense. He would quickly retreat to the gate and step back into the Void. There he would recover and then return here to finish this.

Baku turned once more to face Kita. She was in her customary defensive stance, two handed sword held over her head, ready. Standing up tall he bowed from the waist as he had often seen her do. He then turned his back on her and strode off in the direction of the huge twisting and shimmering portal and his gateway home.

Suddenly one of the insignificant humans nearby shouted out words of power. Baku recognised them. He knew them and he knew what they meant. With sudden certainty Baku realised his end was near. He stopped and looked up. Ahead of him the massive arcane gate which linked this world to the Void shuddered. It began to flex and waver. It warped and twisted. And then it collapsed in on itself.

The gate was gone and Baku was trapped.

*

Kita saw the portal buckle and fall in on itself and knew Darian had succeeded. The gate to the Void was gone. No more of the Writhing Death could pour through into their world. And Baku could not escape.

Taking the initiative she moved swiftly forward, feet hardly touching the floor as the rushed in, her *katana* still held aloft. Reaching Baku, who was stood stock-still looking up to where the gate had been moments before, she decided to show no mercy. She knew given the chance he would show her none – as he had shown none to her father the summer before. Letting out a ferocious *ki-ai* shout, Kita put all her concentration into one staggering blow. She funnelled all the pent up emotion of her father's death at the hands of this monster into the strike. She channelled all the confusion and anger of the last year into the assault. Leaping into the air she focussed every last drop of hatred, rage, anger, and revenge into her sword blow.

Kita's *katana* took Baku across the back of his neck and severed the head. The giant body dropped to one side. The head dropped to the other and rolled in the dirt. The aberration Baku, who had controlled the Writhing Death and who had killed her father, was finally dead at her hands. Her father's memory had been avenged.

Kita looked up to see her friends moving towards her. Tanithil, the slim Lucarcian who knew something about everything and who was a budding telepath. Mosi, the priest of the Light, always wise and dependable, a healer and a pious man. Okoth, the Champion Gladiator of Nubia and the strongest man she had ever known. And Reynard Ferrand, the man who had helped her escape from a slave galley and who she had followed across the empire. The man who had helped her bring the forces of this empire to this place to fight the Writhing Death and fulfil the quest laid upon her father. The man she had fallen in love with. She smiled at them and raised a hand in greeting as if she had not seen any of them in months. Yet they were not smiling back. Instead they all had terrible expressions on their faces. Expressions of fear.

Then she noticed the insects. They had her surrounded. With the death of Baku the invisible wall which had somehow kept them away from her had dropped and without realizing it she was now utterly enclosed. The creatures were not approaching quickly, almost as if they were teasing her, knowing she had nowhere to escape. But slowly and inexorably they came on. Kita knew she could not fight them. There was no way her swords would prevail against the thousands upon thousands of the biting, stinging creatures. She was doomed and there was no way out. Determined to hold true to the Niten code to the end she fixed Reynard with a steady gaze and repeated the code to herself in her head.

Never show pain. Never show fear.

Suddenly a fireball exploded next to her and a wave of intense heat washed over her. Looking behind her she saw a small group of red-robed Pyromancers raining fire down on the remaining insects of the Writhing Death. Leading the fire mages was Wiktor Ebon, their ancient enemy. Behind him were the remainder of the Dread Guard and a group of *Nanuk*, supported by an alarmingly small number of Guild mercenaries.

The Pyromancers moved about the area, sending out gouts of flame and calling down pillars of fire on the remaining insects. Rapidly a gap was made and Kita was able to escape the trap. At Wiktor's command the Pyromancers efficiently split the remaining creatures into zones and simply obliterated them all, group by group.

At last, the job was completed. The last remaining vestiges of the Writhing Death were incinerated. The gate had been closed and every last one of the aberrations which had come through it had been killed or burnt to a crisp.

Closing her eyes, Kita let out a sob of emotion. Kneeling in the dust she put her hilt to her forehead and the tip of her *katana* down into the ground. Taking a deep breath to steady herself she spoke the words she had wanted to say for more than a year.

"Father, hear me now: Your honour is restored, and so too is mine. Rest in peace at last."

Standing up she rushed to Reynard and into his arms. She buried her face into his chest and let go of her self-control. Looking up into his steel blue eyes she felt a tear run down her face. Reynard brushed it softly aside with a gentle touch. "It's over, Kita. You did it."

"*We* did it, Reynard," she corrected. Looking around at her friends, both old and new, she added, "We *all* did."

-Epilogue-

Reynard looked out across the Inner Sea from his balcony high up in the tower of the Azure Palace. The spring rains were lashing down across the bay, driven by a fierce gale blowing out of the east along the shoreline. Whitecaps dotted the seascape as far as he could see and a lonely carrack was fighting its way towards the city and the safely of the deep water harbour far below him. Twirling a glass of Pembrose Red in his hand, he stepped back inside his sumptuous new quarters and out of the rain.

He shut the door behind himself, blocking out the storm. Moving to a nearby mahogany table he put down the glass, picked up a soft linen towel and dried his long blond hair and the stubble which had grown under his chin these last couple of days.

"You look a state, First Consul," said a merry voice from across the room. Reynard looked up to see Kita there before him, smiling. Dressed in simple clothes – a cotton shirt and a pair of loose trousers, covered with a knitted top to keep out the chill – Kita was without her swords for the first time in many a day. Reynard noted the angry scars across her face and reflected that this last year had taken its toll on the group – both physically and emotionally – and that they would never be the same again.

"It's 'My Lord Consul', to you milady," he admonished jokingly. "And I don't think I'll ever get used to it. I'm still coming to terms with the idea of being a Lord," he confided, "Let alone the thought that some idiots voted for me to be the First Consul of the new Republic."

"It is a great honour, Reynard," Kita said, moving gracefully across the floor towards him. "And one you should take seriously."

Reynard sighed. "I know," he agreed, dropping the now wet cloth back onto the table. "And I am trying. But who thought it would be a good idea to put me in charge of the whole of Lucarcia?" he asked rhetorically. "I'm only just about able to control the crew of the *Javelin*, and even then I need my command team to keep me on the straight and narrow."

"Some of the most influential people and brilliant minds on this continent is who," she replied, even though she knew Reynard was not expecting an answer. "And they voted for you because without you this land of theirs would be in the midst of a civil war and overrun by millions of creatures from the Void. You saved them all Reynard."

"It was you, Kita," he responded, taking her hands in his. "I did it all for you. For you and for your father's memory. I knew how much it meant to you and I know how much you mean to me. I could never sit by and watch the anguish and pain eat you away from the inside. I know you too well my dear. Though you try to hide it behind your stoic façade, you cannot fool me. We have been through too much. I've come to know and understand your little idiosyncrasies. I've come to be able to read your moods and your thoughts. I may not be as empathic as dear Tani, but with you I can tell. I just know."

Kita smiled up and him and standing on her tiptoes planted a soft kiss on his lips. "Thank you, Reynard. It means the world to me."

"And now we have succeeded," Reynard stated. "We have defeated the Writhing Death. We have closed the gate to the Void and stopped the aberrations coming through. We have made the lands of Lucarcia safe once more.

The Empire of Lucarcia itself might be at an end, with no emperor to replace the last of his line, but the new Republic of Lucarcia has been born and will stand in its place. We will make this Republic strong. We will make it just. And we will make it prosper." Reynard thought back to their time as slaves in the hold of a galley. "I have seen too much injustice and pain in this land and I will do all I can to replace it with honesty and integrity, with care and love. We can build a better land. We *will* build a better land," he said with conviction.

"And that is why you have been unanimously voted to lead the new Republic, Reynard." Kita replied. "Everyone can see the great passion and energy you have for justice and a better life for all. You will make a great First Consul."

"But I can't do it alone," Reynard said, staring intently down into Kita's eyes. Continuing to hold her hands he looked deeply into the brown orbs in front of him. Then, slowly, he dropped to one knee. "I need you Kita. I love you beyond everything. If I am to help rebuild this land, I have a long, hard road ahead of me. But you have to be there, by my side, or I will not have the strength to achieve it. You are my inspiration, and my solace. You are the reason I wake in the morning and the last thing I think about before I sleep at night.

"Be by my side, always, Kita. Marry me," he finished staring up into her moist eyes.

"No," she replied instantly.

Reynard felt the bottom fall out of his world.

"I mean I will not give you my answer now. Not yet," she continued with a gentle smile and Reynard felt his heart lurch in his chest. "I cannot marry you now, Reynard. There is unfinished business."

"What...?" he asked momentarily confused.

"Lily Jade – the Verdant Queen," Kita explained. "We know now for certain that Lily Jade was behind the whole sorry business on Granita. We know her daughter visited the Great Library in Antissa and recovered a ritual to reopen the gate to the Void. We know Kululu Jade was sent along with us for treacherous reasons and was sent to stop our efforts to close the gate." Reynard nodded in agreement. "But what we don't know," Kita continued, "is why? Why would Lily Jade team up with aberrations from the Void? Is she insane? Is she somehow one of the aberrations herself? For what reason did she open the gate? What did she hope to gain from it? Only when these questions have been answered will I give you your answer, Reynard. Only then will we have closure on this whole business."

Reynard stood to his feet, still holding Kita's hands.

"I guess we'd best get the *Javelin* ready for a trip then."

"Why?" asked Kita. "Where are we going?"

"To Ibini, to visit the Queen."

*

The deep jungles of southern Ibini were soaking wet. The spring rains which lashed the continent at this time of year only seemed to add to the already humid atmosphere and at times it almost felt as if the very air was full of water. Lily Jade walked purposefully on through the thick vegetation, utterly unfazed by the experience. Her mind and her concentration were totally focussed on one thing alone and that was not the weather.

Sliding along behind the Verdant Queen, as she made her way through the thick vegetation, was a towering behemoth. Rising some fifteen feet above the jungle floor, the creature appeared like a giant snake from the waist down and it propelled itself along much as a snake would, by undulating through the vegetation. Its body was four-foot thick at the waist, slowly tapering off as it reached the tail, and full of muscle. From the waist up the creature appeared loosely humanoid, though massive in size and strength. It had two huge arms which ended in claws with opposable thumbs. The immense two-handed sword strapped across its back paid testament to the fact that it could certainly use those claws to grip things, but the razor sharp talons on the ends of the claws indicated that it probably didn't need such a weapon. The chest and shoulders of the creature were human-like and hugely muscled. The face was somewhat a combination between human and snake, but the flat, wide mouth, the tongue which darted out tasting the air and the huge fangs were definitely snakelike. The creature had a flared crest behind its neck, much like the lethal *naja* snake which could be found in this part of the world. The eyes, set in the middle of the head, were utterly human – full of intelligence, cunning and malice.

"This way my lord," said Lily Jade over her shoulder, pushing on through the bush. "This way."

"You have done well, my queen," praised the towering creature, its voice deep and resonating, and slightly sibilant. "You and your offspring have served the Naga well, opening the portal to the Void and letting me back into this world."

"Thank you, my lord," she responded. "But I have done much more than that," she promised, eyes glinting with barely suppressed glee. "Come. See." Pushing on through the jungle foliage Lily Jade continued on down the winding path which led to the valley ahead. Occasionally looking over her shoulder to make sure the giant Naga was still following her she marvelled at how it moved almost utterly silently through the bushes, and somehow, despite its huge bulk it appeared to cause no damage to the foliage and left no easily discernible trail.

"I have started a breeding program my lord," she told the giant snake behind her. "It is still early, but I hope you will be impressed with the results."

"Interesting," commented the Naga Lord. "You were not instructed to do this, but let us see what you have achieved. Never let it be said that the Naga do not appreciate initiative."

"Yes my lord, of course," fawned the Verdant Queen nervously.

Moving further down the slope Lily Jade topped a rise where the jungle opened up a bit. She stopped at the ridge and waited for the Naga Lord to catch her up. As he arrived alongside her she said, "Behold – the results of my efforts!" Gesturing to the clearing below her she smiled and stood aside.

In the clearing were assembled a group of Naga, each looking much like smaller versions of the giant snake next to her. The males and females were clearly distinguishable from each other. The males rose to about eight foot in height and their waists were around two foot in diameter, making them about half the size of the Naga Lord, but still massively powerful warriors. Each carried an assortment of weapons, ranging from spears to tridents to two handed axes and swords. The predominant choice was two handed weapons but a few wielded sword or axe and shield. Alongside these males the females were distinctive by their much smaller physique. They stood no more than five or so feet high, and were much slighter than the males. The occasional one carried a weapon – typically a spear of some form – but most of the females were unarmed. The female Naga had no real need for weapons, as they were all versed in the elemental arts, able to summon raw energy from the Void and shape it to their will. There were perhaps somewhere between fifty and a hundred of the Naga sheltering in the valley.

"Impressive, my queen," praised the Naga Lord once more. "I am pleased with your initiative, though perhaps the numbers here are small. Given that you have had over a year to work on this program of yours, I would have expected greater numbers."

"Yes, indeed," she agreed hastily. "But please, do not judge until you have seen all there is to see," she continued.

The Naga Lord cocked his serpentine head to one side and whispered, "There is more?"

"Oh yes, my lord, much, much more. Come this way please."

Moving across the ridge Lily Jade headed to a place she had prepared in advance. She knew the location she was leading the Naga Lord to would provide the best view of what she had to show him. She was excited and nervous at the same time.

It had been nearly two years since the spirit of Vasukini had first visited her in her dreams. It had been he who had explained to her how she could open a portal to the Void. He had shown her the way to the Great Library in Antissa. He had suggested that she send her daughter there to recover the ritual and then on to Granita to reopen the gate which had been closed some five hundred years before. The spirit of the Naga Lord had prompted her and encouraged her, promising her what she had always wanted: control of the continent of Lucarcia. He would enter the world through the gate with her help and together they would subjugate and enslave the whole empire. Together they would rule and all men would bow down to them. Everything he had promised her had come true. And now, finally he had arrived in the flesh. She was so tense because her life-long goals would soon be realised.

Reaching the spot she stopped just short of the brow of the ridge. She turned to face the Naga Lord as he undulated his way up the rise to where she was standing. "Now, my lord, please witness the complete program I have prepared for you. Welcome to the Breeding Pits!"

The Naga Lord slithered forward a little further so that he could see down into the deep valley beyond. The hillside here was bare of trees – it appeared they had been cut down to make space. And what he saw filled the evil aberration with great delight. As far as the eye could see, from left to right and stretching right across the valley into the distance were eggs. Thousands upon thousands of eggs. Naga eggs.

As he looked on a nearby egg suddenly cracked open and out wriggled a fully grown, eight-foot tall male. The Naga were born as fully functioning adults, already possessing all the cunning and malice of their ancient race. His army was growing right before him. The human had done well.

"Look, my lord, over there to your left," Lily Jade indicated and Vasukini turned his great snake-head to see where she was pointing. In the deep shadows of a grove of acacia tress which had been left standing was a massive form: a Naga Mother. A huge aberration whose only purpose was to create and lay Naga eggs, this particular specimen was immense. And as Vasukini watched it shuddered and rippled and laid yet another egg.

"Come here, my queen," the Naga Lord purred. "Come and stand before me, and look at the incredible fruits of your work."

Lily Jade did as she was bid. Moving in front of the giant snake she stood and looked down on the valley and the huge array of Naga eggs. She felt the huge talons rest upon her arms and then the giant Naga Lord began to softly massage her shoulders. She was amazed at the dexterity and the soft touch those huge and hideous claws could produce.

"You have done all that I have asked and more," congratulated Vasukini, whispering into her ear. "Now there is only one thing left to sort out: your reward." The Naga Lord continued to gently and softly massage the lumps in the Verdant Queen's shoulders. As he did so she shut her eyes and revelled in the feeling of well-being and the knowledge that she would soon begin her conquest of the empire. Soon, everyone would bow before her.

The Naga Lord's talons continued to gently rub and probe at the knots in her shoulders. As they did his huge flat mouth slowly opened and his jaw clicked softly as it dislocated, allowing his mouth to grow extraordinarily wide. His head moved up and over the top of Lily Jade. Then with a single, sharp snap, Vasukini bit the Verdant Queen's head clean off.

"Now we can begin the invasion," he said to himself, swallowing, as her headless body dropped into the earth.

Printed in Great Britain
by Amazon